And then, as Picard stared, the world began to . . . *ripple?*

"*Enterprise* to away team!" The words were out of his mouth before he even realized he was speaking. "Mister Worf, can you hear me?"

Static laced the first officer's reply as it erupted from the intership. "*Worf here, Cap . . . thing happeni . . . own here. We are attem—*" The rest of the response vanished in another burst of electronic squawk.

On the viewscreen, the unnamed planet wavered, and even seemed to expand or stretch for a brief moment, then appeared to pull in on itself, shrinking within an increasing cascade effect before disappearing in a flash of light and leaving only the multihued gases of the NGC 8541 nebula to fill the viewscreen.

"Oh, my god," said Faur. Breaking her gaze from the screen, she turned to look at Picard, and the captain saw her expression of disbelief mirrored on the faces of the other bridge officers.

He forced himself to maintain his composure as he processed what had just happened. Though the nebula beckoned to him from the viewscreen, the planet—and his people—were gone.

STAR TREK
THE NEXT GENERATION®

HEADLONG FLIGHT

DAYTON WARD

Based upon
Star Trek: The Next Generation
created by Gene Roddenberry

POCKET BOOKS

New York   London   Toronto   Sydney   New Delhi   Ushalon

Pocket Books
An Imprint of Simon & Schuster, Inc.
1230 Avenue of the Americas
New York, NY 10020

This book is a work of fiction. Any references to historical events, real people, or real places are used fictitiously. Other names, characters, places, and events are products of the author's imagination, and any resemblance to actual events or places or persons, living or dead, is entirely coincidental.

™, ®, and © 2017 by CBS Studios Inc. STAR TREK and related marks and logos are trademarks of CBS Studios Inc. All Rights Reserved.

This book is published by Pocket Books, an imprint of Simon & Schuster, Inc., under exclusive license from CBS Studios Inc.

All rights reserved, including the right to reproduce this book or portions thereof in any form whatsoever. For information, address Pocket Books Subsidiary Rights Department, 1230 Avenue of the Americas, New York, NY 10020.

First Pocket Books paperback edition February 2017

POCKET and colophon are registered trademarks of Simon & Schuster, Inc.

For information about special discounts for bulk purchases, please contact Simon & Schuster Special Sales at 1-866-506-1949 or business@simonandschuster.com.

The Simon & Schuster Speakers Bureau can bring authors to your live event. For more information or to book an event, contact the Simon & Schuster Speakers Bureau at 1-866-248-3049 or visit our website at www.simonspeakers.com.

Manufactured in the United States of America

10 9 8 7 6 5 4 3 2 1

ISBN 978-1-5011-1131-0
ISBN 978-1-5011-1132-7 (ebook)

Dedicated to the memory of
longtime Star Trek *reader and fan*
Eric Cone
June 29, 1966–September 19, 2016

HISTORIAN'S NOTE

This story takes place in mid-2386, seven years after the *U.S.S. Enterprise*-E's confrontation with the Romulan praetor Shinzon (*Star Trek: Nemesis*) and approximately two months after the events involving the Federation, the Klingon Empire, and the renegade Klingon cult known as the Unsung (*Star Trek: The Next Generation–Prey*).

HEADLONG FLIGHT

PROLOGUE

U.S.S. Enterprise, NCC-1701-D
Stardate 44853.6, Earth Year 2367

Geordi La Forge was feeling lucky.

From the storage container he had brought with him, he extracted two decks of playing cards and a set of poker chips. He placed the items atop the green felt surface that now covered the table in the sitting area of Commander Data's quarters. The chips went to the center of the table, whereas La Forge positioned the cards before the chair in the room's corner, which was Data's preferred seat.

"Tonight's the night," La Forge said, stepping back from the table and adjusting his uniform tunic. "Payback for the beating I took from you last week."

Sitting behind the expansive console that served as his desk, Data swiveled in his high-backed chair. Still dressed in his Starfleet uniform, he now also wore a green eyeshade. Despite a notable lack of emotions, the android still managed to affect a range of facial expressions that seemed to simulate human reactions. In this case, he frowned as though attempting to display confusion or doubt.

"I administered no physical punishment during our last poker session."

La Forge smiled. "Data, I swear there are times when I can't tell if you're being dead serious, or trying to joke with me."

"This would be one of those times."

"Now you're just putting me on."

"Putting you on what?"

Realizing this could go on all evening if he allowed it, La Forge held up his hands. "I surrender." He looked at the table and for the first time realized that there were seven chairs, instead of the usual six. "We've got an extra player tonight?"

Nodding, Data said, "Lieutenant Worf, Counselor Troi, Wesley, and the doctor will be joining us as usual. The captain made a point to mention that he may perhaps 'drop in.' I thought it prudent to reserve a seat for him."

"Really? That's surprising." La Forge pondered the possibility. "How long's it been since he last sat in for a game? Seven or eight months?"

"Nine months, twenty-one days, seven hours, and thirty-seven minutes."

La Forge shrugged. "Like I said." He nodded in satisfaction. "It'll be nice to have him back, though I can't say I've missed not getting my scalp handed to me the way he does it." Seeing Data adopt a quizzical expression, he raised a hand. "Never mind."

Moving away from the table, the chief engineer crossed to where Data had returned his attention to the screens set into his desk. From where La Forge stood, he could see that his friend was poring over what obviously were columns of sensor data scrolling past three different screens at a pace too fast for him to follow. "What are you looking at?"

Data replied, "Sensor readings from our survey mission to the Hecuba star cluster. This is my first opportunity to review the information we collected, both from our own scans as well as the survey probes we launched into the region. Now that we have completed our studies of the area, I am preparing my final reports for the captain and for transmission to Starfleet Command."

"That sounds exciting. There wasn't much to write home about, after all."

La Forge made no attempt to hide his sarcasm, even though he knew Data likely would not pick up on it. The Hecuba star cluster had been first cataloged more than a century earlier by automated deep-space survey probes, and now it along with the surrounding sector was the *Enterprise*'s current focus of exploration. After nearly two weeks of being subjected to intensive sensor scans, the cluster appeared to harbor nothing of any real interest. Still, the engineer was sure astronomers and other scientists would find much to enthrall them once the first detailed sensor data was transmitted back to Starfleet Command.

"While we encountered no unusual stellar phenomena," said Data, "one planet in the Polydorus system shows remarkable parallels to Earth during its Paleoproterozoic Era. The evidence of eukaryotic organisms is very much like what evolved on Earth approximately one point eight billion years ago. There may be other similarities, as well, but such discoveries likely will require a dedicated science team over an extended period."

"At that rate," said La Forge, "I'm thinking we have plenty of time to get someone out here."

"Agreed."

"Besides, we're overdue for a rendezvous at Starbase

198. The captain promised me we'd put in after we took on this last survey mission, and I've been wanting to put the ship through a baryon sweep before we're sent out on anything long-term." The procedure to rid the ship of baryon particles—residual elements that accumulated on and within a starship as a result of extended travel at warp speeds—was routine in most respects, though it did require travel to a starbase with the specialized equipment to carry out the process. Further, it necessitated the crew disembarking the ship for the duration of the sweep. Vessels normally were not required to undergo this procedure at such an early point in their life spans, but the *Enterprise*, during its rather short period of active service, had logged many more hours at warp than other ships of similar tenure. Based on the projections he had formulated, and taking into account the ship's atypical operational tempo, La Forge predicted the *Enterprise* requiring a baryon sweep at approximate intervals of three years.

The challenge, conceded La Forge, was figuring out what to do with the shore leave that came with being a crew displaced by such a sweep.

Who am I kidding? Starbase 198 has at least one working holodeck, right?

Even as he decided to take himself to task for the errant thought, La Forge's reverie was broken by the sound of a yellow alert klaxon. A moment later, the ship's intraship activated, followed by the voice of Lieutenant Worf.

"Attention, all personnel. Sensors have detected an unexplained stellar anomaly. We are changing course to investigate. All on-duty personnel are ordered to their stations. All other duty shifts remain on standby until further notice. Senior staff, report to the bridge."

As Data removed his eyeshade and rose from his chair, La Forge tapped his communicator badge. "La Forge to bridge. Data and I are on our way."

Over the open frequency, Worf replied, *"Acknowledged."*

Eyeing his friend, La Forge said, "Any idea what it might be?"

The android shook his head. "Without information, it is difficult to form a hypothesis."

"I'm betting it's not a nebula."

"That would seem to be a logical assumption, as I do not believe the captain would upgrade the ship's alert status and order the senior staff to the bridge for something of that nature."

La Forge shook his head as the pair exited Data's quarters and proceeded to the nearest turbolift. "You're putting me on again, aren't you?"

"Putting you on what?"

1

HERE
U.S.S. Enterprise, NCC-1701-E
Earth Year 2386

Roused from slumber, Jean-Luc Picard was still rubbing
the last remnants of sleep from his eyes as the turbolift
began decelerating, heralding his arrival at the bridge.
He had but a moment to adjust his uniform jacket
and compose himself before the doors parted and the
sounds of the starship's nerve center filled the lift compartment.

"Captain on the bridge," said Commander Worf,
who was the first to notice Picard emerging from the lift.
Pushing himself from the command chair at the center
of the bridge, the *Enterprise*'s first officer rose to his full,
imposing height at Picard's approach. Seated to Worf's
right, the gamma shift watch officer, Commander Aiden
Lynley, also stood.

"Number One," said Picard by way of greeting, stifling a sudden urge to yawn.

The Klingon nodded. "I apologize for disturbing you,
sir, but given what our sensors have detected, I felt this
was something you would want to see for yourself."

Picard had figured that much upon hearing the alert
siren that had awakened him even before Worf's sum-
mons. The odds of his second-in-command calling for
him in the middle of the night for a routine matter were
nonexistent. Indeed, the Klingon likely had been called

by Commander Lynley, leaving it to Worf to determine whether Picard should be alerted.

"No apologies needed." He noted the blinking status indicators around the bridge. "We'll maintain yellow alert for the time being. What have you found?"

Worf nodded to Lynley, who said, "We've been continuing our sensor sweeps of NGC 8541 as ordered. There was nothing out of the ordinary for the first several hours after gamma shift started, but then we got a change in the sensor readings." He looked over his shoulder toward the starboard bridge stations. "Lieutenant Elfiki, let's see it."

Seated at one of the bridge stations positioned along the bulkhead and facing away from the command well, Dina Elfiki turned in her chair even as the fingers of her right hand played across her console. "Aye, sir."

The image on the main viewscreen shifted from a view of open space to the enormous, swirling mass of ionized gases and interstellar dust designated as object number 8541 in the *New General Catalogue*. It was the seventh stellar phenomenon of this type the *Enterprise* had encountered since beginning its exploration of the Odyssean Pass several months earlier. Like the previous six nebulae, this one seemed to Picard to be rather unremarkable, though the *Enterprise* had, of course, followed through with a full sensor scan of the area and the cataloging of that data for transmission to Starfleet Command. Based on the last report submitted from the astrometrics department heads, the captain had been prepared to order a course set for their next scheduled point of interest.

Such thoughts vanished as Picard beheld the planet centered on the viewscreen.

"It wasn't there until about fifty-two minutes ago, sir," said Elfiki. Rising from her seat, the young science officer moved to the edge of the command well, and Picard briefly wondered how long ago she had been called to the bridge after doubtless being awakened by Commander Lynley. "Based on a review of our sensor scans, it literally just appeared out of nowhere."

His gaze locked on the dull gray, seemingly lifeless body now hanging amid the nebula's swirling cloud of violet gases, Picard crossed his arms. "And you're certain this can't be explained by a sensor anomaly or other interference?"

Elfiki shook her head. "No, sir. Given the problems we've already been having, I triple-checked everything."

"I've had a level-three diagnostic run, Captain," added Lynley, "just to make sure we're not being fooled by a sensor echo or something else in here." He pointed to the screen. "That planet just wasn't here an hour ago, sir."

Stepping closer to the viewscreen, Picard pondered the pale, dead world. Since the *Enterprise*'s arrival at NGC 8541, the nebula had been causing no small amount of trouble for the starship's sensors. The ionization levels either blocked scans or else muddied the readings to an extent that the engineering and science staffs had been required to make continuous adjustments to the equipment to compensate for the interference. The background ionization also hindered the deflector shields and long-range communications while the ship remained within its boundaries. In an attempt to combat these difficulties, Lieutenant Elfiki also had gone to painstaking lengths to devise a course through the nebula that would either avoid or mitigate disruptions to the affected systems. While that effort had been somewhat successful, continuing to scan the nebula often required a choice between clarity of sensor data or risking an interruption of the ship's deflector shields and perhaps its protection against the region's inherent instability. Upon arriving at the nebula and learning to what extent surveying it would hamper his ship's systems, Picard was reminded of the Briar Patch, a volatile area in Federation space that had given him and the *Enterprise* so much grief years earlier. At least here, the ship's propulsion systems did not appear to be suffering adverse effects.

"Could it have been cloaked?" asked Lynley. Along with Worf, the commander had moved to stand behind and just to the left of Picard.

"I'll recheck the sensor logs, Commander," replied Elfiki before returning to her station. "But I didn't notice indications of energy readings consistent with any cloaking technology with which we're familiar." Turning back to her instruments, the science officer set once more to work.

"The power requirements to cloak an entire planet would be staggering," said Picard. "I'd hope they'd also be detectable. Lieutenant Elfiki, what can you tell us about the planet itself?"

Elfiki looked away from her console. "It doesn't have an atmosphere, sir, but our scans have detected artificial structures at a single location on the surface. There's also a significant energy reading coming from an underground location. Scans indicate it's a subterranean nuclear fusion reactor. Pretty decent size, too, a lot larger than you'd think they'd need to power the complex on the surface." She paused, and Picard saw a fleeting expression of nervousness before she schooled her features.

"The readings we're getting would be better if we could get closer, sir."

Picard considered the lieutenant's request as he continued to study the planet, before looking to his first officer. "Number One?"

"We could move closer, sir," said Worf. "We are currently maintaining position five hundred thousand kilometers from the nebula's outer boundary. With the reconfigurations we have made to compensate for the region's effects on sensors and shields, we may be able to cut that distance in half, though it would still expose the ship to increased risk."

Lynley added, "We'd probably have to move even closer, Captain." He gestured to the viewscreen. "The soup in there is enough that our scans would still be pretty muddied at that distance."

"Let's keep things simple for the moment," said Picard. "Mister Worf, cut our distance from the outer boundary by half. We'll take it from there."

The Klingon nodded. "Aye, sir."

With Commander Lynley moving to take over the bridge's tactical station, Picard settled into his command chair as Worf oversaw the efforts of the gamma shift flight control officer, Lieutenant Gary Weinrib.

"Shields are reacting to the nebula," reported Lynley after a moment. "Compensating for the increased effects."

Picard replied, "Very well."

Casting a glance over his shoulder, Weinrib said, "Now holding station at two hundred fifty thousand kilometers from the nebula's outer boundary, sir."

Shifting in his seat, Picard looked to Elfiki. "Lieutenant?"

The science officer was splitting her attention between her console and the main viewscreen. "Readings are better, sir, but still somewhat distorted. I'm instructing the main computer to scrub the scan imagery we're receiving." She frowned. "These readings are odd. It's like the sensors are out of alignment, but that's impossible. I'm not sure . . ." When she paused, Picard watched her lean closer to one of the station's display screens. "I'll be damned."

"What is it?" asked Picard. Rising from his chair, he crossed to Elfiki's station and moved to stand behind her. "What are you seeing?"

Pointing to the screen that had captured her interest, the science officer replied, "Sensors are picking up quantum fluctuations, sir. The nebula's masking most of it, but we're close enough now that we can see some of the effects. I've just rechecked the readings to be sure, Captain. They're definitely coming from the planet."

Picard studied the telemetry feed, as translated by the *Enterprise*'s computer from the raw sensor data to a format understood by mere living beings. Something about the information seemed off to him. "Can you identify a point of origin?"

"That's just it, sir." Elfiki turned in her seat. "It's not coming from a single location on the planet." She shook her head. "I mean, they're being generated from the structures we've already detected, but they're expanding outward to encompass the *whole* planet."

Worf had moved to stand next to the captain. "You're saying the entire planet has possibly shifted from another dimension?"

"I'm saying that's what the sensors are indicating, Commander." The science officer pointed once more to the readings. "These readings are consistent with what we know about interdimensional rifts, as well as shifts between dimensions made through artificial means."

"You're certain?" asked Picard.

Elfiki paused, as though weighing the impact of her answer, before replying, "Yes, sir. I am."

Turning from the science station, Picard again took in the sight of the mysterious world before them, its ashen surface contrasting with the nebula's brilliant indigo hues. Was it possible that the planet itself had come from some other realm of existence? If so, what had brought it here? To what unexplained cosmic forces had it been subjected prior to its arrival here? For what purpose might it have been sent from one reality to another?

"Artificial dimensional shift," he said after a moment, almost to himself. Then, in a louder voice, he asked Elfiki, "Lieutenant, the structures you detected on the surface—what about life signs?"

The science officer consulted her instruments. "Sensor readings are still experiencing disruption, sir, but we're picking up indistinct life signs."

"Captain," said Commander Lynley from where he still stood at the tactical station. "We're being scanned. The sensor beams are coming from one of the structures."

Worf asked, "Any signs of weapons or other aggressive action?"

"Negative." The commander tapped several controls on his console. "Just the scans, and they're fairly weak, especially compared to ours and even with the problems we're having."

Picard said, "So, whoever's down there knows we're here."

"Looks that way, sir." Checking his instruments, Lynley reported, "Now I'm picking up what looks like an incoming communication. The transmission's a bit garbled, but I think it's an automated message that's being repeated at intervals of roughly thirty seconds. I'm running it through the translation processor now." A moment later, he pressed another series of controls. "I've got a portion of it, sir. It's audio only."

Picard said, "Let's hear it."

Lynley entered another command to his console, and the bridge's intership communications system flared to life with a burst of static that faded, leaving only what to Picard sounded similar to wind rushing through a tunnel. Then that sound dissipated and was followed by a male voice.

"You who are receiving this message are likely in proximity to our planet. If that is the case, then please heed this warning: It is dangerous to approach this world. We are trapped here, but the circumstances of our captivity are of our own doing. There is nothing to be done for us. Assisting us is not worth the risk to your vessel or your lives. We—"

Whatever might have come next dissolved into a hiss of static before Lynley silenced the audio. "The rest of the transmission's too garbled, Captain."

For his part, Picard had heard enough. "Whoever's down there said they're trapped because of something they did to themselves. Lieutenant Elfiki, is it possible they're referring to whatever may be responsible for the quantum fluctuations you've detected?"

"If the planet's moving between dimensions," replied the science officer, "then it's possible they're trapped within a containment field or something similar that protects them during the shift. From this distance and with our sensors still experiencing disruption, it's hard to be sure, sir."

"Captain," said Worf, "if we move closer, the risk to the ship could be significant."

Behind him, Picard heard Lynley add, "I have to agree, sir. There's just too much we don't know."

"Well, we can't just sit here and do nothing," said Picard. "Whoever's down there, they know we're up here. We can't turn and leave them without at least investigating and seeing if there's anything we can do." Sensing Worf poising to object, the captain held up his hand. "Your concern is noted and appreciated, Number One, and we will exercise every precaution. For now, let's just have a look."

Staring at the strange new world depicted on the viewscreen, Picard could only hope that he was not making a grave mistake.

2

Resisting the urge to pace back and forth across the bridge, William Riker instead kept his eyes focused on the main viewscreen that was dominated by the orange-yellow mass of the Spindrift Nebula. By itself, the spatial phenomenon was more than sufficient reason to remain in the region while allowing the ship's science department to spend days scanning and studying it to their heart's content. For his part, Riker was more interested in what had apparently been hiding in the nebula until just a few minutes ago, and that now seemed to have disappeared as though never having existed.

Where the hell did you go?

Hearing the aft turbolift doors open, Riker turned to see Data and Geordi La Forge stepping from the car.

"Captain," said the android as he moved down the ramp on the bridge's port side and proceeded into the command well. Behind him, La Forge moved to the work-stations along the aft bulkhead where Lieutenant Worf already stood.

"I'm afraid you missed it, Mister Data," Riker said, waving toward the viewscreen before glancing over his shoulder to the tactical station. "Tasha, let's have another look at it."

Standing at the console immediately above and behind the captain's chair, Lieutenant Natasha Yar nodded. "Aye, sir."

A moment later the viewscreen shifted to show another image of the anomaly, though this time the region of orange gases was dominated by a dull, gray planet.

"Hello," said La Forge. "Where did that come from?"

Riker replied, "That's what we're trying to figure out. Sensors detected it about fifteen minutes ago, but it was in an area of the nebula we'd already scanned yesterday."

"We detected no such planetary bodies during those scans," said Data.

"Exactly, and now it's gone again. It disappeared right after I had Worf call you to the bridge."

Data said, "Intriguing. I assume sensor interference has been ruled out as a cause for not detecting the planet earlier?"

"Yes," replied Riker, "but it won't hurt to double-check. Geordi?"

At the back of the bridge, La Forge replied, "Already working on it, Captain. So far, I'm not seeing indications of any interference we haven't already accounted for." The chief engineer tapped his console. "I'm going over the sensor logs now. Data, you're going to want to see this."

Exchanging glances with his first officer, Riker followed the android up to the aft stations, where he saw that La Forge had already isolated a segment of sensor telemetry and now was gesturing to it.

"See it?" he asked.

Data nodded. "Quantum fluctuations. Such readings might be indicative of a dimensional shift, but I have never heard of such an occurrence on a planetary scale."

"That makes two of us," added La Forge.

Yar said, "We picked up structures on the planet's surface." She reached up to brush aside an errant lock of blond hair. "There were also some pretty significant power readings down there, including what looks like a massive fusion reactor."

"We also detected life signs," added Riker. "The readings were distorted thanks to the nebula, and maybe these quantum fluctuations, but there was definitely somebody down there."

"It is likely that anyone on the planet would have at least some knowledge about this phenomenon," said Data. "That we are unable to communicate with them is unfortunate."

Yar nodded toward the nebula depicted on the viewscreen. "If we think this was done artificially, then it would take a tremendous amount of power for the sort of shift we're talking about."

"Or some force or other power source from wherever the planet originally came from," said La Forge. "Something we can't detect with our own sensors." He shrugged. "All of that assumes we're really talking about some kind of dimensional shift involving an entire planet." He looked to Riker. "I think I'd like to rule out any chance of sensor interference or some other glitch, Captain."

Riker nodded. "Agreed. Run a diagnostic on the sensor array. In the meantime, we already collected plenty of readings. Mister Data, have a closer look at the sensor logs. See if you can find anything else of interest. One thing I want to know right now is whether those quantum fluctuations came from the planet or something else inside the nebula."

"In other words," said La Forge, "are we in any danger?"

"Exactly."

Data replied, "Aye sir," before moving to the console adjacent to La Forge's workstation. After a few moments, the android said, "My review of the collected sensor telemetry shows the quantum fluctuations were confined to the planet. There are no indications that the effect extended into the nebula itself, and current scans show no signs of such readings. Based on this, I do not believe we are in any danger, Captain."

"Good." Riker allowed himself a small sigh as he studied the nebula on the viewscreen. "Is it possible the planet could still be in here somewhere? Could whatever's producing the quantum fluctuations be moving it around within the nebula?"

"Given how little we know about quantum shifts and transdimensional movement," said Data, "it would be premature to rule out such a possibility. Perhaps the properties of the nebula somehow facilitate the transfer. Of course, the only way for us to determine such activity would be to further our exploration of the region, which is made problematic due to the continued interference with our sensors."

La Forge said, "We could deploy some automated survey drones. Say, a half dozen of them to sweep the entire nebula." The chief engineer paused, as though considering his own suggestion. "Along with the sensor data we'd be collecting ourselves, we could probably have a picture of the whole thing inside of twenty-four hours, maybe less."

"What about the nebula's effects?" asked Riker. "Wouldn't that distort the probes' sensor readings?"

Data said, "We could modify each probe's sensor array to compensate for the interference. We may also be able to strengthen their communications systems to augment the transmission of scan telemetry, but that might decrease the speed with which we receive the information."

Turning once more to regard the viewscreen, Riker shrugged. "We're not in a hurry to be anywhere, and I'm guessing I'm not the only one who's curious. How soon can you have the probes ready to launch?"

"I can get the current duty shift to start now," replied La Forge. "If I pitch in and with Data's help, I figure three, maybe four hours?"

Riker glanced to a chronometer on the nearby engineering workstation. "It's not an emergency, but I won't stop you if you want to get started now." He added a small smile. "We can take a rain check on the game and try again tomorrow night."

Nodding, La Forge returned the smile. "Aye, sir. We can do that."

Though he would not say it aloud, Riker had truly been looking forward to returning to the senior staff's weekly poker game. It had taken the other members of the *Enterprise*'s executive cadre quite some time to resume what had been a regular, anticipated pastime in the wake of losing their former captain. The emotional wound caused by the death of Jean-Luc Picard at the hands of the Borg ran deep, and likely would never fully heal. His absence had cast a pall over the entire crew, and it was only in recent months, following extensive repairs to the ship and the resumption of their duties that everyone had begun to feel anything like their old selves again. Riker's promotion to captain in the immediate wake of Picard's capture by the Borg had helped maintain continuity aboard the ship, along with his permanent appointment as the *Enterprise*'s commanding officer once all hope of rescuing Picard was lost, but the pain of loss remained. Although Riker had been training for this job throughout his entire career, earning the posting in this manner was the last thing he had ever wanted. His admiration for Picard ran greater than the feelings he held for his own father. A trusted friend, a gifted mentor, and one of the finest leaders ever produced by Starfleet was gone, and it had fallen to Will Riker to carry on what Picard had begun as the *Enterprise*'s first captain. It was a tall order, and one Riker sometimes doubted he was able to fill. Succeeding Jean-Luc Picard was by itself a formidable challenge, but replacing him was impossible, and Riker had vowed never to try.

"Captain, I have something you need to see."

Riker realized it was Lieutenant Yar calling to him, and that he had been momentarily lost within his own thoughts. He saw that La Forge and Data both appeared occupied with the sensor configurations the chief engineer had proposed, and Lieutenant Worf had moved to take the ops position.

"What've you got?" he asked the security chief.

"I don't know why I didn't detect it at first," replied Yar, her attention divided between him and her instruments, "but I was going back through the logs, and we caught a brief snippet of an incoming transmission." She looked up from her console. "From the planet. It was on a low frequency, and I think the nebula interference just made me miss it, sir. I'm sorry."

Shaking his head, Riker said, "Easy to do in here, Lieutenant. What about the transmission?"

"It wasn't random, sir." Yar pressed a trio of buttons on her console's smooth, touch-sensitive interface. "Whoever sent it was definitely aiming it at us. There's no indication it was transmitting before we discovered the planet. I've been running it through the computer to get a translation, but from what I can tell, we only got a portion of it before the planet disappeared."

Her console beeped and she touched another control. "The computer's got something, sir."

"Put it through, Lieutenant," said Riker.

A moment later, the bridge's intership flared to life, and he heard a string of subdued pops and crackles, which the captain reasoned were artifacts from the weak signal and nebula interference. Then, the distortion faded.

"*. . . dangerous to approach this world. We are trapped here, but the circumstances of our captivity are of our own doing. There is nothing to be done for us. Assisting us is not worth the——*"

Yar said, "The transmission was cut off at that point, sir. From what I'm able to determine, the interruption coincides with our losing the planet on our sensors."

"Their own doing," said Riker, glancing to each of his officers. "What do you suppose that means? Some kind of experiment gone wrong?"

Nodding, La Forge replied, "That'd be my guess, Captain."

"A reasonable assumption, based on the limited information we possess," added Data. "I recommend we continue our efforts at investigation, sir."

His first officer's proposal being entirely expected, Riker offered a small smile of understanding. There was no blaming the android, of course. Now that his curiosity had been piqued, there would be no stopping him. Riker guessed that the rest of the crew likely harbored similar thoughts. Investigating the nebula was their first true exploration mission in months, and he knew that his people were eager to sink their teeth into something more interesting than acting as freight haulers and chauffeurs for diplomats and other Federation and Starfleet officials. Such duties, while necessary from time to time, were not the endeavors for which the *Enterprise* had been envisioned.

So, let's do some exploring.

Who were the people on the planet? How had they come to be there? Were the effects of whatever they had done contained to the single world, or was there a greater danger? These and various other questions presented themselves in no particular order to Riker, who knew that if he left them to run unchecked, his thoughts would consume him until this mystery was solved.

"A mystery."

It took him a moment to realize that he had spoken the words aloud, and now he found himself regarding the quizzical expressions on the faces of his senior officers.

"All right," he said. "Data, you and Geordi get to work on your probes, and see what can be done about reconfiguring or enhancing our sensors." Riker nodded toward the viewscreen. "Let's go find us a planet."

3

———————

HERE
U.S.S. Enterprise-**E**

Leaning back in her chair, Lieutenant T'Ryssa Chen rested her feet on the edge of the console she had commandeered in the ship's stellar cartography computer lab. The workstation was one of ten positioned around the large circular platform that was the holographic emitter array at the center of the room. Hanging in the air before her and a meter or so above the emitter was a three-dimensional, computer-generated representation of spatial object NGC 8541.

"Why can't they give these things better names?" she asked, shifting her position so that she was more comfortable. "I mean, some Starfleet cartographer went to all that trouble calling this region the Odyssean Pass, so why not a little extra love for everything else? Only the important stuff seems to get that sort of attention, while the smaller yet equally adorable things like this nebula right here get ignored." She offered a melodramatic sigh. "It's really quite a tragedy, when you think about it."

Seated at an adjacent workstation, Lieutenant Dina Elfiki looked up from her console and eyed Chen with suspicion. "Did you come down here to help me, or to offer distracting commentary?"

"There's no reason I can't do both." Chen grinned. "You know how much of an incredible multitasker I am."

Despite shaking her head, Elfiki could not help the small smile that crept onto her lips. "There are days I really hate you."

"Is today one of those days?"

"Not yet, but it's early." Returning her attention to her console, Elfiki pressed a control on the interface's smooth surface, the action accompanied by a short, melodic tone. In response to the science officer's instruction, the holographic image of the nebula spun clockwise ninety degrees, offering her and Chen a new view of the mass of gases and other dust and debris contained within the cloud's sinuous, fluctuating boundary. Within the nebula's lower left quadrant as it now faced Chen was a small gray sphere indicating the unnamed planet.

Elfiki said, "We've mapped nearly forty-five percent of the nebula, so that leaves a lot of area to explore." The *Enterprise*'s sensor sweeps of the area had been suspended upon discovery of the planet. "As for this little guy, it ranks up there as one of the most boring places I've ever seen. It's a rock. No atmosphere, no ores worth mining, no frozen or trapped water. Aside from the nuclear reactor powering the complex on the surface, asteroids are more interesting than this thing."

"Maybe that was the point," offered Chen, waving toward the projection. "You have to think that whoever set up shop down there chose this planet for a reason, so perhaps it was because it was a dead, boring hunk of rock. No one or nothing to put at risk, so if anything went wrong, the damage was limited just to the people working there."

"Pretty much what I've been thinking this whole time. That, and it's the sort of place someone like the Romulans or Starfleet Intelligence would love to stick a listening outpost, or maybe a prison. You know, a prime vacation destination."

Chen eyed her friend with a raised eyebrow. "I think you need to take better vacations."

Ignoring the comment, Elfiki entered more commands to her console. "The nebula's still giving our sensors fits, but I've been working with engineering to reconfigure them." She shook her head. "It's slow going."

Gesturing to the computer-generated image of the planet, Chen asked, "What about the facility itself? Anything interesting?"

"I'm sure there is," replied Elfiki. "The energy levels coming from that location on the planet are staggering. From what I can tell, there are two structures, one much larger than the other, that are the source of the quantum fluctuations we've detected. Meanwhile, all of the life-forms look to be contained to the smaller structure, which is situated some distance from its larger cousin."

"Whoever they are," said Chen, "they're not answering our hails. All we've gotten is that same automated message that repeats over and over for us to stay away, and that they caused whatever is happening with the planet. Even if they didn't want our help or it really was too dangerous for us to come closer, where's the harm in just talking to us?"

Smiling, Elfiki said, "Sounds like somebody's itching to act like a first-contact specialist."

"Well, sure. I mean, it is my job, after all." Chen waved a hand to indicate the room around them and—by extension—the rest of the *Enterprise*. "There are only so many odd jobs I can do and so much cross-training I can take on before *I* start to question the wisdom of having a contact specialist as a member of the crew if I'm rarely if ever going to specialize in actually contacting anybody."

It had become a routine, and something of a joke not just to Chen but many members of the crew, that her primary duties as a contact specialist were only ever needed on rare occasions. A significant portion of her time was spent on related yet mundane matters such as composing after-action reports, detailed analysis of whatever new species the *Enterprise* might encounter, and recommendations for next steps to be taken by Starfleet and the Federation with respect to a newly discovered civilization. If the species in question was at a technological level that was deemed below the threshold for authorized formal first contact, Chen's reports had to include any ramifications with respect to the Prime Directive and the effects of the *Enterprise*'s interference in the affairs of a society not yet prepared for the reality of interstellar neighbors.

Those are always the fun ones to write.

"If we can figure out what's up with these quantum fluctuations," said Elfiki, having returned her attention to her console, "maybe we can get them to open up a bit. The first thing I'm going to ask them is what they're doing out here in the middle of nowhere. Did they find a rogue planet and set up their operation here?"

Chen said, "When you told me you were coming down here, you mentioned something about looking for another planet."

"I wanted to rule it out, more than anything else." Elfiki waved toward the nebula's holoprojection. "I doubt there's really another planet hiding somewhere in that soup." The science officer had conjured the idea before leaving the bridge, and well before Chen's arrival in stellar cartography. She had explained it as little more than, "ruling out the obvious," while at the same time using the idea as reason enough to continue the starship's mapping of the region in order to see what else might be hidden here.

"It was a stupid idea," Elfiki added. Grunting in irritation, she pushed away from her workstation and leaned back in her chair, using the heels of her hands to rub at her eyes. "Wow, but I'm tired. I'd only been asleep an hour or so before the call came from the bridge." She sighed. "I thought these things were only supposed to happen on alpha shift."

Chen smiled. "And deny the overnight crews some excitement? That wouldn't be fair, now, would it?" A sudden yawn snuck up on her, and she was just able to cover her mouth. "Sorry."

"Don't start that," said Elfiki as she released her own yawn. Then she turned in her chair. "Wait a minute. I went by your quarters last night, and you weren't there. Or, you at least didn't answer the door." Her eyes narrowed. "Not the first time that's happened, either. So, spill it."

Feigning ignorance, Chen replied, "Spill what?"

"For someone who's half Vulcan, you have a lousy poker face." Pointing an accusatory finger, Elfiki leered at her. "Come on. Everybody on the ship except for the captain's kid knows you and Rennan are back together for real. Actually, the more I think about it, I think the kid probably knows too."

"First of all, yuck." Softening the remark with a mock grimace, Chen crossed her arms. "And second of all, is my poker face really that bad? I've been working on it, you know. With a mirror and everything."

Extending her right leg to play-kick her friend, Elfiki said, "Now I hate you. Quit stalling and start talking. I want details. Specific, explicit details. Nothing left to the imagination. At all."

"You're hopeless, do you know that?" Chen said. "Are you collecting gossip for the rest of the crew, or what?"

"I edit the ship's scuttlebutt newsletter." The science officer indicated for Chen to come closer. "We've been on our way back here for weeks, and you're always off hiding somewhere after hours. Out with it, or else I'll just have to make up something."

Where's the red alert when you need one?

Sighing, Chen resigned herself to the fact that her friend would continue to needle and pester her until she offered up something in the way of salacious information regarding her rekindled romance with Rennan Konya. Her relationship with the *Enterprise*'s deputy chief of security had soured in the months following the Borg Invasion. Konya had carried tremendous guilt due to his own survival of that short yet devastating conflict that had claimed many of his friends and shipmates. The feelings that clouded his mind and darkened his soul had caused him to withdraw from friends and nearly every sort of social situation; instead he had become all but consumed by his duties. His training regimens for the ship's security division had become so intense and unforgiving that some of the junior officers began lodging protests with the chief of security, Lieutenant Aneta Šmrhová. Once she had stepped in and spoken to him as his superior officer and friend, Konya had come to realize what he was doing, and he began attending regular sessions with the ship's counselor, Doctor Hegol Den. That, in Chen's opinion, had been the best thing for

Konya, as she knew the Bajoran's counseling approach was very relaxed, providing an atmosphere that allowed his patients to arrive at their own conclusions and decide on a course of corrective or therapeutic action with little pressure and no judgment from him.

Chen also was aware that Konya still saw Hegol on occasion, though those sessions were far less frequent than they had been a year ago. Though the feelings that plagued him remained, at least now he had ways of keeping them at bay, and over time Chen had watched his happier personality begin to reassert itself.

"What's to know?" she asked. "Like you said, everybody on the ship knows we got back together months ago."

Elfiki grinned. "Sure, but it's what's been happening during those months that we all want to talk about."

"You know it's not like that." Chen leaned back in her chair. "After that business with the Raqilan weapon ship, and after his apology for ending things between us the first time, he wasn't looking to start things back up. Neither was I, but we were still friends, and it was good to enjoy each other's company again."

The *Enterprise*'s recent encounter with two newly discovered societies, the Raqilan and the Golvonek, had seen to it that Chen and Konya ended up working together in close proximity. Their mission had called for them to examine the *Poklori gil dara*, an immense spacecraft constructed by Raqilan engineers in decades to come and sent back through time to the late twenty-third century. Once there, the vessel's mission was simple: prevent the war that had all but annihilated both civilizations and their respective homeworlds. This was to be accomplished by destroying the Golvonek's ability to wage war in the first place, with the *Poklori gil dara* able to do that by obliterating the Golvonek's home planet. Raqilan scientists and engineers had constructed the massive ship by reverse engineering much of the technology found in the wreckage of a "planet killer," an enormous, self-sustaining machine created millennia ago by an unknown, advanced alien race. Starfleet's encounters with such vessels had been few but memorable, but it was the Raqilan's re-creation of the ancient automaton that had so thoroughly impressed Chen. She and Konya had been members of the first away team to board and explore the craft, and Chen had marveled at its construction and how its Raqilan builders had been able to adapt and even improve on some aspects of the wrecked vessel's design.

It was during their excursions aboard the alien ship that Konya had apologized to Chen for his past behavior. Later, after she and their shipmate, security officer Lieutenant Kirsten Cruzen, had come within a hairbreadth of dying aboard the *Poklori gil dara*, Konya had reiterated his apology along with his desire to do whatever was needed to make things right between them. Other than the opportunity to do just that, he had neither requested nor expected anything from her.

"It was his sincerity that did it," said Chen, recalling his obvious relief upon seeing her in the *Enterprise* sickbay after not dying aboard the Raqilan weapon ship. "He was so vulnerable, and so sorry, and so happy to see me." She shrugged. "What can I say? It touched me."

Elfiki replied, "And then you touched him." When Chen gritted her teeth, feeling her cheeks flush, the science officer shifted in her seat, tucking one leg beneath her on the chair. "There it is. Now we're talking."

"Oh, stop it," said Chen. "It was just nice to be able to talk with him again, you know? The old Rennan, the way he used to be, before . . . everything."

Elfiki nodded. "Sure, I get it."

"Then we got to the other stuff."

"Of course you did."

They both laughed at that, and Chen now realized her initial embarrassment at discussing this sensitive topic had faded. "To answer your question, yes. It's very nice to be . . . you know."

"No, I don't know. Tell me more."

Chen's eyes narrowed. "Hang on a second. I'm not the only one with juicy gossip they're not sharing. What's this I hear about you and the gamma shift conn officer?"

"Lieutenant Weinrib?" Elfiki's brow furrowed. "What about him?"

Making a show of rolling her eyes, Chen replied, "You want to talk about horrible poker faces? You're not the only one occupying their off-duty hours with a few extracurricular activities." She bobbed her eyebrows to emphasize her point, earning a blush from her friend. "Uh-huh."

Even on a starship as large as the *Enterprise*, with its crew of well over one thousand people, it was still a tight-knit community. Spending weeks and even months traveling through interstellar space with only one another for company ensured that very little in the way of rumor or idle chitchat went unnoticed. One of the most interesting topics was any romantic liaisons—or the ending of such partnering—between members of the crew, and even though most people exercised discretion, it was almost impossible to keep such knowledge from filtering to shipmates. As for Elfiki and Gary Weinrib, Chen had overheard a couple of unsubstantiated reports of her friend spending time with the lieutenant.

"Don't be that way," said Elfiki after a moment. "It's honestly not what you think. He went through a breakup before we left Earth the first time for the Odyssean Pass. His partner was upset that he'd accepted the mission knowing we'd be out here for months and maybe even years. He wanted Gary to take a ground assignment for a while, and Gary tried to convince him to transfer to the *Enterprise*." She shrugged. "It didn't end well, for either of them. Gary and I have been friends since the Academy, so I guess you could say we're each other's confidants."

Though touched by Elfiki's sensitivity to her friend's emotional needs—which was very much in keeping with the science officer's character when it came to helping others—Chen still could not help a mischievous leer. "You're saying that nothing else was going on between you two?"

Elfiki shrugged, and the blush returned. "No, I never exactly said that."

"I knew it!"

Before Chen could press her interrogation, the sound of the ship's intraship cut her off, drawing the attention of both officers.

"*Worf to stellar cartography.*"

Trading curious glances with Elfiki, the young Vulcan responded, "Chen here. What can I do for you, Commander?"

The *Enterprise*'s first officer replied, "*Captain Picard has ordered an away team to investigate the planet via shuttlecraft. We will attempt to make contact with the peo-*

ple on the surface and attempt to determine whether we can provide assistance."

Finally!

Chen was only just able to quell her enthusiasm and maintain her bearing for propriety's sake. From the moment she had heard about the life-form readings on the planet, she had been hoping for something like this. It was obvious that the captain felt no more could be learned about the mysterious world without direct action. Though she knew Picard to be a prudent, even protective commanding officer, he was not above some risk if he felt the situation warranted it, or if undertaking such risk was for the benefit of others in jeopardy. It was not yet proven that the people on the planet's surface were in any actual danger, but determining that would be the away team's responsibility.

About time, too.

Over the open channel, Worf said, *"Lieutenant Elfiki?"*

"Here, sir," replied the science officer.

"You will monitor our activities from the bridge and provide us with updated sensor information about the planet itself. If you detect anything out of the ordinary, you'll be the one who orders us to abort our mission."

Elfiki frowned, and Chen could tell her friend was not thrilled about remaining behind, even though her role in the upcoming excursion would be of critical importance to the mission's success and possibly the safety of the away team. Despite her evident disappointment, she said only, "Understood, Commander."

"When do we leave, sir?" asked Chen.

"Departure is scheduled for eleven hundred hours." There was a pause, and Chen thought she could hear the Klingon emit a soft groan of disdain before he added,

"We'll be wearing environmental suits. Report to the main shuttlebay for final departure preparations. Worf out."

The communication was severed, and Elfiki shifted in her seat.

"EV suits? With Worf? Yeah, maybe staying back isn't so bad after all."

Chen could not help smiling as she rose from her seat. "Speak for yourself. This is going to be fun."

"No joke, T'Rys," said Elfiki, her tone turning serious. "With all those quantum fluctuations, there's no way to predict what might happen, or even when. Be careful down there."

"I'm always careful."

Maybe not always, but most of the time. A lot of the time. Usually.

Noting Elfiki's accusatory glare, Chen sighed.

"Okay, I'll be careful."

4

ELSEWHERE
*U.S.S. Enterprise-*D

Holding the diagnostic scanner close to his right eye, Geordi La Forge saw the glow in the device's viewfinder shift colors, the change interpreted by his VISOR as red dissolving into blue. Then he heard a telltale beep indicating the scan was completed, and he lifted the isolinear optical data chip up to examine it.

"This one's good to go, too," he said as he inserted the chip into an open slot on the primary processor of the class-1 sensor probe.

As with its five brethren, the probe sat on a worktable in one of the ship's science labs. Like its counterparts, the probe's main access panel had been removed, exposing its internal components. Having verified his modifications to the data chip, he and Data had completed reconfiguring four of the five devices, and it had taken them less time than what he had estimated for the task. So far, everything seemed to be proceeding according to his plan.

Don't jinx it.

With the computer chip returned to its proper place on the processor's data interface junction, La Forge reached back into the access panel and activated the unit's power module. He was rewarded by the entire processor interface coming to life, with its rows of indicator lights blinking in what to the untrained eye were nothing more than random patterns.

"The updated control software appears to be operating well within standard parameters," reported Data from where he stood on the worktable's opposite side, holding a tricorder toward the probe. The compact scanning device was emitting a low-pitched warble as the android studied its readings.

La Forge could not help smiling. "Well within standard parameters? That's all I get?" He shook his head. "Tough room."

Looking up from his tricorder, Data asked, "Was that not the desired result of our efforts?"

La Forge glanced up from the probe's open access panel and regarded his friend. "You're doing it to me again, aren't you?"

"Doing what?"

Sensing a rabbit hole threatening to swallow them both if the current conversational drift was permitted to continue, La Forge opted not to respond. Instead, he offered a small chuckle as he reached for his own tricorder. After a moment verifying Data's scans as well as his own hunch, the chief engineer nodded in satisfaction.

"Okay, that makes number five ready to go." Closing his tricorder and returning it to the worktable, La Forge was caught by the sudden urge to yawn, which he did not fight. Of course, the involuntary movement only served to remind him how the muscles in his back and neck had long ago started to ache.

"You appear fatigued," said Data.

Straightening his posture, La Forge pulled down on his uniform tunic before reaching up to where his VISOR attached to the connection points at his temples. "That's one way to put it." The visual-aid prosthesis had always been a source of mild discomfort, which over time he had learned to ignore or just endure, depending on the circumstances. Long hours and detailed work tended to amplify the effects, and he knew he and Data had already been at this task well beyond their normal duty shift. The headache he was beginning to feel was only amplifying the constant dull ache behind his eyes.

Data said, "If you wish, I can complete the modifications to the last probe while you rest."

"I appreciate the offer, but we're almost done." Stifling the urge to yawn a second time, La Forge rubbed the back of his neck. "How long have we been at this, anyway?"

"Five hours, fourteen minutes, eleven seconds."

Whoops.

Glancing toward the chronometer on a nearby workstation, the engineer released a groan of irritation. "I can't believe I forgot. She's going to kill me."

"Someone is going to kill you?" asked Data.

"I don't mean for real." Pausing to consider his comment, La Forge added, "Then again, anything's possible." He pressed the heels of his hands against the sides of his head. "I ruined everything. *Again.*"

Data regarded him with his best approximation of a perplexed expression. "I do not understand."

"I was supposed to have a late dinner with Lieutenant Ellis, from the astrophysics department."

"Lieutenant Heidi Ellis," replied Data. "She is a recent addition to the crew, and came aboard at Starbase 212."

La Forge nodded. "Right. I met her a day or so after that, and we seemed to hit it off. Dinner tonight was my idea, and I forgot to let her know I might be late, or not even make it."

"Surely, she will recognize that your responsibilities as chief engineer took precedence."

"If only it were that simple, Data." La Forge grunted again. "I guess I just lost track of time."

With the interrupted poker game and the time spent on the bridge getting their first look at the planet, and the hours spent requisitioning and relocating the six probes so that they could be reconfigured for surveying the nebula, it was now well after midnight, and likely too late for him to attempt calling Ellis to apologize for his gaffe.

Way to go, La Forge.

His track record with respect to social interactions had been less than stellar in recent months, and it was something he had decided he needed to improve. His failure to remember his date with Ellis was the exact opposite of moving in the right direction.

Nothing you can do about it now. May as well get back to work.

"Let's finish up and launch these things," he said. "I'll apologize to Heidi and then get some sleep after that. Deal?"

Nodding, Data replied, "Very well."

"But if we're going to do this, then I'm going to need coffee." Stepping away from the worktable, La Forge crossed the lab to the replicator set into the room's rear bulkhead. Within seconds the ship's computer responded to his instructions and a cup of steaming brown coffee materialized on the small, recessed platform. The first taste of the brew, his favored blend and with the exact proportions of milk and sugar he preferred, tasted like heaven.

Not as good as dinner with Heidi, though. Idiot.

"All right," he said, "where were we?"

Data was already standing before the sixth and final probe to be modified and was reaching into its access panel to pull from its information processor three of the seven isolinear chips La Forge knew were inside. Moving to the desktop computer interface he had placed on the worktable's far end, the android inserted one of the compact storage devices into a port on the terminal's base and began reviewing the chip's contents.

Without looking up from the computer interface, he said, "Once the modifications to the final probe are complete, it should require less than twenty minutes to synchronize their individual course trajectories with the main computer and our sensor array and move them into position for launch."

"I can handle the rest of this, you know," said La Forge. "I mean, don't you have something else you need to be doing? In case you've forgotten, you're still the first officer."

"My duty shift ended at the same time yours did. The gamma shift duty officer will contact me from the bridge if something requires my attention. As I do not require sleep, I am able to devote my normally off-duty hours to endeavors such as this. Besides, my duties also include assisting the science and engineering departments as needed and appropriate."

It was true that while Data was not officially listed on the *Enterprise*'s crew roster as a science or engineering officer, his talents in those fields made him an invaluable asset. La Forge could vouch for that, and the pair had made an effective tandem for the past few years, to the point that the very idea of not having the android—his friend—around to help with tasks such as the one now before him was almost impossible for the engineer to imagine.

"I swear," he said, "sometimes I think I'll never get used to seeing you in a command uniform."

Pausing in his work, Data looked down at himself, perusing his red tunic. "It is the proper uniform for the ship's first officer."

"I know." La Forge's gaze fell on the three gold pips on Data's collar, denoting the android's rank of full commander. It was a change that had occurred months earlier, following the Borg attack that had cost the life of Jean-Luc Picard and so many others. Following Picard's capture by the Borg before that vessel began moving through Federation space on a course toward Earth, Vice Admiral J. P. Hanson declared him "a casualty of war" before granting Riker a field promotion to captain and giving him command of the *Enterprise*. At the time, Riker had opted to assign the role of his new first officer to Lieutenant Commander Elizabeth Shelby, who with Hanson had originally come from Starfleet's tactical division to brief Picard about the new Borg threat. Shelby had stayed with the *Enterprise* and been on hand during the starship's first encounter with the vessel that ultimately seized Picard.

When the Borg assimilated the captain into their Collective, they were able to utilize his knowledge of Starfleet defenses and tactics to undermine any attempt at protecting the Federation and Earth. The lone Borg vessel met its fiercest opposition at Wolf 359, where a fleet of starships waited. Using the information gleaned from Picard, the Borg annihilated that fleet before continuing on course for Earth. All may have been lost if not for Shelby, working with Data, who hit on the idea of being able to communicate directly with Picard despite his being controlled by the Borg. Shelby and Data, with Picard's guidance, infiltrated the enemy vessel's onboard computer systems and input a series of commands that essentially put every Borg on the ship to sleep. What they had not counted on was the vessel itself taking defensive action and setting into motion a self-destruct protocol. With no time to spare, Riker was left with no choice but to move the *Enterprise* to a safe distance before the Borg ship was destroyed, killing its entire complement along with Captain Picard.

"Do you ever wonder what things might have been like if Commander Shelby had decided to stay behind as first officer?" asked La Forge.

Data shook his head. "No. The commander's skills and expertise are needed at Starfleet Tactical. Except perhaps for Captain Riker, she is the foremost authority on the Borg. Her knowledge and talents may well be our best option for finding a means of defense against their next attack."

"You think they'll come at us again?"

"It seems a reasonable conclusion, based on their past methods and expressed motivations," replied Data. "Further, we must also contend with the fact that the Borg now have access to all the knowledge Captain Picard possessed about Starfleet's offensive and defensive capabilities. Combating that advantage will prove a daunting challenge." Picard's capture and death was an enormous loss for Starfleet, the true scope of which would not even be known until the Borg decided to make another attempt at conquering the Federation. Closer to home, the loss also had been a tragic blow for the entire *Enterprise* crew, many of whom had been with the ship since its launch with Picard as their first commanding officer.

La Forge sighed. "I know all of that's important, but most of all, I just miss him. Will Riker is a fantastic captain, and he's been amazing at getting all of us back on track, but Captain Picard left some pretty big shoes to fill."

"Your choice of idiom seems to be an indication that you doubt Captain Riker is able to satisfactorily carry out the duties in the same manner as Captain Picard." Data studied him for a moment. "However, your body language and facial expression suggest something else."

"I have no doubt Captain Riker can do the job," replied the engineer. "He's already proven that more times than I can count." Again, he rubbed his temples, just above the VISOR's contact points. The headache was really making itself known now. He looked around the room. "I'm just saying that in a lot of ways, Captain Picard was the heart of this ship. He was her first captain, and they're the ones who usually end up leaving a lasting mark long after they're gone. Captain Riker will make his own mark, too, but . . ." He let the sentence drift away, uncertain how even to complete it. "I'm babbling, now. My brain is turning to mush."

Data said, "Perhaps you should reconsider that rest period, while I complete our work here."

"I'll be fine." La Forge gestured to the probe. "Besides, I have a confession: This is the most interesting thing I've done in months that didn't involve the engines or power relays or any of a thousand other things. It's a nice change of pace."

"That is not the first time I have heard such a sentiment." Though he had once more activated his tricorder,

Data paused in his movement to return to working on the probe. "Geordi, as first officer, one of my duties is to assess the morale of the crew, and to ensure that they are not being overworked or overstressed. However, as an android, I find myself questioning my ability to make such a determination with the same effectiveness as a living being."

La Forge smiled. "I don't think you give yourself enough credit. You always seem to read me well enough. That said, if you find yourself wondering about that sort of thing, talk to Counselor Troi. Keeping tabs on the crew's morale is part of her job too."

"We have had conversations on this topic, and her insight has been most helpful. Indeed, we discussed how the crew was reacting to the discovery of the nebula, and how even a straightforward scientific investigation has been beneficial to, as she described it, 'getting us out of a rut.' I had to consult the linguistic data banks to understand that term, but it seems a most apt descriptor."

Chuckling, La Forge replied, "And that was before we found the planet. You can bet the whole ship's buzzing over a genuine puzzle to solve." He released a long breath. "Long hours or not, it's done wonders for me. After making cargo runs and checking up on colonies and ferrying around admirals and diplomats for months, it's nice to get back to doing what this ship was built to do in the first place."

"Indeed," said Data, "I have even noticed a change in the captain's behavior, which coincided with our receiving the orders to investigate the Spindrift Nebula."

La Forge nodded. "He probably needs this more than anyone aboard. It's good to see him acting more like his old self."

The shift in Riker's demeanor had been displayed in different ways, from his intense curiosity about the nebula and the strange planet it apparently harbored to his promise to the senior staff that he would at long last return to the weekly poker game. In the weeks and months preceding the *Enterprise*'s present assignment, Riker had been all business; professional and supportive of his crew, but maintaining a certain detachment that reminded La Forge of Picard during the late captain's first years in command of the starship. It was as though Riker had erected a shell around himself in the hopes of keeping his duties and responsibilities separated from his personal feelings toward those in his charge, many of whom had become akin to family during their service together. As for the rest of the crew, while they continued to carry out their duties to the best of their ability and in the finest *Enterprise* tradition, their captain's sometimes aloof behavior had not gone unnoticed. Despite the apparent lack of glamour or excitement attached to their survey of the Spindrift Nebula, the change of direction and renewal of the starship's perceived purpose—exploration—had been enough to energize everyone aboard ship, including La Forge, and hopefully the captain, as well.

So let's get on with this.

5

"And you're sure you can handle this by yourself?"

Standing at the entrance to their bedroom, Deanna Troi listened to the voice coming from the computer on Will Riker's desk. Other than the glow of running lights from somewhere along the hull outside the slanted viewing ports forming one wall of their shared quarters, the soft shine of the computer's display was the only ambient light in the room. She watched as the gentle illumination played across Riker's face as he sat behind his desk, dressed in a loose-fitting cobalt-blue shirt and matching pants. His internal struggle to maintain his composure was evident to her, perceived as a rolling wave of emotion as Riker stared at the screen and the owner of the gruff voice barking at him. Though the terminal was angled so that she could not see it, there could be no mistaking Admiral Edward Jellico.

Riker, sitting straight in his high-backed chair, kept his hands folded in his lap. "As I said, sir, my people and I are more than capable of investigating this nebula. If we find the planet and determine it presents any danger to the ship, I'll back off and call for reinforcements." Despite his best efforts, Troi was still able to pick up the slight hint of annoyance in his voice. She stepped from their bedroom, moving so that she could see the screen without being registered by its visual pickup.

If he also recognized the strain behind Riker's words, Jellico chose not to say anything about it. Instead, he offered, *"What have you learned so far?"*

"About the nebula? By itself, it doesn't appear to be anything special, at least according to the sensor data we've already recorded. Still, we're preparing a suite of unmanned probes to conduct a comprehensive sweep, while we concentrate on locating the planet. So far, it's doing a good job hiding from us."

"What are the chances this is something new the Romulans have cooked up?"

Riker replied, "The energy readings we've detected so far aren't consistent with what we know of Romulan technology. That said, my first officer and chief engineer aren't ruling anything out just yet."

"Good. Given that we're still trying to get the fleet up to full strength, this isn't the time to get caught with our pants down."

"Agreed."

"Well, it's nice to know we can see eye to eye on occasion."

Her empathic senses noted Riker's flicker of irritation in response to the comment, and Troi watched him raise his chin ever so slightly, his only concession to Jellico's snide remark. Now able to see the admiral's face on the screen, Troi observed his perpetual scowl. Deep lines creased the admiral's forehead, and there were dark circles beneath his eyes. Edward Jellico's reputation for exacting long hours and hard work from those under his command was well known throughout the fleet, as was his penchant for pushing himself even harder than his subordinates. That was likely even more acute now, given the admiral's current assignment overseeing the

Starfleet Tactical Division, which had become a swarm of activity in the months following the Borg attack.

Troi conceded that such an assignment was perfect for a man like Jellico, who was a demanding officer and, without question, a man who epitomized leadership by example. Having never met him face-to-face, Troi could only guess his motivations to present such an intimidating demeanor. Did he perhaps suffer from a lack of confidence in his own abilities? That seemed inconsistent, at least on the surface. His dedication to duty was indisputable, though his methods could come across as brusque and dictatorial, standing in stark contrast to the poised yet self-assured command style exuded by someone like Riker, or even Jean-Luc Picard before him.

"I'll be transmitting a full report with our latest findings shortly, Admiral, and once we start receiving data from the probes, we'll add that to updates from now on."

"I look forward to reading your report," replied Jellico. *"Starfleet out."*

The communication ended before Riker could say anything, leaving him staring at the Federation seal on the screen.

"And a pleasant day to you too." Tapping the control to deactivate the terminal, Riker spun his chair until he faced Troi, then offered what she could tell was a forced smile. "Hello."

"You knew I was back here?" she asked, crossing the room in her bare feet.

Riker replied, "I don't need to be a telepath, or even an empath, to know where you are. Besides, you bumped the table on your way out of the bedroom." His smile faded as he held out his hand to her. "I'm sorry I woke you."

Taking his hand in hers, Troi allowed him to pull her toward him. "I was already awake," she said. "I heard the call from the bridge."

"He said it was urgent." Rolling his eyes, Riker shook his head. "Everything's urgent with him." Gesturing to the computer, he released an annoyed grunt. "Of course, he's had our preliminary report for at least three hours now, but he waits until after midnight, ship's time, to make that urgent call. He never passes up a chance to remind whoever he's talking to that he's the one in charge."

Based on what she could read from him, Troi guessed that fatigue was perhaps more to blame for Riker's comments than genuine aggravation. "You shouldn't let him bother you so much."

"He's never liked me," replied Riker. Releasing her hand, he pushed himself from the chair and crossed to the replicator set into the room's starboard bulkhead. "Not from the minute I was named captain of the *Enterprise*. Everybody knew that he wanted it, but Starfleet Command gave her to me." Troi waited in silence as he ordered water and a crystal glass materialized on the unit's receiving platform. He drained the glass's contents in one go.

"Do you really believe that?" she asked once he had returned the glass to the replicator. It was easy now to read the feelings of resentment welling up within him, even though he was doing his best to keep them at bay.

Stepping away from the replicator, Riker moved to stand before the viewing ports. He folded his arms, staring at the distant stars. From where she stood, Troi was able to make out part of the Spindrift Nebula off the ship's starboard bow.

"He never told me to my face, if that's what you mean," said Riker after a moment, "but you probably heard the same rumors I did."

She had indeed been privy to gossip and unsubstantiated claptrap that had circulated in the immediate aftermath of the Borg attack and while the *Enterprise* had been assigned to Earth Station McKinley to undergo repairs. Much of the talk revolved around whether Riker, who had already received a promotion and operational command of the starship for the duration of the Borg crisis, would retain the posting or if the prestigious billet of commanding the Federation flagship would be given to another, perhaps more experienced officer. Troi had even been aware of several officers, including Edward Jellico, being considered for the posting. Jellico, at the time in command of the *U.S.S. Cairo*, was believed to have been a leading contender, at least until a small group of senior leaders at Starfleet Command, led by Admiral Alynna Nechayev, put forth their recommendation that Riker be permanently assigned as captain of the *Enterprise*. His noteworthy career and accomplishments to that point had been a prime deciding factor, up to and including his actions against the Borg vessel that had come within moments of destroying or assimilating the people of Earth. Further, the three years Riker had spent under the direct mentorship of Jean-Luc Picard, Starfleet legend and the vessel's original captain, saw to it that no other command-grade officer in the fleet was better prepared to take the center seat of the *Galaxy*-class starship.

"You know he wasn't even due for promotion," said Riker. "Word is that Starfleet Command bumped him up to admiral as a consolation prize." He shrugged. "Naturally, nobody's admitting that, either."

Troi said, "He's one of the few people who can do the job he was given, Will. He has a grasp of tactics that is rare even among Starfleet leadership. Working with people like Commander Shelby and developing long-term defensive plans is perfect for him. Starfleet couldn't do much better than having Admiral Jellico, and right now that's where he's most needed."

His gaze not shifting from the windows, Riker replied, "But Starfleet also needs good captains, and there's no arguing he was one of the best."

"And so are you." Troi reached out and put a hand on his arm, prodding him to turn toward her. "Do you honestly think Starfleet would've entrusted you with the *Enterprise* if they didn't think you were ready for the responsibility? In case you've forgotten, they'd already offered you your own command three times. You were considering the *Melbourne* before the Borg attacked, and you've been captain of this ship for months." She studied his face, noting the doubt behind his eyes and clouding his emotions. "Why this sudden uncertainty? Because of Jellico?"

Riker shook his head, moving to the low-rise couch positioned before the windows. "Not Jellico," he said as he took a seat. "At least, not *just* Jellico. Ever since the orders came through, and with every assignment we've been given, I've had this nagging feeling in the back of my mind that I'm being . . . I don't know. Tested, somehow. *Evaluated*, like Starfleet Command doesn't fully trust me."

He forced another smile, this one accompanied by a small, humorless chuckle. "All that time we were at McKinley undergoing repairs, I couldn't shake the feeling that we were being scrutinized. And after? Look at the assignments we got."

Though she was reluctant to admit it aloud, Troi understood what he meant. Upon completing its refit at Earth Station McKinley and returning to active status, the *Enterprise* and its crew quickly found themselves undertaking tasks that could be described in polite terms as "mundane." With few exceptions, those assignments had kept the starship well within Federation borders, often less than a day's travel from Earth. At the time, Troi confessed to thinking little of it, given the numerous demands for Starfleet resources and the need to pitch in wherever assistance was needed as the fleet worked to overcome the loss of nearly forty starships to the Borg at the Battle of Wolf 359. Only later had she begun to hear the first rumors of Starfleet Command deliberately keeping the *Enterprise* on a short leash. Was the top leadership conducting a very unsubtle review of Riker's ability to occupy the captain's chair, succeeding a man he had admired not just as a commanding officer but also a mentor and friend?

"I know you've been feeling uncertain for some time now." Troi moved to sit next to him. "If it makes you feel better, you hide it rather well, except from me, but it's there."

This time, Riker's smile was genuine. "I never could fool you. Not for a minute."

"Why haven't you mentioned any of this before?"

Riker frowned. "To be honest? I was a little embarrassed by the whole idea. Not just the thought of having a spotlight on me, but my reaction to it." He tapped his chest. "I *know* I'm not some wide-eyed cadet fresh out of the Academy. And I know I've had a solid career to this point. Have I made some mistakes? Absolutely. A few were downright stupid, and there's probably one or two I hope nobody ever finds out about, but otherwise?

I don't need someone else's validation. I'm comfortable with who and what I am."

"But . . . ?" replied Troi, after a moment when he said nothing else. She let the rest of the unspoken question hang in the air between them.

"Yeah." Riker cleared his throat. "But, let's be honest: Jean-Luc Picard set the standard for commanding this ship. He casts a long shadow, and deservedly so. I learned more from three years serving with him than I did the rest of my career. If I'm worried about anything, it's not living up to the example he set, or giving anyone—especially Jellico—a minute's doubt that his trust in me was misplaced. I can deal with everything else, but that?" He shook his head. "I'd never forgive myself, and I think others feel the same way."

It was the first time he had mentioned any of this to Troi, and his emotional unrest was palpable. It washed over her own senses like water lapping at a lake's edge. She also read his attempts to control or even dismiss those troubling feelings, though whether that attempt was for her sole benefit or his own she could not tell.

"I think you're being unfair to yourself," she said after they sat in silence long enough that she could feel him relaxing. "First, there are people at Starfleet Command who believe in you and have full faith in your ability to command this ship. If they didn't, they wouldn't have lobbied for you. We're talking about the *Enterprise,* Will. There's too much history and prestige attached to the name for it to be just given to anyone. It has to be someone who's earned that opportunity, and who can be trusted to represent Starfleet and the Federation to an entire galaxy. You are that person, Will Riker. Don't ever forget it."

Riker offered another uncertain smile. "Well, when you put it that way . . ."

Ignoring his attempt at humor, Troi pressed, "Then there's the crew. Every single one of them elected to remain aboard after our refit. They had opportunities to transfer to other ships or assignments, and they chose to stay here, with *you* as their captain. I can't think of a more convincing display of commitment than that."

"You're right," replied Riker, and when he said it Troi read the conviction behind the words. "On that, you are absolutely right. I'm a little ashamed to admit that I doubted that, even for a second." He rubbed his forehead. "I can be an idiot sometimes."

Troi shifted her position on the couch so that she could lean against him and lay her head on his shoulder. "Yes, you can."

The comment elicited the desired response, and Riker laughed for the first time. It was a genuine laugh as he slipped his arm around her.

"There's something else," he said. "I never did thank you."

"For what?"

"Sticking with me." Riker used his free hand to indicate the room around them. "I was never happier than when we were together, and it was a mistake for me to leave you on Betazed."

Troi laid a hand on his thigh. "You did what you had to do at that point in your life. Your entire career was still ahead of you. I never faulted you for that."

"I'm just glad we had a chance to correct that mistake." Riker laid his hand atop hers. "Having you here with me, I mean *here, with me*, means more to me than anything."

Moving in with him was a decision Troi had not undertaken lightly. Their past history notwithstanding, she had wrestled with how the crew might perceive their relationship. As ship's counselor, she was responsible for the well-being of everyone aboard, be they crew or the spouses, partners, and children of those who had chosen to bring their families on what was to be the *Enterprise*'s long-duration assignment far from home.

Despite her misgivings, there was no denying that they each enjoyed the other's company. Their first night together, a few weeks after the ship had been returned to active status with a mission to ferry Federation diplomats to a conference on Pacifica, had brought back all the passion and vivacity they had enjoyed during their relationship on Betazed. It was as though no time had passed, leading them both to wonder what they had been thinking by electing to maintain a respectful "distance" from each other upon learning they would be serving together on the *Enterprise* under Captain Picard. Thinking back on it, Troi conceded that reluctance had been silly and a waste of time. Once they navigated that initial hurdle, it was as though they had never been apart.

Will we stay together this time?

It was a question Troi had kept to herself, not wanting to dwell on past decisions and feelings. Though she had been heartbroken at his departure all those years ago on Betazed, she had known from the beginning that William Riker would always be a man driven by his ultimate goal of one day commanding a starship. Even though he had expressed his own doubts after being offered command of the *U.S.S. Melbourne* just prior to the Borg attack—worries that he had somehow become complacent or even "comfortable" during his tenure aboard the *Enterprise*—she knew that his true nature would ultimately assert itself, with that passion to excel unable to be denied.

Would he have taken another starship command if Picard had survived? Riker had never offered any thoughts on that subject, and Troi had not asked, and it was no longer relevant. What mattered was that Will Riker now commanded the vessel that carried with it the most honored name and legacy in Starfleet. Was he up to the task?

Yes, Imzadi. *Absolutely.*

And what of her and Riker? Troi knew only time would tell, but for now she was happy. He was happy, and they were happy together.

That was good enough.

The soft, melodic tones of the ship's intraship disturbed their relaxed silence, followed by the voice of the ship's first officer.

"Data to Captain Riker."

Troi shifted her position on the couch as Riker straightened his posture, likely by reflex.

"Riker here."

"I apologize for disturbing you, sir, but you asked to be informed when Commander La Forge and I completed our modifications and launched the sensor probes. All six are away and proceeding to their programmed coordinates to begin their sweeps."

Nodding, Riker replied, "Excellent work, Mister Data. How long until we have any useful information sent back to us?"

"The probes will begin transmitting as soon as they reach their intended starting points and commence their individual surveys, but it will likely be several hours before

I have anything comprehensive to report to you." After a brief pause, the android added, *"Unless we find the planet sooner, of course."*

"Of course," echoed Riker. "Keep me informed. I'll be on the bridge no later than oh-six-hundred hours."

"Understood, sir. Data out."

The communication ended, and Troi used that opportunity to lean back on the couch and against Riker. "Oh-six-hundred hours? That's quite a while." She allowed a bit of teasing to creep into her voice. "How are you planning to pass the time?"

"I was thinking I might try to get some sleep," replied Riker, but his expression told her he knew he was only playing his part in her little impromptu game.

"Think again."

6

HERE

T'Ryssa Chen shifted in her seat, trying to adjust the leg of her environmental suit. Was it too short? Had she somehow gotten a suit that was too small for her? That should not be possible, she decided. There was no way the *Enterprise* computer would have made such an obvious error.

Maybe you're just nervous. Quit fretting.

"*You okay?*"

Looking up from where she had continued to fuss with her suit, Chen stared through her helmet's transparent faceplate and saw the *Enterprise*'s deputy security chief, Lieutenant Rennan Konya, regarding her with no small amount of amusement.

"I'm fine, I guess." Deciding that the suit fit her as intended, she straightened her leg and twisted her foot until she felt the material shift around her lower leg. A glance to the control pad on her left wrist told her that her antics had not compromised her suit's internal pressure.

Satisfied—for the moment, at least—she made a show of looking around the interior of the shuttlecraft *Spinrad*'s passenger compartment. "You, me, environmental suits, and a shuttlecraft. Is it just me, or is this becoming something of a habit?"

Konya directed his eyes toward the compartment's overhead as though giving serious thought to the question. *"Now that you mention it, you do seem to keep coming up with excuses to get me into enclosed spaces with you."*

Sitting next to Konya, Lieutenant Kirsten Cruzen said, *"If you two are going to be like this the whole time, I'm walking the rest of the way."* Another member of the ship's security detachment, she had volunteered to accompany Konya on the away mission. A very dependable officer, and far tougher than her appearance might imply, Chen had liked Cruzen from early on, and the two had worked together on previous away missions. They had even saved each other's lives, which tended to do wonders for strengthening the bonds of friendship.

So, we've got that going for us, which is nice.

"That'd be a neat trick," said Chen, nodding toward the shuttlecraft's rear pressure hatch. "That first step is a real attention-getter."

Cruzen shifted in her seat. *"It'll be worth it, for the peace and quiet."*

"Sounds like a plan," offered Konya. *"How's that old saying go? In space, no one can hear you—"*

The rest of the lieutenant's comment was lost as the *Spinrad* shuddered around them. Internal lighting flickered, and Chen noticed a momentary warbling in the shuttlecraft's engines before their omnipresent hum returned to its normal pitch and the illumination steadied.

"Hello," said Cruzen.

Seated in front of them in the compact vessel's cockpit, Lieutenant Commander Taurik turned in his seat so that he could look over his shoulder. *"My apologies for the disruption. We appear to be encountering a form of electromagnetic interference."*

"I'm starting to wonder if this was such a great idea," said Chen.

To Taurik's left, Worf added, *"We are attempting to compensate, but you should be prepared for the turbulence to continue."*

With quantum fluctuations continuing to emanate from the mysterious planet, coupled with the interference coming from the NGC 8541 nebula, the use of transporters had been ruled out. Commander La Forge and his team of engineers were working on methods to compensate for those difficulties, but it would be a time-consuming process. To that end, La Forge had elected to remain on the *Enterprise*, sending Taurik in his stead.

"It is possible that I erred when opting to eat before our departure," said Doctor Tropp. Sitting to Chen's left, the Denobulan's complexion looked pale behind his helmet's faceplate, and she noted that he was holding one hand to his midsection.

"You're not going to be sick, are you?" asked Konya, his eyes narrowing.

Tropp cleared his throat before replying, *"It is certainly not my intention, though one cannot always predict these sorts of things."*

"Doctor," said Worf from the cockpit, *"if you are ill, we will have to return to the* Enterprise.*"*

Holding up a hand, the Denobulan replied, *"No, Commander. That will not be necessary."* He reached to the control pad on his wrist and tapped a sequence on its recessed keys. *"I am adjusting the mixture of my life-support system to increase my oxygen intake. That should remedy the issue."* A moment later, Chen watched Tropp seem to relax and settle back into his seat.

"Better?" she prompted.

The doctor nodded. *"Yes, thank you. If the issue persists, I have remedies in my medical kit."*

Worf glanced over his shoulder. *"You are certain, Doctor?"*

"Yes, Commander. Please do not allow me to hinder our mission."

Appearing satisfied, the first officer turned back to his controls. *"Proceeding on course."*

The *Spinrad* chose that moment to shake a second time, followed by a new low rumbling that seemed to course along the shuttlecraft's hull.

"For a planet with no atmosphere," said Cruzen, *"this one puts up quite a fuss."*

Without diverting his attention from his console, Taurik replied, *"The electromagnetic disruptions we are encountering appear to emanate from the subterranean power source we detected earlier. Sensor readings from the* Enterprise *were inconclusive, but now that we are closer the origin is evident. These readings do not indicate a naturally occurring phenomenon, but instead an artificial origin. I suspect our flight difficulties will only increase the closer we move to the surface."*

"That's not very encouraging," said Konya.

Over the open communication channel, Captain Picard said, *"Number One, we're attempting to track your course to the surface, but our sensors are still encountering their own interference. I'm leaving it up to you to continue or abort the mission at your discretion."* The open channel emitted static, indicating the continuing problems with the quantum energy and its ability to interfere with communications as well as sensors and transporters.

"*Understood, Captain,*" replied Worf, and Chen thought she detected the smallest of pauses, as though the Klingon were weighing his options, before he added, "*The turbulence we are encountering is within tolerable levels, Captain. I recommend we proceed, at least for the moment.*"

"Very well. We'll continue to keep this channel open. Commander La Forge is working on clearing the remaining interference. Are your sensors picking up anything new from the surface?"

Taurik replied, "*We are able to scan the surface structure we detected during the* Enterprise's *initial sensor sweeps. There is still some interference, but readings show an internal atmosphere approximating Class-M conditions.*"

"That's a relief," said Cruzen, tapping her environmental suit's chest plate. "Maybe we'll be able to peel ourselves out of these things."

Taurik continued his report. "*Power readings are growing more intense as we approach the structure, sir.*"

"What about life signs?" asked the captain.

"*Readings are indistinct, though we are able to confirm that the structure is the only location on the planet within our sensor range that indicates life-form readings.*" The Vulcan added, "*This does not rule out the possibility of areas shielded from our sensors, either as a natural effect of the interference we are experiencing or as a deliberate countermeasure.*"

"We're having the same problem, Commander," said Lieutenant Dina Elfiki over the channel. "*Commander La Forge and I are still working to reconfigure the sensors, but it's slow going.*"

Picard added, *"In other words, proceed with caution, Spinrad."*

The shuttlecraft trembled around them again, and this time the effect was sufficient that Chen reached for the edge of her seat in an attempt to steady herself.

"Inertial dampers and artificial gravity systems just experienced a power fluctuation," reported Taurik. The Vulcan's left hand was moving across the main console in front of him while his other hand moved to the interface panel on the bulkhead to his right. *"Routing power from noncritical systems to compensate."*

As though responding to his report, another tremor rattled the *Spinrad* and another shift in the drone of the compact vessel's engines coursed through the passenger cabin.

"Propulsion systems are now reacting to the interference," reported Taurik.

Holding on to his own seat, Konya said, *"All right, now* my *stomach is starting to get queasy."*

Tropp said, *"I have a treatment for that, Lieutenant."*

"Kidding, Doc."

"Increasing power to deflector shields and modulating their frequency," said Taurik. Chen watched his fingers move across several controls on his console, and a moment later the rough ride began to level out.

"Excellent work, Commander," said Worf.

The engineer replied, *"It is a temporary measure, sir. Modulating the shield frequency allows us to mitigate the interference, but not completely protect us from it. According to our sensor readings, the effects will continue to increase as we maintain our descent toward the surface."*

"Mister Worf?" prompted Picard, and Chen heard the concern in the captain's voice.

"We are maintaining course and speed, Captain," replied the first officer.

A beeping tone from the console caught the attention of everyone, and Taurik indicated a new flashing indicator.

"Power readings from beneath the surface, sir. They appear to be rising. The increase is slow, but steady. I am unable to establish a sensor lock on the source of energy output."

Worf replied, *"Continue to monitor those readings."*

"I can do that, sir," said Chen, Curious as to what she might be missing, she moved from her seat and shifted to one closer to the cockpit. She reached for the compact workstation behind Taurik and activated its control interface.

"Power levels are definitely increasing," she said after instructing the console to tie into the shuttlecraft's sensor array. "Some of these readings are topping the scale. I've never seen anything like them." She pulled up another scan. "Commander Worf, the sensor clutter is starting to clear up a bit. I'm able to get a better look at the surface structure and the life-form readings. There's an area at the structure's far end that looks like it might be a landing bay." With a tap of her controls, she sent the information to the cockpit's center console.

"The entrance appears to be a reinforced pressure hatch," said Taurik after a moment. *"I am detecting an atmosphere beyond that door, and what appear to be small craft with chemical fuel–based propulsion systems. If it is a landing area, then it likely requires a depressurization sequence before the hatch can be opened."*

Cruzen asked, *"So, do we get out and knock?"*

"Are we certain the people inside are even able to respond to our presence?" asked Tropp.

"*That is a very astute question,*" replied Taurik, "*and one for which I do not yet have an answer.*"

Worf said, "*We will maneuver closer and see if there is a reaction to our approach.*"

Straining to look past the first officer and his console and through the *Spinrad*'s forward viewing ports, Chen was just able to make out the jagged peaks of dark mountains, which would be all but invisible if not for the computer-enhanced displays, the shuttlecraft's exterior illumination, and perhaps any external lighting from the structure they were approaching. However, Chen was sure she was noticing . . . something else.

"Where's the light coming from?" she asked.

Taurik replied, "*Uncertain. With no sun, there should be no natural ambient light, but the entire surface appears to possess an odd luminosity. My only theory is that it must be an effect of the nebula, or perhaps the quantum fluctuations and other electromagnetic readings we are detecting.*"

"What about radiation?" asked Worf. "*Are we in any danger from exposure?*"

Checking the readings for herself, Chen replied, "Doesn't look that way, sir."

Over the intership, Lieutenant Elfiki said, "*We're double-checking the readings, but so far you're in the clear.*"

Even with the *Spinrad*'s inertial damping systems, Chen still imagined she felt herself pulled to one side as Worf guided the shuttlecraft in an arc and maintained the vessel's descent. The mountains filled the forward viewing port now that the shuttle had dropped below the taller peaks, and Chen saw the unmistakable curves and straight angles of an artificial structure looming in the near darkness.

"There we go," Chen said, only then realizing that she

had risen from her seat in order to afford herself a better look through the cockpit's canopy. As expected, she could see light sources—both interior and exterior—at various points along the construct's surface, illuminating the ground and nearby foothills. It was not a single building, but instead a series of smaller structures positioned close together and connected by conduits that Chen assumed were access tunnels. The exterior walls of each building rose straight from the ground, with flat roofs topped with what might be equipment clusters.

"Be it ever so humble," she said, to no one in particular. "Somebody calls this place home."

"We're close enough now that somebody could be looking out a window and see us," said Konya, and Chen turned to see that he had moved from his own seat and was now standing behind her.

Another tone sounded in the cabin, this time from Chen's workstation, and she shifted her stance so she could examine the new indicator. "Commander Worf, the power levels are continuing to rise, and now sensors are showing an increase in the rate at which they're building."

"Could it be a reaction to our presence?" asked the first officer. *"Some kind of defensive measure?"*

"I don't think so, sir." Chen reviewed the sensor telemetry again. "I'm not seeing anything that could be construed as a weapon, or any sort of shielding. The structures look to be fairly robust, but they're just . . . well . . . sitting there, sir. No real protection against the elements or attack or anything."

Cruzen said, *"Which is pretty weird when you think about how truly alone they are all the way out here, however many light-years from wherever they're supposed to be."*

"Sure," said Chen, "in *this* dimension, but if they're from a different one? For all we know, there's an entire solar system surrounding us on some parallel plane of existence. How's that for crazy?"

"My head hurts just thinking about it," replied Konya.

A rapid sequence of alert tones made them all turn their attention to the cockpit, where Taurik was pointing to another indicator on his console. *"An incoming communication, sir. From the surface."*

Worf said, *"Captain Picard, are you receiving this new transmission?"*

"Affirmative, Number One, but the signal is very weak and laced with interference. As you're closer, you may fare better with a response."

"Aye, sir." Gesturing for Taurik to open the appropriate frequency, the first officer raised his voice. *"This is Commander Worf of the* Starship Enterprise, *representing the United Federation of Planets. We are here on a peaceful mission of exploration, and we detected your planet and its energy readings. We also intercepted your earlier communication. If you are in distress, we are prepared to offer assistance."*

The first response to his call was a burst of static, which was replaced by a steady hum laced with a stream of hiss. That also dissolved in favor of what to Chen's ears sounded like a female voice.

"Unidentified vessel, you are in great danger. We urge you to leave us immediately for your own safety. There is nothing you can do for us in the time rem—"

The rest of the response was lost amid a new burst of static just as the *Spinrad* rocked with sufficient force to send Chen and Konya tumbling backward into the shuttlecraft's passenger compartment. A quick hand grasping the edge of her workstation kept Chen from falling to the deck, but Konya suffered the indignity of tripping over Doctor Tropp's feet and dropping onto his back.

"*Lieutenant!*" snapped the Denobulan, who was already leaning forward and reaching to assist the security officer.

Holding up a hand, Konya said, "*I'm fine, Doc. Wounded pride, is all.*"

"What's happening?" shouted Chen over a new alarm that had begun blaring inside the cabin. Then her eyes fell on her console's sensor readings. "The subsurface power readings are spiking!"

Around them, the shuttlecraft's entire frame was shuddering in protest as every light and console indicator flickered. The steady thrum of the *Spinrad*'s engines deteriorated into a chaotic fit of coughs and sputters, and her stomach lurched as the artificial gravity wavered for a frantic moment before returning to normal.

"*Spinrad, what's your status?*" asked Picard over the comm channel.

Taurik, his gaze fixed on his controls, tapped a control and the klaxon stopped. "*The quantum fluctuations are intensifying and beginning to interfere with our onboard systems.*"

"*We need to move away from the power source,*" said Worf, who was already moving his hands across his own console. "*Increasing power to thrusters.*"

Chen dropped back into her seat, one hand gripping her console as she used the other to call up a status report for the shuttle's onboard systems.

"*I'm starting to think we may have a problem,*" said Cruzen.

Another alarm sounded, and Chen scanned the cockpit console to locate its source, but then the cause for the alert became obvious as the *Spinrad*'s engines died.

"Impulse drive is offline," reported Worf.

Taurik said, *"With only maneuvering thrusters, we will be unable to achieve escape velocity."*

"What about the warp drive?" asked Konya. Chen cast a glance over her shoulder and saw that he had pulled himself from the deck and returned to his seat.

"No," replied Taurik. *"Quantum fluctuations are strong enough that they would interfere with our ability to generate a subspace field. Further, given our proximity to the planet's surface, attempting such an action would be inherently hazardous."*

Another wave of power fluctuations coursed through the shuttlecraft's interior. Lights and consoles flickered, and the *Spinrad* seemed to drop several meters and list to port before regaining its attitude. Chen turned in her seat to see Tropp looking toward the cockpit. Concern clouded his features.

"What about landing?" asked the Denobulan.

Worf said, *"That may be our safest option, assuming we can maintain power and control."* Without looking away from his console, he called in a louder voice, *"Everyone assume crash positions. We will attempt to land close to the structure."*

Pushing himself from his command chair, Picard stepped closer to the forward conn and ops stations, his gaze riveted on the bridge's main viewscreen and the image of the planet depicted upon it. He imagined he could see the shuttlecraft *Spinrad*, attempting to maintain control as Worf and Commander Taurik endeavored to bring the tiny vessel to a safe landing.

"Mister Worf?" he prompted.

The first officer's voice boomed through the intership, *"All power systems are being disrupted. We are making our final descent now."*

"We've still got a sensor lock on them, Captain," said Lieutenant Aneta Šmrhová, the *Enterprise*'s chief of security, from where she stood at the main tactical station behind and just to the left of the captain's chair. "Their course is erratic, but they're holding steady for a controlled landing."

"Mister La Forge," said Picard, without looking from the screen. "Transporters?"

Working at one of the bridge's rear engineering stations, Geordi La Forge replied, "Not from this distance, Captain; not with the elevated quantum fluctuations and electromagnetic interference."

"Can we move closer?" asked Lieutenant Dina Elfiki, turning in her seat at the science station. "The planet has no atmosphere, after all."

Lieutenant Joanna Faur looked first to the young science officer before turning her attention to Picard. "It'd be risky, sir. We'd be subjected to the same interference the shuttlecraft's dealing with."

"But only for a few moments," countered Glinn Ravel Dygan, the young Cardassian exchange officer who currently manned the ops station to Faur's left. "If we modulate our deflector shield frequency in a manner similar to what Commander Taurik did with the shuttlecraft, we should be protected long enough to descend to a safe transporter distance."

Picard turned toward La Forge. "Geordi?"

"It could work," replied the chief engineer, "but it'd be a hell of a rough ride, and that's before we'd have to drop the shields to beam them out of there." He nodded to Dygan. "It would only have to be for a couple of minutes."

For the briefest of moments, Picard considered the notion that it had taken just about that same interval of time for the *Spinrad* to encounter its own difficulties, but he quickly dismissed the errant thought when he heard Worf over the speakers, his voice laced with static.

"Spinrad *to* Enterprise. *We are on the ground. The shuttle itself has sustained damage, but life-support systems are functioning, and we have no significant injuries.*"

"Stand by, Number One," said Picard. "We're putting together a retrieval plan." He looked to La Forge. "Make your preparations."

Šmrhová reported, "We've still got a lock on them, sir, though the sensor readings are really muddled now that they're on the surface."

"Captain," said Elfiki, "sensors are also picking up a new spike in the quantum energy readings. I'm . . ."

She paused, and when she said nothing else after a few seconds Picard turned to see her hunched over her controls, leaning toward one of the station's display monitors and tapping rapid sequences of commands to her console.

"Lieutenant?" he said.

Shaking her head, the science officer replied, "I'm having to recalibrate to properly measure the readings, sir. They're off our normal scales."

"Is the away team in any danger?" Picard asked as he moved toward her.

"I'm not sure, but I don't know if I'd want to stick around down there for any length of time. I've never seen anything like these readings, sir."

"Mister La Forge," said Picard, "your shield modifications?"

His attention on his station, the engineer replied, "Still working on it, Captain."

Not good enough, Picard decided. "We'll just have to make do. Full power to the shields. Route from nonessential systems, if necessary, at your discretion." Stepping closer to the conn station, he said to Faur, "Lieutenant, are you ready?"

She nodded. "As ready as I'll ever be, sir."

Picard was unable to resist a small smile. "Make it s—"

"No!"

The cry of alarm made Picard turn to where Elfiki had spun in her seat, pushing herself away from her station. "Captain, the quantum flux! It's the planet. The entire planet is starting to shift out of phase!"

"What?" Returning his attention to the viewscreen, Picard stared at the planet, the image of which seemed not to have changed at all. It hung there, lifeless, against the backdrop of the nebula, as though doing its level best to dissuade anyone or anything in taking any sort of interest in it.

And then, as Picard stared, the world began to . . . *ripple?*

"*Enterprise* to away team!" The words were out of his mouth before he even realized he was speaking. "Mister Worf, can you hear me?"

Static laced the first officer's reply as it erupted from the intership. "*Worf here, Cap . . . thing happeni . . . own here. We are attem—*" The rest of the response vanished in another burst of electronic squawk.

On the viewscreen, the unnamed planet wavered, and

even seemed to expand or stretch for a brief moment, then appeared to pull in on itself, shrinking within an increasing cascade effect before disappearing in a flash of light and leaving only the multihued gases of the NGC 8541 nebula to fill the viewscreen.

"Oh, my god," said Faur. Breaking her gaze from the screen, she turned to look at Picard, and the captain saw her expression of disbelief mirrored on the faces of the other bridge officers.

He forced himself to maintain his composure as he processed what had just happened. Though the nebula beckoned to him from the viewscreen, the planet—and his people—were gone.

But to where?

7

ELSEWHERE
U.S.S. Enterprise-D

Riker strode into the observation lounge to find the rest of his senior staff already assembled. Standing at the viewscreen set into the room's far wall, Data turned and nodded in greeting as the rest of his officers rose from their chairs in deference to their captain.

"As you were," he said, motioning for everyone to keep their seats as he moved to the chair at the head of the conference table. To his right, the ports making up the room's aft wall offered an unfettered view of the Spindrift Nebula and the curtain of uncounted distant stars. It would be so easy to get lost in the wonder and beauty on display before him, even without the interesting mystery it had deposited at his feet.

Settling into his chair, Riker took in the faces of his officers—Data, Geordi La Forge, Natasha Yar, Doctor Katherine Pulaski, and Deanna—exchanging nods with each of them and even sparing a small grin for Wesley Crusher. Like Deanna and very much unlike the rest of the senior staff, the young man wore typical civilian attire that offered mute testimony to his status not as a member of the *Enterprise* crew but instead a Starfleet technical advisor given a long-term assignment to the starship.

"Wes," said Riker, "good to see you. Thanks very much for pitching in to help Data and Geordi." According to the reports Riker had received from Data and La Forge, Crusher had been assisting with data collection from the automated probes in the nebula for the past several hours, working through the night in order to afford the chief engineer some much-needed rest.

Nodding, Wesley replied, "No problem, Captain. We've been receiving data from the probes for the past couple of hours, but so far nothing interesting has popped up. There's no sign of the planet. At least, not yet."

"What about the nebula itself?" asked Riker. "Surely we've got enough information now to know whether it poses any danger to us or the ship."

"The nebula's background radiation levels are well below any level that might pose a potential risk," said Data. "The *Enterprise*'s hull will provide ample protection in that regard."

Pulaski added, "I've reviewed Mister Data's reports on this, and I concur. Even if we end up needing to send someone outside the ship in an EV suit, they would be protected, and I can increase that protection with hyronalin to counter any effects of possible radiation exposure."

"Good." Riker nodded, pleased that at least one potential source of trouble was off the table. "So, the crew is safe, but our equipment is still a bit hampered in here."

"That's correct, sir," said La Forge. "Sensors are the biggest issue, but the nebula would also interfere with different systems to varying degrees, depending on the situation. We've been able to counter most of the problems with communications, but something like the transporter would be trickier. As for the sensors, that's a bit of an ongoing battle, but we're making progress there too." He nodded to where Data still stood at the viewscreen. "We figured out a few things while reconfiguring the probes, and now we're applying those ideas to the *Enterprise*'s sensor array."

Riker replied, "That's a lot of work in a short time. I appreciate everything you've both done."

"We didn't do it all by ourselves," said the chief engineer, gesturing to Wesley. "Wes was a big help." For his part, the younger man sat in silence and offered a slight, graceful nod, even though his cheeks blushed with momentary embarrassment.

La Forge's compliment was not unique. It was a common observation Riker had heard from numerous crew members almost from the beginning of his tenure aboard the *Enterprise*. He, Wesley Crusher, and the boy's mother, Doctor Beverly Crusher, had come aboard the newly commissioned starship at the same time, having first met on Deneb IV while awaiting the vessel's arrival. It had become obvious in rather short order that Wes, then just a teenager, was a gifted young man with a bright future and all but limitless potential. His grasp of science and engineering concepts far surpassed that of his peers, and his thirst for learning was unquenchable. Even Captain Picard, who had admitted to Riker his discomfort with being around children and his concern with being responsible for a ship filled with families, found himself taken with the boy. Riker was certain at least some of that came from Picard's previous relationship with Wesley's parents, and the tragic circumstances surrounding the death of the boy's father, who, like his mother, had also been a Starfleet officer.

It seemed for a time that Wes might follow in his parents' footsteps and pursue a Starfleet career. Picard had encouraged Wesley, offering the boy access to a course of study and areas of the ship that would assist him in his preparations to one day attend Starfleet Academy. This had culminated in the captain bestowing upon him the provisional rank of "acting ensign," which afforded him even greater opportunity to assist members of the crew and to partake in assignments pertaining to the operation and even safety of the *Enterprise*.

However, it soon became obvious that for all his talents, Wesley Crusher had no real yearning to become a Starfleet officer. Deanna had been the first to see that, and had talked first to him and Doctor Crusher, who in turn had discussed it with Picard. Rather than expressing disappointment, the captain instead supported the young man's decision and made sure that he continued to benefit from his time spent living on the *Enterprise*. In short order, Wesley's technical knowledge and expertise saw to it that he became an integral part of the crew, assisting the engineering and science departments on numerous tasks, including more than a few emergencies. When Doctor Crusher elected to leave the ship after only a year in order to serve as the head of Starfleet Medical, Wesley chose to remain aboard. His talents and contributions eventually convinced Starfleet to authorize him for service as a fully sanctioned civilian technical consultant. As much as anyone on the ship and perhaps more than most, he had taken Captain Picard's death hard. Like every other member of the crew, he had chosen to remain aboard the *Enterprise*, continuing to serve it and Starfleet as though driven by the need to honor the man who once had commanded this starship, and who had sacrificed everything to protect it.

"I guess we can inform Starfleet to extend Mister Crusher's contract a little while longer," said Riker, punctuating the comment with a broad grin that earned him a few polite chuckles. Once that moment had passed, he leaned forward in his chair and rested his forearms on the conference table. "All right, so the planet's still playing hide-and-seek with us. Either our sensors are really fouled up, the damned planet is somehow moving within the nebula to stay hidden, or else it's just not here anymore. I'm not buying the idea that our sensors are that ineffective, and I think we all know planets don't really move the way this one would have to to keep us from finding it. That leaves option number three, and I'm betting even the sensor data we've collected so far will at least support the theory." He raised his head to look to where his first officer remained at the table's far end. "Any chance you can prove me wrong, Mister Data?"

The android shook his head. "I am unable to do so, Captain, as the sensor readings are supporting a hypothesis I have been formulating: The residual quantum fluctuations we detected suggest a form of interdimensional shift has taken place that has somehow affected the entire planet. However, our sensors have detected nothing that might suggest a naturally occurring phenomenon is responsible."

"I'm no scientist," said Lieutenant Yar, "but that sounds like it'd have to be one very large shift, which would require a lot of power to pull off. That would line up with the energy readings we detected coming from the planet."

La Forge replied, "That's our thinking too. That underground fusion reactor they have must be huge, along with whatever technology was constructed to produce the dimensional shift in the first place."

"That does raise a few questions," said Troi. "If we are talking about an artificial mechanism, then who built it, and why?"

Yar nodded. "I was thinking the same thing."

"I know the Romulans are an easy choice for something like this," said Riker, "but we've already ruled them out, based on the residual energy signatures. Any other viable candidates? I doubt the Klingons would be devoting time and energy to something like this. What about the Cardassians?"

"Cardassian technology is not consistent with the readings we have detected," replied Data. "Also, given the current state of their military, it seems unlikely that they would be expending resources toward an effort of this type."

Riker shifted in his seat. "Fair enough. One can never be sure when it comes to them, especially these days."

The Federation had been dealing with fallout from its conflict with the Cardassian Union for nearly two decades. The border and territorial skirmishes, while costly to Starfleet and Federation interests, had caused a much greater level of instability for the Cardassians. It had been years since any major engagements, and it was only months ago that an actual truce had been enacted, bringing the hostilities to a formal end. Now the two interstellar powers were dealing with the ramifications of the armistice, and there were those on both sides who doubted the treaty would hold.

I guess we'll see what we see.

"The level of technology required to accomplish such a feat would seem to limit the number of potential responsible parties," said Data.

"Here's an interesting thought," said Pulaski. "Could

it be us? Some kind of classified Starfleet research and development project we've found by accident?"

Reaching up to stroke his beard, Riker replied, "I'll admit I considered that, but only a little while ago. I wish I'd thought to ask Admiral Jellico something along those lines during our last conversation." That, at least, would have made it worth his while after the admiral had roused him from sleep with his supposedly "urgent" request for an update. "However, I'm betting Data and Geordi can rule that out."

"The power signatures and other readings we took aren't consistent with anything we've got," said La Forge. "I guess that doesn't absolutely rule out some kind of highly classified effort, but I'm having a hard time believing we couldn't at least find something to connect to Starfleet or at least some form of technology we're familiar with."

Pulaski said, "It wouldn't be the first time Starfleet's pulled something like this, you know."

"I've heard stories." Though he said nothing else, Riker knew about such things all too well. He had even been involved in such a project, years ago at the beginning of his Starfleet career.

His final hours as an ensign aboard the *U.S.S. Pegasus*, and the mutiny that had ensued aboard that starship, still found ways on occasion to haunt his dreams. The uprising had occurred after an explosion in the ship's engineering section, which revealed that an experimental phased cloaking device had been installed. A direct violation of the Federation's peace agreement with the Romulan Empire, the Treaty of Algeron, this new cloaking technology was intended as a Starfleet countermeasure to be used in any future dealings with the Romulans. The tactical advantages presented by such technology were obvious, but the consequences of its existence becoming known to the Empire were dire.

Members of the crew, including members of the ship's senior staff, believed they had been duped by illegal orders issued by the *Pegasus*'s commanding officer, Captain Erik Pressman. They attempted to relieve Pressman of his command, and the situation quickly devolved into a firefight throughout the wounded ship, with Pressman and those loyal to him forced to leave the *Pegasus*. During the skirmish, Ensign William Riker, only months removed from his graduation from Starfleet Academy, found himself defending his captain from what he perceived at the time to be riotous mutineers. He and eight other officers, including Pressman, were able to flee the ship in escape pods, and they watched, helpless, from a distance as the *Pegasus* was consumed by a massive explosion. A warp core breach? Had the damage to the vessel's engineering section been that extensive? A sensor sweep of the area showed no sign of a disaster beacon, meaning that the truth behind the starship's destruction might forever remain a mystery.

Only in the aftermath of the ship's loss did Captain Pressman inform Riker about the truth behind the accident, along with its larger ramifications with respect to Federation relations with the Romulans. There would be inquiries, the captain explained, and it was important that the information provided to Starfleet be as factual and accurate as possible. Riker recalled being confused by Pressman's instructions. How could he lie? So secret was the phased cloak project that he had not known anything about it until after the explosion, and only then because the ship's first officer had taken Pressman to task for the accident. To this day, owing mostly to strict orders and the thick veil of secrecy under which the entire project was shrouded, Riker had never said anything to anyone about his assignment to the *Pegasus*, but he often wondered what had happened aboard the ship during those final, dreadful moments.

Maybe it's better to just not know.

The audio signal for the intraship sounded, followed by the voice of Lieutenant Worf.

"Bridge to Captain Riker. Sorry to disturb you, sir, but one of the sensor drones has detected something new."

Exchanging glances with his staff, Riker pushed himself to his feet, and everyone followed suit. "On our way."

The door leading to the short passageway that connected the observation lounge to the bridge parted at Data's approach and the first officer paused at the threshold, allowing Riker to be the first to exit. Upon entering the bridge, Riker's first action was to glance to the main viewscreen, which continued to display an image of the Spindrift Nebula.

"What've you got, Lieutenant?" he asked.

Standing at the tactical station located on the elevated platform just behind the captain's chair, Worf nodded toward the viewscreen. "Captain, probe number four detected a similar, weaker series of quantum fluctuations coming from the area it was sweeping. Its onboard computer automatically adjusted its course to investigate and found this."

The Klingon officer entered a string of commands to his console, and a moment later the image on the viewscreen shifted. Though the backdrop provided by the nebula looked largely the same, Riker recognized the change in perspective as well as the density of the gas clouds that masked the view of distant stars. Of greater interest to the captain was the odd, cylindrical object now drifting at the center of the screen.

"Hello, stranger," said La Forge, who had moved to one of the bridge's rear workstations. Glancing over his shoulder, Riker saw that the chief engineer was calling up whatever program or process he and Data had created to oversee the sensor probes and their activities.

"Any guesses?" asked Riker.

Data, now standing next to La Forge, replied, "It appears to be an unmanned vessel. Sensors indicate it is three point seven meters in length and one point six meters in diameter, and its outer shell is composed of a substance for which there is no record in the ship's computer banks."

"Some kind of drone or buoy?" asked Wesley, who had descended the ramp from the back of the bridge and was now standing just behind the unoccupied flight controller's station.

"Looks like it," replied La Forge. "It's broadcasting some kind of communications signal, but I have no idea who the intended recipient might be, and it gets better." Turning from the workstation, he moved to stand next to where Yar had relieved Worf at the tactical station while the Klingon returned to the ops position. "If I'm reading this sensor information correctly, that thing's in a state of flux. In fact, the sensors were having trouble at first deciding if it's even there, but I think I've got it sorted it out now. It's definitely there, but it's like it's caught in the midst of an interdimensional shift."

Shifting his gaze to Data, Riker asked, "Can you confirm that?"

"I am attempting to do so, Captain," replied the android, "but the quantum fluctuations emanating from the device appear to be interfering with the probe's sensors. I have instructed the probe to remain at what I believe is a safe distance, which would have an effect on the quality of scans it conducts. However, the *Enterprise*'s sensor array would provide better returns, if we were to move closer."

"Let's do that, then," said Riker. "Mister Crusher, you mind taking conn?"

The younger man smiled. "Not at all, sir."

Sliding into the flight controller's seat, Crusher offered Worf a silent nod as they both set to their respective tasks, with Wesley taking on the responsibility of maneuvering the *Enterprise* deeper into the nebula as La Forge sent him the proper coordinates. Moving at one-quarter impulse power, it took only moments for the starship to cover the distance separating it from the sensor probe and the mysterious object it had found.

"The closer proximity is proving most helpful," said Data, and Riker turned to see his first officer engrossed in the information streaming across the engineering workstation's primary display. "A dimensional shift does appear to have occurred, but the effect on this device is most unusual. According to our sensor readings, the object is holding steady at a point where it has only partially transitioned from our dimension." He turned from the console. "Based on the available information, I theorize that this device is deliberately occupying a fixed point between at least two separate dimensions."

"What about that communication signal?" asked Yar. The security chief was propping herself against the tactical station with one hand, her stance allowing her to lean toward the railing behind the captain's chair.

La Forge replied, "We've got the computer working on it, but it doesn't seem to be aimed at anything in our vicinity. It's on such a low-power frequency that it'd take years—maybe decades—for someone to pick it up, and even then it's a long shot." He paused, his gaze shifting to the viewscreen. "It might be transmitting to something in that other dimension, though."

"It is even possible that the object is interacting with more than two dimensions," said Data.

Having taken her customary seat in the chair next to Riker's in the command area, Troi asked, "If the planet we're looking for has also shifted from our dimension, could the buoy somehow be in contact with it?"

"That is an intriguing possibility, Counselor," replied the first officer. "The signatures from the quantum fluctuations it appears to be generating are similar to what we recorded from the planet, though on a much smaller scale. An examination of the device's internal components could prove most enlightening."

"Yeah," said La Forge, "but the trick is that because it's locked in this odd phase shift, we can't scan inside it. The only way we'd likely have a chance is if it shifted completely back to our dimension."

Riker descended the ramp on the bridge's port side and made his way to his chair. "Any chance we could find a way to make it complete that shift?"

"Perhaps," said Data, "but without more information, we cannot know whether such action might have a detrimental effect, either on the buoy or anything else in the immediate vicinity."

"Let's try to avoid that, then," offered Pulaski, who had been standing quietly at the back of the bridge, observing the proceedings. The doctor now was moving to the command area and, without waiting for an invitation, took the seat normally reserved for Data. "I know we decided these odd fluctuations didn't pose a danger to the crew, Captain, but that was before we started talking about messing around with alien technology that's obviously doing some strange things."

Riker said, "Your concern's appreciated, Doctor. We're not going to be charging blindly into anything. We've taken our time to this point, and I don't see any reason to alter that. Data, Geordi, Wes: You three continue your investigation. I want to know who or what that buoy is talking to." Glancing at the chronometer set into the arm of his chair, Riker saw that it was close to eleven hundred hours, shipboard time. "Mister Data, what time is it at Starfleet Headquarters?"

Without hesitating, the first officer replied, "Oh-two-fifty-one hours, sir."

Releasing a small chuckle that made Troi and Pulaski regard him with similar expressions of surprise, Riker smiled. "Middle of the night. Seems like the perfect time to update Admiral Jellico."

Troi said, "Will, really?"

"Really."

"You're an evil man, Captain William Riker," added Pulaski, and he heard the note of approval in her voice.

"Evil?" Riker shook his head. "No. Just obeying orders and keeping my superiors informed."

8

ELSEWHERE

"Ow."

Blinking several times in rapid succession did nothing to alleviate the visual chaos that seemed to be dominating T'Ryssa Chen's vision, and that frenzy was now manifesting itself as a headache that felt as though her skull might come apart. She started to reach for her temples, realizing in midmotion that she was still wearing her environmental suit, and her helmet and faceplate remained in place.

"Is everyone all right?" asked Worf, who like Taurik had moved from the *Spinrad*'s cockpit into the shuttlecraft's passenger compartment.

Shifting in her seat, Chen saw the *Enterprise*'s first officer assisting Doctor Tropp from the deck back to one of the bench seats, while Taurik was offering a hand to Lieutenant Konya. Beyond them near the shuttle's rear hatch, Lieutenant Cruzen was examining the control pad on her EV suit's left wrist, as though inspecting it for damage. Her right hand was pressed against the side of her helmet as though she, too, were trying to massage her head.

"You know how we take shore leave on some planet?" said Cruzen, now apparently satisfied that her suit or its controls had not been compromised. *"We drink too much of the local spirits instead of sticking with synthehol, and we end up with headaches that could split fault lines?"*

Groaning as he allowed Taurik to pull him to his feet, Konya replied, *"Yeah?"*

"I wish I felt that good right now."

Konya offered a rough, dry laugh, followed by a cough. *"Copy that."* Turning in his seat, he cast a look at Chen. *"You okay?"*

Hearing the mixture of professional and personal concern in his voice, she nodded. "I'm fine. You?"

"I'll live. Lucky you, right?" He ended the question with a smile. Though he tended to avoid displays of affection in public, and certainly while on duty, Konya did allow himself the occasional deviation, which often had the effect of embarrassing her. Right on schedule, she felt her cheeks warming in response to his infectious grin and even the mischievous leer he directed her way. She reached over and punched him in the arm.

"Behave yourself."

Having regained his feet, Tropp asked, *"Is anyone else suffering ill effects from . . . whatever that was?"*

Other than bruises as well as head and muscle aches and—in Konya's case—a sprained wrist, which the doctor was able to treat in moments with the help of his medical kit, there were no other serious injuries. After verifying that the shuttlecraft's internal atmosphere had not been compromised, Worf instructed everyone to remove their helmets, which afforded Tropp the opportunity to administer analgesics and anti-inflammatory agents to everyone.

"Any idea what happened?" asked Chen as she rubbed the sides of her head. The medication Tropp had given her acted fast, but she was still experiencing residual pain. "The last thing I remember was everything spinning and then my vision going to hell."

After the somewhat harrowing landing to which Worf and Taurik had brought the *Spinrad* on the planet's surface, there had barely been time to assess damage and injuries before everyone aboard the shuttlecraft began experiencing what Chen could only describe as an odd vertigo. A sensation not unlike nausea swept over her, and she even felt herself break out in a cold sweat as wind seemed to howl in her ears. Light and color flooded her vision, washing away everything and everyone around her. The entire effect faded within seconds, leaving her panting and partially blinded until her awareness returned, and Chen found herself staring at her equally bewildered and disheveled shipmates.

Once more seated at his controls in the *Spinrad*'s cockpit, Taurik replied, "Based on the surge in power levels from the subterranean facility as well as the spike in quantum energy readings, coupled with our apparent inability to contact the *Enterprise* even though our communications equipment is undamaged, I am beginning to believe that we have experienced an interdimensional shift."

Cruzen, having risen to her feet, made her way to the front of the passenger area. "You're saying we're still here on the planet, but in a different dimension?"

"No," replied Chen. Though she was listening to Taurik, she also was examining scan data from her own workstation behind the cockpit. "Our sensors are still functional—at least to a point—and I'm not picking up any sign of the *Enterprise*, but there's something else." She pointed to a collection of information scrolling past on one of her console's display screens. "The nebula's not there, either."

"Want to run that by us again?" asked Konya.

Instead, Taurik replied, "NGC 8541 no longer appears on any of our scans."

Worf said, "You are saying that the planet itself has moved from one dimension to another?"

"Based on the available information," said the Vulcan engineer, "that is the most likely explanation. I am still unable to get a sensor lock on the source of the quantum fluctuations. It is there, but it is as though it is protected by a force field or other scattering technology. Were the shuttlecraft capable of flight, we could ascend to orbit and attempt to gain a fix on our position using the stellar cartography database in the onboard computer, but I am afraid that without repairs to our propulsion system, that is not a viable option at this time."

"Any chance we can make some repairs ourselves?" asked Chen. "You're a pretty good engineer, last time I checked, and I'm not exactly a slouch in that department. Between the two of us, we should be able to jury-rig something, right?"

Taurik seemed to consider the possibility before shaking his head. "Given sufficient time and tools, we might be able to devise a temporary solution that would allow us to attain orbit and perhaps attempt to contact the *Enterprise*. My preliminary examination of the damage to our systems leads me to conclude that such a solution is beyond our current capabilities. However, I have not yet had the opportunity to examine the engines from outside. Doing so will require us to don our suit helmets and depressurize the shuttlecraft interior." He turned to Worf. "With your permission, Commander?"

"We will all go," replied the first officer. "Konya and Cruzen, draw phaser rifles from the weapons locker and establish a secure perimeter outside the shuttlecraft." He pointed in what everyone now knew was the general direction of the group of buildings several hundred meters south of the *Spinrad*'s current position. "Just in case. Everyone else will carry standard sidearms. Set phasers to stun, and . . . we shall see what happens."

The security officers exchanged glances, and Chen knew what they were thinking. Along with the interference already being experienced with transporters, sensors, and even communications, the quantum fluctuations permeating the planet's surface were also having an adverse effect on phasers. Lieutenant Elfiki had been the one to break that good news as part of the away team's final briefing, warning them that the weapons would be unreliable at best.

"Unreliable is better than nothing," remarked Cruzen at the time.

Given the limited number of life-forms on the surface and the apparent absence of anything resembling weapons that could pose a threat to the shuttlecraft or even the *Enterprise*, Worf had expressed confidence in the team's ability to carry out their mission. If a Klingon warrior could handle it, Chen decided she could, as well.

It took only moments for the away team to put on their helmets and reestablish the seals of their individual EV suits before Taurik keyed the controls to remove the atmosphere from the shuttlecraft's interior. With a final nod from Worf to proceed, the engineer pressed another key on his console.

"Opening rear hatch," he called out, and the team turned their attention aft as the heavy door that formed the *Spinrad*'s aft bulkhead began to lower. Chen was not surprised to see the near darkness that greeted them, broken only by the shuttle's exterior lighting and illumi-

nation from the distant cluster of buildings. Then she realized that she had expected to see something else.

"Hey. That odd luminosity we saw before? What happened to it?"

Carrying an open and activated tricorder in his gloved hand, Taurik replied, "*Interesting. I am detecting no residual energy or radiation signatures that might account for that effect.*"

"*We can investigate that later,*" said Worf, "*after we ascertain the damage to the shuttle.*"

Taurik turned toward the *Spinrad*. "*Understood, Commander.*"

"I can help with the inspection," said Chen, reaching for the tricorder that rested in its holster on her left hip. She had only given the shuttlecraft a quick visual once-over after disembarking, scrutinizing the dents and tears in the compact vessel's port warp nacelle. She had predicted that much, judging from the broken, uneven soil surrounding them, from which jutted portions of rocks and boulders of varying shapes and sizes. Behind the *Spinrad* and extending for several dozen meters, she saw the trail carved into the ground by the shuttle as it had come in for its rough landing. The newly plowed soil rested on either side of the shallow ditch, and Chen saw bits of crystal and other minerals mixed in with the pale dirt.

"*I'm in position twenty meters in front of the shuttle,*" reported Konya, and Chen shifted her stance so she could see where he now stood, wielding the phaser rifle he had withdrawn from the *Spinrad*'s weapons compartment. His tone indicated he was all business now, his attention focused on his responsibilities and the safety of the rest of his team.

"I've got our backs," said Cruzen, and Chen saw that the security officer had moved in a straight line from the *Spinrad*'s rear hatch and now was standing with her own phaser rifle at the same approximate distance from the shuttle as Konya. The weapon was cradled in the crook of her right arm as she studied a tricorder in her left hand, searching for signs of anyone approaching.

Her attention once more on the shuttlecraft's port nacelle, Chen used her tricorder to confirm her initial damage estimate. "There's some minor buckling over here, but I think we can work with it."

Though he was on the other side of the shuttle, Taurik's voice still sounded loud and clear in her helmet speakers. *"The starboard nacelle has ruptured. I am afraid repairing it is beyond the limits of the resources we have available. However, if the port nacelle has not suffered significant damage, we should still be able to achieve orbit and return to the* Enterprise.*"*

Chen's tricorder warbled as she pointed it at the *Spinrad*'s port nacelle. "We'll want to run a full diagnostic on it just to be sure, but so far I'm not seeing anything that's a deal breaker." She caught sight of Taurik stepping around the shuttle's slanted bow, his own tricorder aimed at the side of the craft.

"Though there is some minor structural damage as a consequence of the landing, I am detecting no signs of a hull breach." He reached to adjust one of the tricorder's settings. *"The deflector shield emitters on the underside are also damaged."*

"All things considered," said Chen, "we were pretty lucky."

Tropp said, *"A testament to the flying skills of both Commander Worf and Mister Taurik."*

"*Heads up, everybody,*" said Cruzen. "*We've got company coming from the structures.*"

That didn't take long, thought Chen. The rest of the away team moved to where Cruzen was standing, facing away from the *Spinrad* and toward the cluster of buildings. Despite the low lighting, Chen was able to make out a half-dozen figures walking across the rocky, uneven ground.

"*Six of them, six of us,*" said Konya, who, unlike the rest of the team, had elected to take up a position near the shuttlecraft's open rear hatch. "*Coincidence?*"

Cruzen, her tricorder still in her left hand, had adjusted her grip on her phaser rifle so that its barrel now lay atop her left arm with her right hand on its grip, ready to fire if necessary. "*They're not armed. Not even a knife or club. They're wearing a type of environmental suit, but not as advanced as ours. Instead of atmospheric regenerators, they're simply carrying tanks with whatever it is they're breathing.*"

"*You already determined that Class-M conditions exist inside the structure,*" said Tropp.

Taurik replied, "*That is what our scans indicated, Doctor.*"

"*Since it looks like we're going to be here a while,*" said Cruzen, "*maybe we shouldn't be too picky.*"

Worf, moving to stand in front of the rest of the away team, said, "*Lieutenant Cruzen, lower your weapon. Mister Konya, maintain your position. Everyone else, keep your phasers holstered.*" Chen almost offered a remark about the first officer's very un-Klingon attitude toward the new arrivals, but thought better of it.

Time and place, Lieutenant. In her head, Chen

thought she could hear Captain Picard offering the gentle reminder.

The approaching group stopped with several meters separating them from the away team. All of them appeared humanoid, at least so far as their environmental suits allowed. The protective garments were bulky, comprised of a gray material that Chen guessed was thick and possessing of several layers, with the extremities terminating in oversized boots and gloves. None of the suits possessed any patches or identifying symbols or markings, and each person wore a large rectangular pack on their back, with a tube running from it to the back of the wearer's helmet. The helmet itself consisted of a large transparent globe, the back half of which was covered by the same material as that used for the suit.

One of the group members, the apparent leader, held its hands up to its chest, crossing them at the wrists before bowing slightly at the waist. At least to Chen, the gesture seemed obvious.

Welcome?

"Lieutenant Chen," said Worf. *"You are our contact specialist."*

He left any addendum to that sentence unspoken, and Chen realized that was her cue to join him at the front of the group. She glanced at him, hoping her expression conveyed at least some of the uncertainty she felt.

Use your brain, T'Rrys.

Holding up her tricorder, she displayed the device to the new arrivals and also showed them her open and empty right hand. With her thumb, she keyed a control on the unit to activate its scan feature.

"Okay, their suits have communications equipment. It's just not as sophisticated as ours. The frequencies they use are pretty low, but our transceivers should still be able to adapt." After providing the correct frequency to the rest of her team, Chen deactivated the tricorder and returned it to its holder on her hip. She then looked to Worf, who nodded in understanding before turning to face the other group.

"Are you able to hear me?" he asked. *"I am Commander Worf, first officer of the* Starship Enterprise *and representing the United Federation of Planets. We are here on a mission of peaceful exploration and intend no harm toward you."*

The reaction among the visitors was immediate as they began looking to one another. Then the group's leader stepped forward and extended its arms away from its body in an obvious signal of greeting.

"Welcome to our world, travelers."

It was a female voice, Chen realized. At least, it had been rendered by the communications system's universal translation protocols as feminine, and it was familiar.

"You're the one from the message," Chen said. "You warned us to stay away."

The new arrival nodded. *"Yes, that was me. I am Nelidar."* She motioned to the rest of her group. *"We call ourselves the Sidrac, but you appear to represent more than one species."*

With Worf prompting her to continue, Chen replied, "That's correct. Our Federation is a group of more than one hundred fifty worlds and civilizations." She indicated the away team. "Just in our group, we represent five different planets." Pointing first to Worf, she proceeded in turn. *"Qo'noS*, the Klingon homeworld. Betazed. Denobula. Earth, and in my and Commander Taurik's case, Vulcan." Pausing, she smiled. "Actually, I'm part human, so I represent Earth as well."

"Incredible," said Nelidar, and Chen heard the genuine amazement in her voice. Then her expression faltered. *"Your Federation sounds quite remarkable, but it is regrettable that you have found yourselves here on our world."*

Worf asked, *"Is this your homeworld?"*

Shaking her head, Nelidar replied, *"No. This is—or rather, was—Ushalon, an uninhabitable planet in the star system where our world, Elanisal, is located. It was only through our own hubris and error that this is no longer the case."* She regarded Chen and the others with sadness. *"You should have heeded our warnings, travelers."*

"I don't think I'm liking the sound of this," said Cruzen.

"What are you saying?" asked Worf. *"The dimensional shift is not under your control?"*

Nelidar regarded him with sadness. *"Not any longer. This world no longer has a home, and now you are trapped here with us."*

HERE
U.S.S. *Enterprise*-E

Picard stalked the bridge, unhappy. He had quit counting the number of times he had circled the room's perimeter, his gaze taking in every console, each screen, and every indicator. Nothing was overlooked, to the point that he could tell when even a single status light or gauge changed between his rounds. Each of those was a reason to stop and examine the information being relayed to a particular workstation or processed by one of his officers, and each time brought further disappointment.

What happened to the planet? Where are my people?

Around him, his officers were immersed in whatever task demanded their attention, doing their best to provide answers to those very questions, which their captain had been asking for the better part of an hour.

"Mister La Forge," said Picard as he completed yet another circuit and found himself once more standing before his chief engineer at the back of the bridge. "Anything?"

Shaking his head, La Forge sighed. "Not yet, sir, but I'm convinced that what we saw was an interdimensional shift that sent the entire planet . . . somewhere. I just don't have the first damned clue where that somewhere is." He indicated the bridge's main viewscreen. "It could be right there, but occupying space in a completely different dimension, or it could have been transported to another area of space. We just don't have enough information yet, and unless or until that planet comes back, we're not liable to get much more."

"Do you believe it might come back?" asked Picard.

La Forge shrugged. "No reason to rule it out, sir. We're reviewing the sensor logs we took of the area before and after it appeared the first time, and working up what we hope might be a rough timeline. It'll be a lot of guesswork, at least until the planet shows up a second time, and hopefully it gives us some kind of pattern we can work with."

It was not much, but it was more than nothing, and for now that was good enough for Picard. "Make it so," he said, reaching out to pat the other man on his shoulder. "I know this is a challenging task, Geordi, but I'm glad you're the one overseeing it."

"Then this probably isn't the best time to tell you that Taurik or Lieutenant Chen are usually the ones better at the numbers and calculations, sir." The engineer forced a smile. "We'll find them, Captain. We'll find all of them."

The man's conviction was heartening, Picard decided, and he had no intention of dampening his chief engineer's enthusiasm. "Use whatever resources you feel are necessary." He looked to the viewscreen and the innocent, almost serene image of the NGC 8541 nebula. "That planet is out there, somewhere. Sooner or later, we'll find it."

"Maybe sooner, sir."

Both men turned at the sound of Lieutenant Dina Elfiki's voice, and Picard saw the science officer rising from her chair as though intending to move toward them. Seeing them looking at her, she motioned to her console. "Sensors just found something, Captain."

Crossing to the science station, Picard asked, "What is it, Lieutenant?"

"More quantum fluctuations, sir," replied the science officer, who had retaken her seat. "Much weaker, and not as widespread, but still there. It would be easy to miss if we hadn't recalibrated the sensors to be on the lookout for this kind of thing. Plus? There was something else." Calling up a display of information, she pointed to one column of streaming text.

"I'll be damned," said La Forge, who had moved to stand next to Elfiki, opposite Picard. "A communications signal?"

Elfiki nodded. "Looks that way, sir."

"A signal from what?" asked Picard. "And to whom?"

Leaning closer to the console, La Forge had begun interacting with another of the station's displays. "It's hard to say from this distance, sir. The sensors are still muddled, but it looks like the source is some kind of metallic object, a little under two hundred million kilometers from our current position, toward the center of the nebula."

He tapped another control, and an image of the object in question coalesced into view on the compact screen. Though the feed was fraught with static and other artifacts belying the interference the sensors were enduring, Picard was still able to make out a cylindrical shape, along with an assortment of antennae and other attachments that reminded him of a sensor or communications buoy of the type often deployed by starships—including the *Enterprise*—when venturing into previously unvisited regions of space. How many such objects had they left behind them as they continued their exploration of the Odyssean Pass?

Too many to count, but that's not really important, just now.

"I don't recognize the technology," said La Forge. "It doesn't look like it belongs to anybody we know."

Picard asked, "Can you intercept the signal?"

Frowning, the engineer replied, "It's a bit choppy from our current distance, but if we were to get closer we might be able to do something."

"Relay those coordinates to conn," ordered Picard.

It took only minutes for the *Enterprise* to maneuver to the prescribed location, with La Forge and Elfiki continuing to refine the starship's sensor array. After a few more adjustments and the distance separating them from the mysterious object now considerably smaller, the image on the bridge's main viewscreen was much improved, including the metal cylinder displayed in sharp relief.

Except that it was not.

Picard, having moved to stand with his arms crossed in front of the conn and ops stations, studied the odd object as it seemed to fade in and out of existence, like a faulty transporter beam or holographic projection.

"Is it caught in some kind of phase variance?" he asked. "Or the midpoint of a dimensional shift?"

Once again manning the engineering station at the back of the bridge, La Forge replied, "Looks that way, Captain. The flux readings are low, but holding steady. If I didn't know any better, I'd think it was deliberately holding a fixed position in the midst of a phase shift."

"It's definitely an unmanned probe or buoy of some kind," reported Lieutenant Elfiki. "It's far too small to be a lifeboat, and a bit too big for something like a quantum torpedo. We're not detecting anything that might be a weapon, though because of the phase variance and the resulting quantum fluctuations, I'm having a hard time getting a good look at its interior. I can't tell if our scans are being reflected back, or just passing right through the thing. It's like the sensors don't even know for sure."

La Forge turned from his station and stepped into the bridge's command well. "One thing we *do* know for sure." He pointed to the viewscreen. "The quantum energy readings coming from that are consistent with what we picked up from the planet."

"And what about the communications signal?" asked Picard. "Could it be some form of contact with the planet?"

"It's as good a guess as any, sir."

The engineer returned to his work, leaving Picard to stare at the odd metallic object on the viewscreen. Who had built it and put it there, and for what purpose? Would it lead him to the mysterious planet and his people?

As good a guess as any.

No, Picard decided. It was better than a guess. It was hope.

9

ELSEWHERE
Ushalon

With a sigh of relief she did not even attempt to suppress, T'Ryssa Chen removed her EV suit's helmet and felt cool air play across her face.

"These are nice and all," said Rennan Konya as he pulled his own helmet from his head. "Particularly with how they tend to keep you from dying in a poisonous atmosphere or vacuum, but that doesn't mean I have to like them."

Beside him, Kirsten Cruzen replied, "It doesn't help that you always end up smelling like feet when you take yours off."

Konya smiled. "I hardly think I'm the biggest offender in that department."

"You might want to take a poll when we get back to the ship." Cruzen placed her helmet on a shelf set into the gray metal wall of the room into which the away team had been guided upon entering the largest of the buildings. "I was thinking of starting a betting pool."

Though she had observations of her own to lend to the discussion, Chen curbed that urge as she took note of Worf and Taurik at the other end of the room. They had removed their EV suits, leaving them dressed only in the gray, form-fitting coveralls that were normally worn beneath the heavier garments. Thinner than regular duty uniforms, the coveralls bore no rank insignia or other accessories except for the communicator badge each officer affixed to his chest. Phasers and tricorders hung from carriers on their hips.

"Lieutenant Konya," said Worf, "you and Doctor Tropp will remain with our equipment."

While Tropp merely nodded in acknowledgment, Konya replied, "You want me near that doorway, sir?" He waved toward the passageway leading from this room, beyond which Chen could see a larger chamber. Standing along at the threshold of that entry was Nelidar, as though waiting for them to remove their EV gear.

"Yes," replied Worf. "Keep your phaser holstered for now. There is no need to foster any . . . ill will."

"Aye, sir."

For her part, Nelidar seemed unperturbed by the exchange. With her pale white complexion, lack of visible body hair, and piercing, cobalt-blue eyes, the Sidrac appeared almost ghostlike as she seemed to hover near the doorway. Everyone Chen had seen was slight of build, almost gaunt in appearance. A quick tricorder scan had shown this to be a facet of their physiology, rather than a consequence of malnutrition. The Sidrac were long limbed, with three fingers on each hand along with an opposable phalange as the innermost digit. It apparently was a Sidrac custom to dispense with footwear indoors, and Chen observed that Nelidar's feet were thin. She walked on her toes while the bones of her feet appeared to comprise the lower portion of her legs, giving her lower extremities an almost feline aspect. Like the other Sidrac, Nelidar wore loose-fitting light-blue garments that to Chen looked like pajamas.

We're casual, here on the planet from another dimension.

The room in which they now found themselves was little more than a collection of equipment lockers. At

Worf's direction, the away team had staged their suits on the floor where they would remain visible, while everyone would carry their weapons and other equipment. Chen noticed that neither Nelidar nor other Sidrac—either those who had accompanied her outside or anyone else inside the complex—had remained to guard their new guests during this process. Instead, they had moved to another room to remove their own suits, and now that Nelidar had returned, she seemed anxious to escort them around, rather than apprehensive.

Hopefully that's a good sign.

"I hope you are comfortable," said Nelidar as Worf led the team from the changing area. "Despite our differences, we appear to have similar environmental needs."

Worf nodded. "We are fine. Thank you."

Both Tropp and Taurik had scanned the structure's interior once the away team was inside, verifying that the air contained nothing that might be harmful. Though the oxygen content was somewhat richer here compared to normal Class-M conditions, it was well within tolerable levels for humanoids, and Chen realized that she felt more alert and energetic after a few minutes breathing the Sidrac's atmosphere.

With Nelidar leading the way, the away team entered a larger, high-ceilinged chamber. The walls and floor were composed of an ash-gray metal, with most of the bulkhead space devoted to displays and consoles that were arrayed with clusters of multicolored controls, indicators, and other gauges. Most of the larger displays and interfaces were labeled with a flowing, curling script. Another set of consoles and workstations was arranged in a horseshoe pattern at the room's center, each offering a view of the large oval display screen set into the chamber's forward wall. The screen was inert at the moment, but numerous other screens on the floor and wall stations were active, depicting images or streams of information in the same eye-catching script. Along the walls to her left and right, Chen observed a pair of catwalks with spiral ramps at each end that descended at a gentle angle toward the floor. The backless chairs positioned before the different workstations offered concave seats and padded knee rests for the eight Sidrac working here. Five females and three males, their individual movements made them appear to be not so much working at computer consoles as playing musical instruments. From her vantage point, Chen saw a handful of the display screens and different stations, with a mixture of the beautiful Sidrac script as well as streams of shifting color. Was that a form of information exchange?

I can't wait to get a closer look.

As much as the room interested her, it was the source of the complex's massive quantum energy readings that now had her attention. The surreptitious scans Chen had taken with her tricorder after changing out of her EV suit had piqued her curiosity. The power levels were unlike anything she had seen before, but the area was either shielded or else the energy fluctuations were simply interfering with her ability to get a closer, more detailed look at the subterranean area's interior.

"This place is beautiful," said Cruzen. Looking over her shoulder, Chen saw the security officer providing subtle protection for the away team at the back of the group. Her right hand rested on the pommel of the phaser on her right hip, and for a brief moment Chen wondered if the damned thing would even work. She and Konya had both returned their phaser rifles to the

Spinrad's locker at Worf's order after the initial meeting with Nelidar and the others on the surface. It was not that the Klingon had come to trust their hosts, but instead had decided against providing the Sidrac easy access to a weapon of such power.

Turning to face the away team, Nelidar said, "This is our observation room. From here, we oversee all the operations taking place throughout this entire habitat."

"And what exactly is it that you observe?" asked Taurik.

"Our quantum-field experiments, primarily, but also the complex's energy production facility, life-support, communications, and other mundane features that serve to keep us alive here." Nelidar pointed to the banks of equipment lining the walls to either side. "What you see here is the result of many years worth of research, followed by several more years spent constructing this facility, all for the sole purpose of expanding our knowledge and understanding of the universe around us." Lowering her arms, she clasped her hands before her. "We do explore as you do, with vessels that travel between the planets of our star system, but I suspect our efforts in that regard are less sophisticated than what you are used to encountering."

Worf said, "We have encountered numerous species with varying levels of technology."

"Then you would very likely be unimpressed with my people, Commander. For example, we have not yet achieved an ability to propel a vessel faster than light." Nelidar smiled. "The simple fact that you are standing here tells me that you have solved this puzzle."

Uh-oh.

Chen forced herself to maintain her composed expression. Had the *Enterprise* inadvertently violated the Prime

Directive, now that she and the others had made contact with a species that had not yet achieved warp-capable space travel? Perhaps not, as Nelidar and her companions had contacted the *Enterprise* first. Of course, a case could be made that insufficient steps were taken to mask the starship's presence from detection, but there was also the mitigating factor that the Sidrac had warned the ship of danger and to stay away, thereby justifying an attempt to render assistance. The permutations of a possible Prime Directive transgression were enough to make Chen's head hurt, and she decided that someone back home would have to deal with working it all out. She and her companions had other matters demanding their attention just now.

"So," said Worf, "you have been experimenting with quantum energy."

Nelidar nodded. "Oh, yes. It has been an interest of mine since childhood. The first experiments with quantum-field generators were undertaken while I was an adolescent receiving my formative education, and I knew even then it was a field in which I wanted to work. The idea of constructing a particle accelerator was one that had been discussed by leading scientists for years, but there were concerns about the instability of building such a structure on our homeworld." She once more extended her arms, gesturing to the room around her. "Therefore, the decision was made to build a large-scale collider here on Ushalon, the planet adjacent to our own."

"The underground facility," said Chen. "The source of all the quantum fluctuations we've detected."

"Exactly. A quantum-field generator of such size and power requires a dedicated energy production and support facility, so we decided to construct the entire complex here on Ushalon, well away from our homeworld." Nelidar's expression softened. "The complex is powered using a fusion reactor, and while we took every conceivable safety precaution, it was not enough to alleviate the worries of politicians and those who lacked the proper science and engineering knowledge. As it happens, their concerns were not completely unfounded."

Taurik said, "Are the quantum shifts this planet is experiencing deliberate?"

Offering a small, sad smile, Nelidar replied, "Yes, though we certainly exceeded our wildest expectations by a rather wide margin."

She indicated for them to follow her, and they moved to the room's far end, where another open doorway waited. Beyond the portal was a smaller room, outfitted with a trio of computer consoles, work spaces, and display screens, though none of the other Sidrac were working at these stations. Moving to one of the consoles, Nelidar slid her thin hand across its dark, smooth surface and the panel illuminated to reveal a touch-sensitive interface with rows of colored controls. She tapped a violet circle and the display monitor mounted to the bulkhead above the console activated.

"A group of our civilization's leading scientists first postulated the theory of other dimensions that might exist in parallel to our own. It was not the first time such a notion had been offered, but usually such ideas were confined to fiction. It has only been in recent generations that the hypothesis was given any credence by our scientific community."

The screen depicted a two-dimensional star map. As

the presentation continued, additional maps began to materialize above and below the original graphic. Then that image shrank and moved to the screen's upper right corner before the rest of the screen was dominated by a picture of an immense metal construct surrounded by walls of unyielding rock.

"Our particle accelerator," explained Nelidar. "It is located deep underground and is a self-contained facility that operates autonomously in large part. Except for maintenance or repairs that require on-site work, the complex was designed to be overseen from here."

"It looks most impressive," said Taurik.

Nelidar said, "It is the culmination of many years' work, and the knowledge we gained from its use has been wondrous. Insights into the origins of the universe, the limits of the physical laws that govern that universe, and how or if other universes exist in parallel to our own." She shook her head, and Chen saw the Sidrac's obvious passion. "It is my life's work, and it never fails to astonish me." Refocusing her attention on the away team, she said, "It occurs to me that perhaps I am speaking of things with which you are already quite familiar."

"Your theories are not unfounded," said Worf. "We have had our own encounters with other dimensions and parallel universes." The Klingon paused, and Chen heard a mild grunt of annoyance. "Such experiences have proven . . . troublesome at times, but we also have a large scientific community who feels that studying these dimensions offers us greater insight into our own. Based on personal experience . . . I have my doubts."

Nelidar laughed at that. "We must seem like children to you."

"Not at all," said Chen. "It's one of our strongest beliefs that every civilization must proceed at its own pace, acquiring knowledge and developing technology as it best suits their needs and desires."

Hey. You almost sounded like a contact specialist just then.

"Unless one acquires knowledge and then develops technology without first considering the wisdom of doing so." Turning back to the console, Nelidar touched another control, and the image on the screen shifted to depict a squat, cylindrical object standing on a metal platform that in turn rested on a rocky plain. The device was supported by a quartet of spindly legs and had a trio of large globes affixed to its top. It reminded Chen of the history texts she had read as a child and later at the Academy, which had pictures of unmanned probes and landing craft created by humans and other species during their earliest days of space exploration.

"After the first experiments with the quantum-field generator provided compelling evidence of other dimensions," said Nelidar, "attention turned toward seeing if there might be a way to reach across the barriers separating those realities from our own. With the belief that each dimension possesses its own unique and identifiable quantum signature, it was thought that replicating that signature using the field generator and channeling the resulting energies could create a connection between our reality and the targeted dimension." She pointed to the screen. "Probes like this one were constructed with the idea that they could record information from the other dimension and return it to us, either as transmitted data or else when the probe itself was retrieved."

Cruzen, who had been standing near the doorway—

perhaps, Chen decided, so that she might guard the away team's rear—said, "Obviously you succeeded."

"Not at first," countered Nelidar. "We conducted three tests, all of which ended with the probe being destroyed, but even those failures provided us with information that then was used to refine the quantum-field process. That was what made our fourth attempt a success."

On the screen was footage of the probe standing on its platform, then being enveloped within a sphere of bright white glow that obscured the device. When the light vanished, the probe was gone.

Nelidar said, "We started receiving telemetry from the test drone almost immediately. It had arrived within a nebula, and the probe's onboard cameras were able to take pictures of it as well as the star patterns as they appeared from its perspective, and when we decoded the transmissions with those images we observed that they were completely different from the stars visible from our own world. That was our first indication that movement between realities was not simply a matter of transitioning between dimensions while occupying a fixed point in space. Once we verified the quantum signature that was different from the one consistent with our dimension, we knew without doubt that our experiment had succeeded. However, we reserved our celebrations until after a second test was completed, with another probe being sent to an altogether different dimension." Once more, the Sidrac's enthusiasm seemed on the verge of getting the best of her. "That was when we realized the enormity of what we had done."

"NGC 8541," said Taurik. "The nebula we were exploring when we found this planet."

Nelidar replied, "Yes, exactly. The second probe also arrived in a nebula, albeit one composed of different gases and other properties. However, there were sufficient similarities between the two nebulas that we began to theorize that such spatial phenomena harbor characteristics that lend themselves to what we had begun to call 'dimensional transference.' In order to prove that, we expanded our testing until we successfully sent a total of five test probes, each to its own destination and able to verify its target dimension's unique quantum signature. All five probes arrived within a different nebula or similar interstellar cloud."

"Intriguing," said Taurik. "There have been several hypotheses formed that cover similar ground, and we have encountered more than one spatial phenomenon possessing similar properties that facilitated dimensional and even temporal transition."

"Temporal transition?" Nelidar's eyes widened. "That is astounding, though I suspect that if your scientists are like ours, they caution against such research for fear that we might somehow corrupt our history and alter the course of our future." She shook her head. "It sounds like so much fantasy to me."

Chen exchanged looks with Worf and Taurik, but said nothing on that topic. Instead, she asked, "So, you had several successful tests, but I'm guessing this planet being one of the test objects wasn't part of the plan."

"You are correct, Lieutenant."

Another graphic materialized on the screen in response to Nelidar's command, depicting five star maps, each with a yellow circle marking a different location.

"Our knowledge of the probes' positions within their respective dimensions was limited, but it was enough for us to continue with new experiments. Using these five points as coordinates, we constructed a series of more robust drones for transfer to the other dimensions. Fitted with special communications equipment, they act as beacons, transmitting signals from their position back to us."

"You created a network," said Worf.

Again, Nelidar smiled. "Exactly. Each beacon's signal is detected by the quantum-field generator, allowing for the precise transition of objects. In two cases, we programmed the probes to maneuver away from the nebulae in which they arrived, and we were still able to maintain signal clarity. So, while the nebulae themselves seemed helpful with the transition process, they are not essential, at least not while we maintain contact with the beacon itself."

Cruzen said, "Like a transporter lock." Then, as though realizing she may have offered hints about a technology the Sidrac did not possess, the security officer hastily added, "Or a targeting fix?"

Nice save, Kirsten.

"That is an apt comparison," said Nelidar. "There definitely are similarities to a weapons targeting system, though our intentions were far less martial in nature. It was our intention to use the five beacons as the first stage in a test network, to see whether an object could be shifted between each of the dimensions, first in sequence and then based on generating a specific quantum signature. Our initial tests were successful, with our test drone moving between different beacons in the network, crossing back and forth from one dimension to another." She paused, and Chen again noted the obvious pride Nelidar had taken from what she and her colleagues had accomplished.

Nelidar continued, "That was when our problems began. During one of our experiments, a malfunction in the energy distribution center of the generator's support complex triggered a massive power feedback. This produced a tremendous surge of energy that overloaded the generator's control system, and the resulting outpouring of quantum energy was enough to shift Ushalon itself through the rift we had opened. It required some time for us to realize what had happened, but finding the beacon in that other dimension removed all doubt."

"And now you are unable to control the dimensional shifts," said Taurik.

"Correct, Commander." With apparent hesitation, Nelidar reached for the console and pressed another lighted indicator, and a new computer-generated graphic appeared on the screen. Now it depicted what Chen took to be Ushalon as the planet moved in random fashion and at sporadic intervals between each of the five beacons still displayed on the schematic.

"The power surge created another problem," said Nelidar, "in that it somehow shifted the field generator itself with the rest of the planetoid. We can see it, and we can detect its energy readings, but we cannot access it directly, and neither can we interface with the support facility's control processes. It is as though an invisible barrier now exists between us."

Taurik said, "That would explain the continual quantum fluctuations and the difficulties I have experienced when attempting to scan the field generator."

"And without an ability to control the process or reach the underground complex," said Chen, "you can't stop the shifts."

"Not since the accident," said Nelidar. For a moment,

she closed her eyes. "Eighty-two cycles. The shifts occur at irregular intervals, so we do not know how long we will remain in any one dimension, or even which one is our next destination. Our attempts to predict the shifts have been futile."

Taurik held up his tricorder. "Using the information from the computer simulation, I have determined that the accident occurred approximately one hundred twenty-six days ago."

"Four months?" Cruzen shook her head. "Damn."

"The generator continues to draw energy," said Nelidar. "We have made attempts to interrupt the power flow, but even that has proved unsuccessful. We can study the readings and make calculations based on our data, but we are unable to attempt to alter or stop the process. So long as that continues, Ushalon and everything on it will simply keep shifting between the five dimensions."

"At least until there is some kind of mechanical malfunction," said Taurik, "though I am reluctant to consider the ramifications of such an event."

With a grim smile, Nelidar replied, "Nor are we."

"Can't you evacuate the planet?" asked Cruzen. Still standing near the doorway, the lieutenant gestured toward the computer screen. "Surely you have some kind of spacecraft that would let you leave if necessary."

Nelidar said, "There are twenty-four of us here, and we do have sufficient craft to transport our entire team away from Ushalon, but where would we go? While the planet moves within the network established by our beacons, none of those probes is in our own dimension." She held out her arms. "This planet was always intended to be the anchor point for the network. We cannot even launch a new probe with the hopes of sending it to our dimension, because we are unable to access the field generator and target the proper quantum signature." She shook her head, and for the first time Chen heard defeat in the Sidrac's voice. "We are trapped here, forever."

"Perhaps not," said Worf. The Klingon stepped forward. "If we were able to make contact with our ship, our people may very well be able to render assistance." He indicated Taurik. "We have some very talented engineers and scientists among our crew."

"He's right," said Chen. "Maybe our finding you makes this your lucky day." She could not wait to hear what Commander La Forge thought of this.

Nelidar said, "You are the first who have attempted to make contact with us, but we know our presence in other dimensions has not gone unnoticed."

10

ELSEWHERE
Earth Year 2266

Sarith was tiring of this particular game.

She paced what deck was available within the confines of the *Bloodied Talon*'s bridge. Like the rest of the combat vessel Sarith commanded, the control room was designed for function and durability, not comfort. There were few luxuries to be found aboard even this, one of the Romulan Empire's most advanced warships. This only served to heighten Sarith's feelings of restlessness, given the distinct lack of activity or anything of interest currently taking place aboard the ship or—so far as she could tell—anywhere else in the known universe.

Am I being punished?

"Status report," she said, more to alleviate her boredom than in the hopes of hearing anything that might deviate from the responses she had received to her last six identical queries.

Standing at the bridge's weapons control console—one of four workstations arrayed around the control hub at the center of the room—N'tovek turned to face her. Like the other centurions manning stations on the bridge, he wore the gold helmet that was the normal uniform accessory denoting a low-ranking subordinate.

"There has been no change in any of our scan readings, Commander. We are continuing our observations."

Of course you are. What else are you going to do?

"Are you certain the sensors are functioning normally?" Sarith already knew the answer to her query, but this exchange, useless as it was, helped to occupy another few brief moments.

N'tovek nodded. "I have verified complete functionality, Commander, as well as confirmed that our cloaking field is not interfering with scanner effectiveness." As he always did when addressing her, he stood at ramrod attention, offering his responses in crisp, formal fashion. Though every member of her crew paid her the proper respect due her rank and station, N'tovek always added another layer to such interactions. "I can repeat the inspection if you wish."

You could certainly use the practice.

Sarith almost gave voice to the cross thought, catching herself only at the last moment. Chastising him in such a manner before his peers would only embarrass him, and she considered such tactics poor leadership. It was not the centurion's fault that nothing had materialized on the ship's sensors. As with everyone else aboard the *Bloodied Talon*, he was at the mercy of whatever forces were at play here. With respect to any perceived shortcomings in N'tovek's ability to carry out his responsibilities as both a weapons and a sensor control officer, Sarith had already discussed the matter with his immediate superior. She was confident that with proper training and supervision coupled with the centurion's genuine, demonstrated desire to excel at his duties, N'tovek had the potential to become an acceptable if not noteworthy officer.

There was also the indisputable fact that he had proven himself useful and talented in other areas, precisely none of which had any bearing on his effectiveness as an officer of the Romulan military. Indeed, there were those, her senior staff and other officers included, who would take great exception to her having engaged a subordinate in a personal relationship. Discretion had been key in that regard, and N'tovek understood that the time they shared in private would offer no influence or protection for him should he fall short in any of his duties. At least, he seemed to understand this, even after the discussions regarding his professional deficiencies. If anything, the counseling session had served only to make him even more eager to please her away from the bridge.

This could be dangerous.

She realized she had not yet responded to N'tovek, and that she instead was staring at him. Forcing away the thoughts that had distracted her, Sarith motioned toward him.

"That will not be necessary, Centurion. Attend your station."

N'tovek offered the expected salute before turning back to his controls, allowing Sarith to continue her circuit of the *Talon*'s bridge. She stepped to the sensor control station, and the centurion manning that post moved aside in order to afford her a better look at one of the console's compact display screens. Studying the image of the blue-green nebula displayed upon it, she released a small sigh.

"All things being equal, it is rather striking." She glanced to the centurion as she spoke the words, and the younger officer, Darjil, nodded.

"Yes, Commander."

"Have you learned anything new about it?"

Darjil shook his head. "No, Commander. Though its gas concentrations do have a destabilizing effect on our sensors, the nebula appears to contain no special properties that present a danger to the ship."

Reaching for the console, Sarith activated the control that allowed her access to the volumes of data collected by the *Talon*'s sensor array and stored within the memory banks of the ship's computer. It took her only a moment to call up the directory of files pertaining to the mysterious object they had found hiding within the nebula's dense gases.

"What of the automated probe?"

"Our research is ongoing, Commander. Despite all our efforts to date, we are still unable to determine the device's origin, or access its internal systems. We have analyzed the communication signal it continues to broadcast, but it is unlike anything we have encountered before."

Sarith knew from the status reports she received that Darjil had taken a keen interest in the device since its initial discovery by ship's sensors nearly two weeks ago. That find had come just days after the *Talon*'s first encounter with the odd rogue planet that seemed to also be hiding within the nebula. Studying the planet and the probe had commanded all of the centurion's waking hours regardless of whether he was on duty. Though Sarith only understood some of the dense information packed into the detailed reports, it was obvious that Darjil comprehended the scope of what they had stumbled upon and was doing his level best to convey the importance of the discovery to anyone who would listen.

"The communication signal," said Sarith. "You've been able to confirm that it is broadcasting beyond our dimensional plane?"

As though uncertain of his own answers, Darjil replied, "Based on the available data and following a series of calculations using the ship's computer, that is my best hypothesis at this time. I apologize for our lack of progress, Commander."

"Your effort has not gone unnoticed or unappreciated, Centurion," said a new voice, and both Sarith and Darjil looked to see Subcommander Ineti.

The *Talon*'s second-in-command had entered the bridge through the service corridor at the rear, pausing at the threshold as was his habit while taking in the scene around him. Standing with his hands clasped behind his back, the older officer missed nothing as he subjected the bridge to his scrutiny. His blue eyes radiated an intensity that seemed to bore through everything they saw. Deep lines on his face and white hair cut in a typical male officer's style marked him as a Romulan of distinction, bearing mute testimony to a long career spent in uniform.

Every centurion on duty seemed to focus even greater attention on their instruments, each making an obvious effort to avoid the subcommander's withering gaze. Sarith suppressed an urge to smile as Ineti, apparently satisfied that his subordinates were carrying out their duties per his expectations, finally turned and made his way around the bridge's central control hub toward her. For his part, Darjil seemed to have frozen in place, staring straight ahead and saying nothing at Ineti's approach.

"Your reports have made for fascinating reading, Centurion," said the subcommander. "There can be no doubt that they are the result of many hours of dedicated research. That you were able to make them understandable for a battered old soldier such as myself is also to be commended. It is good to see you devoting your off-duty time to such constructive pursuits."

Sarith forced herself not to chuckle at Ineti's last comment. As her second-in-command, it fell to him to oversee the crew's conduct, as well as their training. It was a responsibility for which Ineti was perfectly suited, given the even-tempered, almost paternal demeanor in which he comported himself. Though he could and would apply discipline with all the force and conviction that was required for a given situation, he preferred the role of mentor, constantly overseeing those under his command and teaching them how to improve themselves not just as soldiers of the Empire but also Romulans. He almost never raised his voice when issuing instructions or orders, tending instead to speak in deliberate, thoughtful tones, which did more to instill obedience and even fear in his subordinates than any overt displays of emotion. However, it was the misguided soul who confused Ineti's measured approach to leadership as weakness. Sarith had observed that phenomenon more than once, and it almost always required her to exit herself from the immediate area lest he or his unwitting subordinate hear her laughing.

As for Darjil, Ineti had taken a greater interest in the centurion's activities of late, as part of a larger initiative aimed at redirecting the focus of the crew's younger members toward beneficial endeavors, rather than some of the more wasteful activities that seemed to occupy their off-duty hours. Darjil in particular had become something of a personal reclamation project for the subcommander. Rather than taint the centurion's service record with unflattering entries pertaining to disciplinary action, reductions in rank, or other penalties, Ineti instead had counseled the young Romulan on his deficiencies as well as establishing guidelines and a schedule for improving his performance.

Knowing Ineti as she did, Sarith was certain her second-in-command saw great potential in Darjil, provided he was guided at this early, influential time in his budding career. Other officers might have been satisfied to level punishments on wayward subordinates, but not Ineti. He favored teaching and perhaps salvaging what had already been a significant commitment of time and resources on the part of the Romulan Empire to train and prepare new centurions for military service, and see a return on that investment.

"What else have you learned?" asked Sarith, deciding to provide Darjil with a respite from Ineti's unrelenting gaze.

The centurion replied, "I believe the drone device is in communication with the planet and that the transmission is a means of maintaining a connection between the two points. It is possible that whatever causes the shift somehow uses the transmission as a tether. That might explain the consistency in the odd energy fluctuations we are so far unable to identify."

"If that's true," said Ineti, "then perhaps the planet's arrival and departure can be predicted somehow."

"That is my belief, Subcommander. If these events can be forecast, then it would give us the advantage we have been seeking."

Sarith nodded in approval. Such a revelation and their ability to capitalize upon it would be just the opportunity she had been seeking since receiving this assignment. Her mission here was a simple task, at least in theory. After an unmanned reconnaissance probe had discovered the planet drifting within the Lirostahl Nebula, the *Bloodied Talon*—accompanied by a pair of escort vessels, the *N'minecci* and the *Jarax*, to provide any necessary additional personnel and other support—had been instructed to monitor the region and learn all that was possible about the mysterious planet that seemed to disappear and reappear at random intervals for no discernible reason. This had hampered her ability to achieve her other objective: making contact with the life-forms that had been detected on the planet, learn the nature of the planet's odd qualities, and seize control of the installation and any equipment or other technology that might be causing the phenomenon to occur.

So far, there were no indications that anyone on the surface had detected the *Talon* or the escorts, thanks to each ship's cloaking device. Following an examination of their initial sensor readings of the planet, Sarith had been prepared to send down a scouting party from one of the escort vessels, but that notion was halted when the planet disappeared before her eyes. Unless and until the duration and frequency of the world's movements could be predicted, she was unwilling to risk members of her crew or the other two ships.

"What about the people?" she asked. "Have you learned anything about them?"

Darjil shook his head. "No, Commander. The planet itself does not correspond to anything in our stellar cartography database. As we believe it to be nomadic in nature, with no links to any star system in this region, that makes identification most difficult. As for the life-forms recorded by our sensors, they do not correspond to any known species. The energy readings we detected coming from the subterranean complex are also unfamiliar."

"A most interesting puzzle for us to solve," said Ineti.

Scowling, Sarith replied, "The praetor does not care about puzzles, or games, or whatever other childish pursuits to which this might be compared. He wants answers to his questions, and he has tasked me with providing them. I do not expect his patience to be long-lasting in this regard."

More than anything, it was the planet's technology that had so enamored Praetor Vrax. The elder Romulan leader had been so intrigued by the mystery Sarith presented him in her constant stream of reports that he had taken the unusual step of contacting her directly, rather than sending instructions via intermediaries as was normal. Given the sheer number of links in the chain of command that separated Vrax from her, the contact was unprecedented. Sarith wondered if the praetor's interest and his willingness to break with protocol was because her mother, Toqel, who currently served as a proconsul to the Romulan Senate, was an advisor charged with ensuring Vrax and the other members of the ruling elite were provided with all manner of military advice and perspective. Sarith hoped that was not the case. There already were an intolerable number of rumors in circulation, implying that she had obtained her command of the *Bloodied Talon* through familial connections and favoritism rather than her own merits. She had expended a great deal of energy fighting such unsubstantiated tripe and taken great steps to prevent even the merest hint of impropriety.

The hushed allegations had followed her from the beginning of her career, intensifying as she continued to advance in rank and position. The *Talon*'s original first officer had at least possessed the fortitude to confront her with such accusations face-to-face, offering Sarith the unparalleled opportunity to have him removed from the ship's crew and replaced with an officer she trusted with her life, Ineti. She had known the subcommander since childhood, when he had served with her father. Like Praetor Vrax's, Ineti's career and accomplishments dated back to the war against Earth and its allies, before those adversaries had come together to forge a new alliance as the United Federation of Planets. Ineti, her most trusted confidant, had never questioned her abilities or her achievements, and she knew he would serve at her side until death took either or both of them. It was Ineti who had advised her on more than one occasion to ignore the rumors, for they were the blathering of lesser officers unworthy of her notice or respect. Instead, she should take the energy she otherwise might spend worrying about the hearsay that was beyond her sphere of influence and concentrate instead on serving the Empire to the best of her ability.

You know why you are here, and you have been given a task. Complete it.

"I would prefer my next report for Fleet Command to contain something more than an update about our continuing efforts and lack of progress," she said. "If this technology does allow for transfer between dimensions, then the value to the Empire would be immeasurable. Think of the resources available to the wielder of such technology, unreachable by our enemies."

"Indeed, Commander," replied Ineti. "The implications are staggering. We would be a power without equal in the galaxy. Given our present circumstances, that is a most desirable goal."

Sarith offered a grim smile. "That is putting it in the mildest possible terms, my old friend."

Though there existed no formal declaration of hostilities with the Federation, both sides knew that the truce between the two powers, forged out of the conflict fought against Earth and its own coalition of sympathizers—the Vulcans, the Andorians, and the Tellarites—was fragile. Since the end of that war, the involved parties had seemed content to remain on their own side of the thin ribbon of space separating the territories. That was but a line on an interstellar map, and Sarith knew that there were those within the halls of government and military power who seethed at the restrictions placed upon all Romulans by a demonstrably lesser people. Even Vrax, as calculating and patient a leader as anyone who ever had held the title of praetor, had long ago begun to chafe at the Federation's unbridled arrogance as it continued its expansion efforts. Their ships ventured to the very brink of violating the so-called "Neutral Zone" at the edges of Romulan space, as though daring a wayward ship commander to violate the tenets of the peace treaty. A string of observation stations, arrayed along that border, maintained constant vigil as they stalked Romulan ship movements with unrestrained glee. Such insult was only exacerbated by the knowledge that their observers performed these acts of voyeurism from territory that had been surrendered as part of the treaty stipulations to which the Empire had agreed in order to end the Great War.

No longer content to be the object of such unchecked curiosity and aware that the other concerns far from the Empire may be requiring the Federation to focus attention elsewhere, Vrax had agreed to a bold proposal presented by members of the senate. The objective was straightforward: Probe the Federation's borders in order to assess their current level of technological prowess and determine their strengths and weaknesses. Did an opportunity exist to reclaim valuable territory ceded to the humans and their collaborators as a consequence of the war? There was only one way to find out.

The first such test had already taken place, with another vessel dispatched to the border. That ship, according to the reports to which Sarith had been privy, had been successful in determining the Federation Starfleet's current capabilities. Further triumph had come in the form of destroying three of the Starfleet observation outposts, as well as one of their premier battle cruisers after its commander had demonstrated the temerity to follow the Romulan ship into the Neutral Zone. From the reports Sarith had read, what had followed was a remarkable battle of tactical acumen and sheer will as the two vessels faced off against each other, before the Empire's ship emerged victorious. Even now, Federation diplomats were falling over themselves in their haste to make amends, assuring Praetor Vrax and the Romulan Senate that the incident was isolated, the result of a rogue commander who had disobeyed orders and taken it upon himself to violate the treaty. Anxious to avoid war, they were promising a full accounting of the incident. Sarith suspected such humility would be short-lived, with the Federation now awakened to the reality that the Romulan Empire had neither forgiven nor forgotten past transgressions.

That could have been me. It could have been my ship and crew.

Perhaps it would be, one day, Sarith knew. On the other hand, the battle could just as easily have gone in the Starfleet captain's favor, resulting in the loss of a celebrated Romulan commander and his vessel. There were worse things than dying in service to the Empire in order to maintain the security of the Romulan people, including her family. Every officer always was aware of that possibility. Such was the burden of duty. However, there was something to be said for living to continue carrying out one's duty for another day.

Today, for example.

"Continue your research, Centurion Darjil," said Sarith, after a moment. "Keep Subcommander Ineti informed of any new developments. Notify the sensor officers on the other ships to maintain their observations as well. If and when anything changes, I want to be ready to act." She had already conferred with the commanders of the *N'minecci* and the *Jarax*, notifying them that their sensor crews were to be put at her disposal until further notice.

The young officer nodded. "Yes, Commander."

As they moved away from the centurion and allowed him to return to work, Ineti said in a soft tone, "Somewhere, out there, perhaps in a realm unreachable to us, awaits a great prize." His voice had taken on that musing, contemplative quality he adopted when he decided the time was appropriate for sounding like the wizened mentor to which she likened him. "Delivering it to the praetor would do much to secure your standing within the Empire, and silence those who would doubt you."

"I am well aware of that, my friend." Sarith was all too aware that fate had provided her an unparalleled opportunity.

She just needed to be ready to seize it.

11

Though the ready room had been his for nearly a year now, Riker had yet to take true ownership of the small inner sanctum.

Leaning forward in his chair, he rested his forearms across the polished surface of his desk and contemplated this space. Though it was intended as a secluded workspace for the ship's captain while still allowing easy, direct access to the bridge, Riker found he could not get comfortable in this room. It had its uses, of course, such as for private conversations with members of his senior staff, or simply a temporary refuge where he might shrug off the stresses of command for a brief time. So far, he had been unable to relax here, feeling as though he might be missing out on some activity or other concern unfolding on the bridge.

How did you do it, Jean-Luc? How could you just set it all aside, even for five minutes?

These were questions Riker had asked himself more than once. Jean-Luc Picard, a private and deeply contemplative man in most respects, had found some measure of serenity here. When the *Enterprise* was involved in a specific mission or task, Picard had often eschewed his personal quarters during off-duty hours in favor of seeking brief rest periods here. This was also where he spent the bulk of his time tending to ship's business, such as taking advantage of the quiet and solitude in order to complete the latest in an unending string of reports for Starfleet Command. With that, Riker could sympathize, as he forced himself to avoid glancing in the direction of his desktop computer terminal and the incomplete status update displayed upon it. Perhaps if he ignored it long enough, the report would finish writing itself before enabling its own transmission to Admiral Jellico back on Earth.

I'll just sit here and hold my breath.

Though Riker had written his share of similar correspondence during his tenure as the *Enterprise*'s first officer, the volume and scope of the administrative burden placed upon a starship captain had to be experienced in order to be fully appreciated. It seemed axiomatic that the amount of paperwork required of any Starfleet officer increased in direct proportion to an individual's rank.

So I should probably avoid ever becoming an admiral.

The door chime sounded, breaking Riker from his reverie.

"Come in," he called out, and the doors parted to reveal Deanna Troi. As was her habit, she was dressed in professional civilian attire rather than a Starfleet uniform, in this case a teal-blue dress, with her communicator badge serving as the only hint to her formal billet aboard the ship. Like many ship's counselors, Troi believed that opting for a more relaxed choice of ensemble when carrying out her duties allowed her patients to relax in her presence, removing much of the inherent formality that came with the uniform. Captain Picard had agreed with her views on this subject soon after her arrival aboard the starship, and Riker had never seen a reason to change that position.

"Hi," he said, smiling as he straightened in his seat. Seeing her always made him feel better.

Troi stepped into the room. "Everything all right?" Without waiting for an invitation, she availed herself of the low couch positioned along the ready room's forward bulkhead, beneath an artist's rendering of the *Enterprise* soaring through interstellar space.

"Everything's fine," replied Riker. "Just taking a short breather." Forcing himself to look at his computer terminal, he added, "Another report for Admiral Jellico. I'm having a hard time coming up with new ways to say we have nothing new to report. I'm thinking I may just change the time stamp on the last message and send it again, just to see if he notices."

Though she offered a polite chuckle, Troi still shook her head. "I don't think that would go over very well with the admiral."

"Don't look at me. It was his idea." Riker nodded toward the large globe-shaped aquarium occupying the room's back corner. Swimming in and around the plants and rocks contained within the tank was Livingston, the lionfish that had been Picard's companion here in the ready room almost from the beginning of the late captain's tenure aboard the *Enterprise*. Picard had never explained his reasons for keeping the fish. After Riker assumed command, it had taken him some time to realize he had never thought to broach the subject while Picard was alive. Perhaps it was because whenever he was in this room, on the other side of the desk, it was always for a larger purpose. It was a rare occurrence that Picard and Riker spent any sort of quiet time here, simply talking about things that had no bearing on their individual responsibilities.

How did that happen?

Though most of Captain Picard's personal belongings had been removed from the room during the *Enterprise*'s refit and repair work while docked at Earth Station McKinley and delivered to his brother, Robert, on Earth, a few items remained. In addition to Livingston, there was also Picard's prized copy of *The Globe Illustrated Shakespeare*, containing all of the written works created by the seventeenth-century human playwright. The *Enterprise*'s first captain had held Shakespeare in high esteem, and Riker had heard him quoting from one of the ancient plays or poems on more than one occasion. Positioned under a glass cover near the ready room's door and turned to what Riker knew was one of his former captain's favorite passages from the play *Hamlet*, it was a memento that seemed to personify Jean-Luc Picard's diverse interests and passions. Robert Picard had insisted that Riker keep the enormous tome as a gift, telling him that the very essence of what made his brother the man he was could be found tucked within the book's pages.

"Are you ever planning to bring any of your own things here?" asked Troi.

Sensing the question was being asked not just as his lover but also his counselor, Riker offered a knowing smile. "If you're asking me whether I'm reluctant to replace Captain Picard's stamp with my own, the answer is . . . maybe a little." To this point, he had been content to keep the ready room strictly as office space, but now that Deanna had posed the question, he realized he was overcorrecting so far as his desire not to supplant his predecessor. "Sometimes I come in here, and I wonder what he would say or do about a particular issue." He laughed. "I don't know. Maybe I'm hoping I'll gather divine inspiration or something."

Troi said, "We all do that in some fashion. There's nothing abnormal about that, so long as you maintain a proper perspective."

"Fair point." Swiveling in his seat, Riker started to raise his legs so that he might rest them on the desk, then stopped himself. Recalling unpleasant memories of his first hours as captain of the *Enterprise*, he said, "When he was taken, and after I received the official promotion, I came in here, looked right at this chair, and asked him what he would do in our situation." He rested his hands on the chair's arms. "I didn't get an answer, of course. At least, not from him, but no sooner did I ask the question than Guinan showed up." He smiled again. "She has that habit, you know."

"I do," replied Troi. "There are times I worry that she's better at my job than I am."

The gentle humor was allowing Riker to relax, and it was something he welcomed. "I don't think you have anything to worry about, but what she said then was something I needed to hear, at least right then. I didn't know how to fight Picard and to be the captain this ship needed." He tapped the desktop. "I told her he wrote the book on this ship, and she told me I had to throw that book away. It hurt to hear that, but she was right."

"She was right within the context of that situation," replied Troi. "You needed to sever your feelings for Captain Picard in order to defeat him and the Borg. But that's over now, and he's gone. They can't use him against us anymore."

"Can't they?" Riker frowned. "They still have his knowledge; everything he knew about Starfleet tactics, they took it from him."

Troi crossed her arms. "We'll devise new tactics. We'll

change those things that can be changed, and new Starfleet captains will come up with new ideas; things the Borg can't yet anticipate. In the meantime, you still have to be Will Riker, and part of who you are is what you learned from Captain Picard. Before, you had no other choice but to cut yourself off from everything he meant to you. Now you have the time to integrate those things back into your life and into your leadership. That's normal, Will, but you're fighting it. Yes, you're the captain of the *Enterprise*, but you're not allowing yourself to *be the captain*. Part of that is taking what you learned from the man who prepared you for that role and making it your own."

She was right. Riker had been resisting such feelings, for months. Part of it was concern that he might somehow bring dishonor to his friend's memory, though he knew on an intellectual level that was not possible. Picard had handpicked him as his potential successor and spent three years preparing him for this day. Yes, Riker had been offered command of the *U.S.S. Drake* even prior to accepting the assignment as the *Enterprise*'s first officer, and had chosen the latter because be believed it represented an unparalleled opportunity to serve beside one of Starfleet's most respected captains. He turned down two subsequent promotion offers, first for the *Aries* and later the *Melbourne*. The *Aries* mission had held great appeal for him, in that it involved a long-duration voyage to an uncharted area of the galaxy, embodying everything that had drawn Riker to Starfleet in the first place. Upon further consideration, however, neither assignment carried with it the prestige of serving on the *Enterprise*.

That, and if I'd taken the Melbourne, *I'd be dead now.*

The bitter thought came unbidden as he remembered

seeing the swath of devastation left by the Borg following Starfleet's engagement with the intractable adversary at Wolf 359. The *Enterprise* had found the wreckage of thirty-nine starships, including the *Melbourne*, adrift in space. Tens of thousands of lives snuffed out in moments by the single Borg cube, which had cut through the armada almost without effort as it continued on its course toward Earth. How close had Riker and the *Enterprise* crew come to being listed among the dead?

But they had not died. They were here, and Riker knew he had a job to do.

"You're right," he said, affirming his earlier thought, "and I promise I'll work on that." He gestured around the room. "It just occurred to me this is the perfect place to practice my trombone."

Smiling, Troi replied, "Having heard you play, I agree."

Any chance at a retort was cut off by the sound of the intraship, followed by Data's voice. *"Bridge to Captain Riker."*

"Go ahead."

"We have made progress in our attempts to interface with the alien buoy, sir."

Riker felt a jolt of fresh energy coursing through him as he pushed himself from his chair. "On my way."

With Troi following him, he exited the ready room to find Data, La Forge, and Crusher standing at the rear bridge stations. Lieutenant Worf occupied the ops station in front of the command area, sitting next to Ensign Sariel Rager at the conn position. Ascending the ramp to the upper bridge deck, Riker offered a nod to Lieutenant Yar at the tactical station before moving to join the other officers.

"What've you got?"

"Our attempts to interpret the buoy's communications signal have yielded some success, Captain." Data looked to Crusher. "It was Mister Crusher who made the breakthrough."

Riker offered the younger man an appreciative nod. "How far did you get?"

"We were able to access and download a portion of the buoy's communication log," replied Crusher. "Some of the data's encrypted, and other portions of the packets were corrupted, most likely due to the buoy's state of quantum flux. However, we were able to wash some of it through the computer and the universal translation protocols, and we found something very interesting."

Without waiting for further prompting, Crusher tapped several controls on the engineering workstation's smooth, touch-sensitive panels and the console's larger display screens began displaying a graph, with a line describing peaks and valleys as it moved across the image. At two points along its path, Riker noted the icons corresponding to time stamps beneath the graph. He recognized the significance of both marks.

"When the planet appeared and disappeared?"

La Forge replied, "Right. There's a definite change in the signal that corresponds to the planet shifting into and out of our dimension."

"We found additional log entries that suggest other spikes in conjunction with earlier transitions," said Crusher. "There's no real pattern or consistency to the readings, at least not from what we've found so far, sir. From the looks of it, the shifts occur at completely random intervals."

Riker pondered this. "So, there's no way to predict when the planet will show up again?"

"No, sir," said Data, "but the information at our disposal suggests the planet will return, even if we are unable to forecast the next such occurrence."

La Forge added, "That doesn't mean we're giving up, sir. There's still a lot of data to sift through."

"We're not totally in the dark, though," said Crusher. "The changes in the communication signal are still something we can monitor. Watching for the deviation would give us at least a little advance warning that a shift's coming."

Crossing his arms, Riker reached up to stroke his beard. "All right, then. At least now we've got something to look forward to. Tasha, if we move to a point between the buoy and the planet's expected point of arrival, can you maintain a sensor lock on both areas?"

The security chief replied, "With our current sensor configuration and along with the automated sensor probes we've still got out there, we've got good coverage of both targets, sir."

"Outstanding," said Riker. Then, raising an eyebrow, he looked to Data. "Make it so." La Forge and Crusher smiled in response to the gentle directive, and even Yar turned from her station to regard him with a knowing expression.

That felt pretty good.

Having listened in silence to the conversation, Troi asked, "What about the people on the planet? Will we be able to contact them?"

"Our analysis of the sensor data we have collected suggests contact through standard communications protocols should be possible," replied Data. "However, it may be prudent to prepare a message for delivery as soon as the planet reappears, just in case another dimensional shift occurs before we have an opportunity to establish a dialogue with the planet's inhabitants."

Riker said, "Let's hope for the best, but plan for the worst. Mister Data, you and I can compose that message. If we can establish a dialogue and they can tell us what's going on, there might be something we can do to help them." He exchanged glances with each of his officers. "At the very least, this has the potential to be one of the more interesting first contact situations we've ever had."

"And that's saying something," said La Forge.

A previously unknown species, perhaps hailing from another dimension? What were they like? How had they come to be in their current situation? Were they a potential ally, or a threat? Whatever the answers to those questions, there was no denying the *Enterprise* had stumbled upon something interesting here.

And now, we wait.

12

Picard awoke, startled. It took him a few seconds to recognize the main room of the quarters he shared with Beverly Crusher and their son. Other than dim light from the table lamp next to the sofa he now occupied, and the computer on the nearby desk, the room was cloaked in darkness. He reached for the back of his neck, rubbing away the ache from having dozed with his head resting against the sofa cushion. Blinking several times, he forced away the vestiges of fitful sleep that had managed to seize him, if only for a short time.

Though he started to move, he caught himself upon realizing that he was not alone on the sofa. Curled up beneath a blanket, feet resting on Picard's lap and the top of his head just visible as it rested against the opposite armrest, was his son. René Jacques Robert Francois Picard was deep in the sort of slumber that only small children seemed able to manage. Listening for a moment, Picard heard the boy's soft snoring. He smiled before looking down at the padd in his lap.

"Of course," he said in a low voice. "Now I remember."

According to René's mother, the precocious four-year-old had been missing his father's presence earlier in the evening, owing to Picard's wanting to be close at hand while the investigation continued for the missing planet and the away team. The whereabouts and condition of Commander Worf and the others weighed heavily on him, to the point that he realized he was beginning to worry the rest of his crew with his constant stalking of the bridge. He had retreated to his ready room, content to let Commander La Forge and Lieutenant Elfiki continue their work without his constant if well-meaning requests for updates, but so consumed was he by the current situation that he had all but forgotten the time until Beverly contacted him. Only then did Picard realize that he had missed the story time he regularly shared with René each night before the boy went to bed. It was not the first time, but it was the second night in a row for this oversight. With that in mind, and after leaving things in the capable hands of Lieutenant Commander Havers and the beta shift crew, Picard returned to his quarters with plans to spend a brief respite with René before resuming his vigil on the bridge.

As for the book, though René was capable of reading it himself, he still loved the sound of his father's voice when reciting it aloud. Picard glanced at the padd and the book's text as displayed on its screen cover. The story involved the exploits of a group of exceptional children representing different planets, living and working at a special academy that had been constructed on an asteroid, where they encountered all manner of excitement and danger. According to the *Enterprise*'s daycare facility supervisor, Hailan Casmir, René had been fascinated by the stories, and Picard had since learned that several adventures with the characters were available for viewing as holographic adaptations. Searching his memory, Picard was certain he recalled a promise to his son for them to conduct "an away mission" to the holodeck for further investigation.

Looking across the room to the desk, Picard was unable to make out the chronometer displayed on the computer screen. "Computer, what time is it?"

In its usual feminine voice that still sounded loud enough to rouse the dead, the *Enterprise*'s main computer replied, *"Current ship's time is zero one twenty-seven hours."*

Picard eyed René, but the boy seemed undisturbed, and he could not help smiling. He felt a momentary pang of envy at his son's ability to sleep through almost anything. It had been quite some time since Picard himself had managed so well. In fact, the longer he sat here, the more guilt he felt that he had dozed at all.

"You're not going back to the bridge, are you?"

Turning toward the sound of the voice, Picard saw Beverly Crusher standing in the doorway leading to their bedroom. She wore an off-white silk sleeping gown and a matching robe, and her long red hair was pulled back into a ponytail. The heaviness of her eyelids was the only telltale sign that she had just awakened.

"I will be shortly, yes."

"You need your rest, Captain," she said, adopting her best chief medical officer's tone as she stepped farther into the main room. "Commander Lynley can handle things for a couple of hours."

Picard sat up straighter on the sofa. "Commander Lynley?" Only then did he realize that he had moved René's legs. For his part, the boy did not seem to care. Then Picard nodded in comprehension. "Yes. Gamma shift is on duty now." He had been asleep for nearly four hours, far longer than he had anticipated. "I need to check in." He started to move from the sofa, but Beverly held up a hand.

"Commander Lynley would've called if there was anything to report, Jean-Luc."

With a small sigh of exasperation, Picard replied, "Beverly, I have people who are missing. I can't just sit here."

Beverly crossed her arms. "And what exactly can you do that your crew can't?"

Rather than fight, Picard allowed a small chuckle. "Nothing, but there's more to it than that. You're a certified bridge officer, Beverly. You know how this works." Now fully awake, he eased René's legs from his lap and rose from the sofa. He had removed his uniform jacket, opened his tunic's high collar, and rolled up his sleeves, and he was in the process of putting everything back into its proper place when the intraship chose that moment to beep.

"Bridge to Captain Picard," said Commander Aiden Lynley.

Shaking her head, Beverly moved to the sofa. "Saved by the bell." She added her own smile to the end of her comment, and Picard understood the remark had been meant as gentle teasing.

"Picard here," he said. "Go ahead, Mister Lynley."

"Sorry to bother you, Captain, but you asked to be notified if we had anything new to report."

"You have something?" Picard moved to the table in the corner of the room's dining area, where he had hung his uniform jacket across one of the chairs.

The gamma shift watch officer replied, *"Commander La Forge and Lieutenant Elfiki have been continuing their research of the buoy's communications signal, sir. They're starting to put together a plan and would like to brief you."*

Casting a glance toward Beverly, Picard said, "I'm on my way, Commander. Picard out." Before he could offer any further comment to his wife, she held up her hand.

"I know, Jean-Luc. Believe me. I'm worried about them, too, but I'm also worried that you and the others aren't getting enough rest." Then the doctor's tone returned. "I'd hate to start pulling rank around here."

Picard nodded, accepting the gentle advisory in the spirit with which he knew it was intended. "Acknowledged and understood. I'll be back as soon as I can."

Stepping onto the bridge, Picard was surprised to see not only Commander La Forge and Lieutenant Elfiki, but also Glinn Ravel Dygan standing at the rear workstations. The Cardassian exchange officer's dark, bulky uniform stood in stark contrast to the rest of the bridge crew's regulation Starfleet attire.

"Good morning, sir," said Commander Aiden Lynley as he rose from the command chair. "I hope you were able to get some rest."

Picard cocked his eyebrow. "Have you been consorting with the ship's chief medical officer to ensure this old captain gets his beauty sleep?"

"No, sir," replied the commander, smiling at the question and Picard's knowing look. "I'm really not that brave."

"But you'd do it if she asked you?"

Lynley's grin widened. "Probably. As I said, sir, I'm *really* not *that* brave."

"That makes two of us. As you were, Commander."

Joining the trio of officers waiting for him at the engineering station, Picard asked by way of greeting, "Have you been working here all this time?"

La Forge shook his head. "No, sir. We took a break a couple of hours ago, and our plan was to reconvene later this morning."

Gesturing to Dygan, Elfiki added, "This is all his fault, sir."

The stoic Cardassian's eyes widened and he turned to Picard. "I apologize, Captain. I meant no disrespect or offense."

"I'm kidding, Ravel," said Elfiki. Realizing she now had become the object of scrutiny from Dygan as well as Picard and La Forge, the young science officer indicated the engineering console with a wave. "Why don't you explain what's got us all up here in the middle of the night."

Dygan moved closer to the workstation. "Yes, well, first I must say that I am aware that this is outside the scope of my normal responsibilities, but I confess that I have been most curious about the sensor readings we have received, both from the planet we seek as well as the buoy we later found. To that end, and because I was having difficulty sleeping, I took it upon myself to begin studying the sensor data we have collected to this point, in an attempt to discern a pattern that would allow us to predict when or if the planet might return." He tapped a series of controls on the console. "While examining our readings of the buoy's communications signal, I found evidence of an alteration with that signal's frequency and strength that immediately preceded the most recent dimensional shift."

The image on the workstation showed a computer-generated representation of the signal transmission, and Picard observed the minor spike with a time code noting the point at which the planet had disappeared. There were no other such variations in the data stream.

"We only have the one example," he said, "but you're sure of your findings?"

Dygan nodded. "Absolutely, sir. If and when the planet reappears, we should be able to record a similar deviation in the signal, and perhaps at that point a pattern will begin to emerge that will allow us to predict the frequency of such events."

"Until or unless the planet comes back, it's still a theory," said La Forge, "but it's one I like."

Elfiki nodded. "Me too."

"Indeed." Eyeing the Cardassian, Picard said, "You did this during your off-duty hours, Glinn Dygan?"

"Yes, sir. Once I began researching the data, I became . . . enamored with the process. After I arrived at a preliminary hypothesis, I contacted Lieutenant Elfiki for corroboration, who in turn notified Commander La Forge."

The chief engineer added, "And I'm the one who told Commander Lynley to wake you up, sir."

"I appreciate your initiative and willingness to assist, Glinn Dygan," said Picard, making a mental note to add an appropriate citation in the officer's service record and the next report he would file for Starfleet Command regarding the exchange program.

Dygan had been with the *Enterprise* for nearly four years, and what had begun as a temporary experiment had turned into a long-term assignment following Cardassia's signing of the Khitomer Accords. There had been some concern about his posting to the starship in the immediate wake of President Nanietta Bacco's assassination and the early implication of Cardassia as the responsible party, but Dygan's performance and commitment to his assignment had never wavered, and even when Picard and the *Enterprise* had been given their orders for a long-duration exploration of the Odyssean Pass, the young Cardassian had with great enthusiasm volunteered to extend his tour aboard the ship. Starfleet as well as both the Cardassian and Federation governments saw the potential such an opportunity presented, and with Picard's endorsement approved the request. In the time he had been with the ship, Ravel Dygan had distinguished himself while serving as one of the *Enterprise*'s operations managers, overseeing all of the ship's systems and keeping the captain informed as to their status. Officers in that role often possessed engineering or science backgrounds, supplementing those departments as appropriate to a given situation. Dygan had immersed himself in those responsibilities from the outset, undertaking several courses of study as well as training across multiple areas of ship operations. The reports from his department head and other supervising officers had all been glowing, and Picard had even discussed with the Cardassian the idea of joining Starfleet, so that both parties might continue to benefit from his presence on a permanent basis.

"There's more," said Elfiki. "Once Ravel showed us what he'd been up to, the three of us started tossing ideas around. We think with some reconfigurations to our communications array, we might be able to tap into the buoy's signal."

Picard frowned. "Even though the buoy itself would appear locked within a state of transdimensional phase?"

"We didn't say it'd be easy," replied La Forge, "and to be honest, we're not entirely certain it'll even work. But, if we could access that stream, we might be able to contact whatever's on the other end of that signal. The logical target is the planet."

"And the away team," added Elfiki. "If we can find a way to piggyback onto that signal, there's a chance we can send our own transmission through to the other side; one our people can receive with their communicators."

Dygan said, "And let us not forget the people already on the planet. If they were in distress, we may be able to render assistance. However, I suspect that any degree of long-term assistance will require us to have a better understanding of the planet's movements between dimensions."

"Maybe the buoy's signal is even part of the process," replied Elfiki. "If we could figure that out, maybe there's a way to alter that signal and . . . I don't know . . . force a shift?" Even as she spoke the words, she shook her head. "No, scratch that, at least for now. We have no idea what effect that might have on the planet or anyone on it."

"No," said La Forge. "Don't scratch it. Let's just move carefully on it until we get more information. For now, our priority should be establishing communications with anybody on the planet." He sighed. "With luck, Taurik's getting a chance to investigate the equipment or whatever it is that's causing the shifts in the first place." He paused, his gaze dropping to the deck for a moment before he added, "We know they landed without too much trouble. Here's hoping the locals are looking after them. After all, they did warn us to stay away for our own safety."

Picard nodded. The tone of the message received from the planet's surface—to him, at least—seemed to have been one of concern, rather than malevolence. His gut told him that the people on the planet were somehow victims caught up in whatever consequences had befallen their activities there. He hoped there would be an opportunity to learn the complete circumstances surrounding the planet, as well as to help those who might be in trouble.

"Geordi, take whatever steps you feel are necessary and prudent to establish a connection with the buoy's signal. Glinn Dygan, continue your research and attempt to find some pattern we can use to predict the planet's reappearance."

"Aye, sir," replied the chief engineer. "We'll get right on it."

Eyeing the three officers, Picard asked, "All this, because you couldn't sleep?"

La Forge shrugged. "We do some of our best work when we're not sleeping."

13

ELSEWHERE
Ushalon

The alarm, a series of four electronic tones repeated in rapid succession, filled the passageways and echoed off the metal bulkheads. All around the observation room, T'Ryssa Chen watched as the Sidrac engineers and scientists, eight of them in total, moved to different workstations around the large chamber.

"Another shift is imminent," said Nelidar as she led the away team into the room, gesturing for them to remain in a corner away from the consoles or other equipment that her people might need.

"If this transposition is like all of the others," she continued, "then there should be no problems."

Standing at the rear of the group, Kirsten Cruzen replied in a voice only Chen could hear, "There's always a first time."

Chen stepped to her left, the movement enough to give her an unfettered view of the observation room and its Sidrac staff. There was an obvious purpose to their movements, but Chen saw that everyone seemed to conduct themselves as though their motions were well-practiced and carried out almost without conscious thought.

That makes sense. How many times have they gone through this?

"The quantum energy readings are spiking," reported Taurik from where he stood next to Worf at the head of the group, holding his tricorder in his left hand. "These levels are very similar to what we recorded soon after our landing." The engineer had taken the initiative of tying his tricorder to the *Spinrad*'s onboard computer, allowing him remote access to all of the shuttlecraft's systems. This included the ability to configure and employ the compact vessel's sensor array.

"Energy levels are approaching target levels," reported one of the Sidrac engineers, a male whom Nelidar had identified as Livak.

Another scientist, a female named Pevon, called out, "All systems optimal."

Cruzen asked, "That's good, right?"

It was bizarre, Chen decided, to stand and watch the Sidrac team go about their tasks, knowing that they were in reality observers with no influence over what was happening around them. They, along with the away team, could only watch and wait to see how the process played out. What if the field generator experienced a malfunction while in the midst of carrying out the shift?

Let's not dwell on that too much.

"Field generator at maximum output," said Livak, just before a large orange indicator set into the wall at the front of the room began to flash.

Nelidar turned to the away team. "This is it."

"Does anyone feel sick?" asked Chen. "Disorientation, nausea, anything?" Instead of the sensory overload she had endured during the previous shift, now she felt only mild discomfort. There seemed to be no issues with her vision or hearing this time, and neither was she sweating or out of breath.

"Nothing like last time," replied Cruzen.

Taurik said, "I am feeling no ill effects. My tricorder

is detecting a new energy signature, emanating from within this structure. It appears to act as something of a damping field, perhaps reducing the severity of adverse reactions to the quantum shift."

"That's a nice touch." Chen's attention had been drawn to the banks of computer equipment lining the observation room's far wall, where several rows of status indicators and gauges were illuminated or otherwise displaying various bits of information. None of it made any sense to her, but the Sidrac engineers were taking it all in, and none of them seemed alarmed. The familiarity of this process for all of them was evident, leaving only Chen and her companions to worry.

For the first time, she perceived bright light intruding at the edges of her peripheral vision, and a dull hum now sounded in her ears. Then she saw the workstations and the people around her begin to stretch and ripple. Her stomach heaved and Chen thought she might have to sit down, but she felt a hand on her arm. It was Cruzen, whose expression seemed to have paled as her eyes widened.

"I take it back," said Chen. "This isn't nice. At *all*."

Cruzen started to say something, but Chen lost her words in the howl that roared in her ears. Color drained out of everything before a bright flash made her close her eyes. She reached up to block the illumination's source, but it surrounded her. Somewhere nearby she heard someone—possibly Cruzen—saying something she could not understand.

And then it was over.

The light faded, along with the assault on her hearing, and the nausea that had threatened to wash over her also was gone. Not nearly as pronounced as the first time they had experienced the shift, the effects this time were easier to shake off, and Chen observed that her companions all looked to have weathered the transition in similar fashion.

Worf, his Klingon countenance fixed, placed a hand on Cruzen's arm. "Are you all right, Lieutenant?"

"I'll be okay, sir," replied the security officer, her hand still pressed to her stomach. "That was fun, but I'd really rather not make it a habit."

"Now for the big question," said Chen. "Where are we?"

Stepping away from the group, she moved to where Nelidar stood at the forefront of the U-shaped arrangement of workstations, watching over her colleagues as they already were immersed in various tasks. On the far wall, the banks of computer stations had calmed down, their array of status lights and indicators now idle or dark. Nelidar, noticing her, offered a grim smile.

"We appear to have successfully completed another transition." She gestured to her people. "They are conducting our usual review of all systems, looking for problems or anything else requiring our attention, but so far all appears normal."

Chen asked, "Which dimension did we shift to?"

Gesturing to another of her female companions, Nelidar replied, "Bidani is ascertaining that now."

The other Sidrac engineer looked up from her console. "According to the quantum signature, we have arrived at target location three."

"Having moved from target location one," said Chen, recalling the details from the information Nelidar had shared with the away team as part of her extended explanation of the network established by the Sidrac scientists and their communications buoys. "And location five before that." Location five was the one she wanted to hear, as that dimension was where the *Enterprise* waited.

Location five was *home*.

Still, Chen could not help but be intrigued by what this represented. Before them was yet another plane of existence, separate from their own. How similar was it to the dimension they had left behind? What wonders awaited them here, and what might they find if they were to go exploring? The possibilities were astounding, she knew, and the opportunity presented by the Sidrac technology was too great to ignore.

Maybe someday, after we get home, and possibly figure out how to better control the process?

"All systems are optimal," reported Livak, who had risen from his seat and moved away from his station as he approached Nelidar. "The quantum energy output has declined as expected."

"For now, anyway," said Chen. "Right?"

Nelidar replied, "That is correct. As always, we will monitor the energy readings in order to prepare for the next transition."

Movement to her right made Chen turn to see Taurik approaching them, his tricorder once more open and activated.

"I have had the *Spinrad*'s sensors conducting active scans throughout this process," said the Vulcan. "With the data we are collecting, we can analyze the field generator's output and perhaps find a way to circumvent it, or at least disconnect it from the primary power source. The challenge will be doing so while avoiding a future transition."

"Yeah," said Chen, "I'm thinking we don't want to be messing around with the machinery while sailing between dimensions."

Taurik nodded. "Indeed." His tricorder beeped, and he studied the unit's compact display, and Chen saw how his right eyebrow rose as though he was surprised by the readings.

"Trouble?" she prompted.

"Perhaps." Looking up from the tricorder, he turned to Worf. "Commander?"

Along with Cruzen, the first officer moved to join Taurik and Chen. "Yes?"

"The shuttlecraft's sensors have detected three ships in proximity to the planet, sir." He paused, looking at his colleagues before adding, "They are not in orbit, but seem to be maintaining station within scanning range. Our sensor readings indicate they are Romulan vessels."

"Uh-oh," said Cruzen.

Worf scowled. "You are certain?"

"Yes," said the engineer. "There is something else. If the readings are accurate, the ships appear to be of a design and level of technology we would consider obsolete. One vessel is a *Vas Hatham*–class warship, accompanied by two smaller, *Mularr*-class escorts."

"The Romulans haven't used ships from either of those classes for almost a century," said Cruzen. "Is there anything to indicate they might be restored or refurbished? Maybe it's not Romulans, but civilian freight haulers or someone else who got lucky at a surplus depot."

Taurik replied, "According to the *Spinrad*'s sensors, the vessels appear to be in perfect working order and possess armaments and other features consistent with ships in the prime of their operational life cycle. All three ships are cloaked, but the shuttle's scans were still able to detect them, suggesting outdated stealth technology."

"So," said Chen, "either somebody's pulled a couple of antique ships out of mothballs and taken them for a joyride, or . . ."

"Or it is possible that in addition to our dimensional shift, a temporal transition has also occurred." Taurik's right brow arched again. "Intriguing."

Standing next to Chen and listening to the exchange in silence to this point, Nelidar asked, "Temporal transition? Are you suggesting we have moved to a different point in time?"

"Perhaps not in the strictest sense," offered Taurik, "though I am at present unable to offer further analysis, as this not a situation for which I have any comparison."

Cruzen crossed her arms. "What he means is that this is all pretty new to us, and that's saying something."

"You indicated the ships were not in orbit," said Worf, "but they were in scanning range. That implies they may have been waiting for the planet to reappear in this dimension." Turning to Nelidar, he asked, "Have you detected anything during your previous shifts to suggest the planet was being observed?"

The Sidrac shook her head. "No, not at first. However, during the past few visits to this location, our scans did detect peculiar energy readings, which we at first thought might be an orbiting vessel, but we were unable to confirm that, and neither did anyone answer our attempts to communicate."

"Romulans wouldn't have answered," said Cruzen, "and their cloaking technology likely shielded them from your scans, at least enough to confuse your readings."

Nelidar frowned. "So, you are familiar with these . . . Romulans?"

"Afraid so," said Chen, "though where we come from,

their technology is much more advanced than what we seem to have here."

Worf grunted. "If the Romulans have been monitoring this region for some time, then they will be aware of the planet's behavior. It is possible they are observing from a distance in an attempt to predict the planet's appearances in this dimension, and if they have scanned your field generator and other technology, they likely will want to investigate further."

"And unlike us," said Cruzen, "they're not very friendly."

"They would not harm us?" asked Nelidar, but Chen could see that she already suspected the answer to her own question.

"If they feel there is a strategic advantage to be gained by seizing your technology," replied Taurik, "most Romulan military commanders have no compunction about killing anyone who might present resistance." To Worf and the others, he said, "If they are observing the planet, then they likely know that they are unable to access the field generator directly. However, I do not expect that to dissuade them indefinitely."

Worf nodded. "Agreed. The Romulans may be coming. We must be ready."

ChR *Bloodied Talon*

Examining the sensor readouts for herself, Sarith was still struck by disbelief.

"Where could it have come from?" she asked, pointing to the computer-generated image of the mysterious craft sitting on the surface of the equally enigmatic world that had chosen to appear just moments earlier.

"I do not know, Commander," replied Darjil, once again standing at stiff attention, having stepped away from his station to give Sarith clear access to the console. "I have rechecked the sensor logs, and it was not there during our previous scans. It is as though it materialized from nothing."

Scrutinizing the odd little ship, Sarith realized it looked at once familiar and alien to her. "It resembles a Starfleet shuttlecraft," she said, more to herself than Darjil or anyone else, "and yet there is something about it that seems wrong."

"If anything," said Ineti, who had moved to stand next to her, "it looks more advanced than anything we have seen. Perhaps Starfleet has been fielding new shuttle designs, but I find it hard to believe this would escape the notice of our spies."

Considering this, Sarith said, "Unless there is something about this particular vessel that makes it of heightened value to Starfleet. Some experimental propulsion or weapons system, or perhaps even a cloaking device of their own."

"There have been no indications that the Federation has made any attempts at cloaking technology," said Darjil.

"And you are informed as to the latest developments in Starfleet tactical research, Centurion?" Ineti's question was enough to make the younger Romulan bow his head.

Properly chastised, Darjil said, "My apologies, Subcommander. It was not my intention to speculate aloud."

"Never mind that now," snapped Sarith. Her enthusiasm at being given another opportunity to study the odd planet had been dampened by the realization that someone, somehow had landed near the cluster of buildings that was the only sign of life on the surface. Had the Earth people somehow found a way to best them, even here in this remote region of unclaimed space far from their borders?

Impossible.

She motioned to the sensor display. "What can you tell me about the craft?"

Darjil replied, "It does bear a resemblance to known forms of Starfleet shuttlecraft, Commander, but its propulsion and weapons systems appear far more advanced than anything on record."

"Perhaps our agents behind enemy lines are not as effective as their reputation suggests," said Ineti. "If something like this has escaped their notice, what other Federation secrets have they failed to uncover?"

It was generally suspected, if not outright believed, that Romulan agents had for some time been conducting all manner of clandestine surveillance of Federation and Starfleet interests. No one in any position of military or civilian authority had ever officially confirmed such allegations, but the sort of information given to ship commanders and other military leaders by the government gave credence to the notion. Rumors abounded of covert operatives skulking deep behind enemy lines, some even embedded as children after being surgically altered to appear human and living in secret for years until such time as they worked their way into positions of influence or access within Starfleet or the Federation government. Similar initiatives had been perpetrated against other adversaries and parties of interest to the Empire, but Sarith had never seen any evidence of such agents working within the Federation. If true, it would be a triumph of intelligence gathering, and while she suspected such activities were taking place, they were closely guarded secrets. The cost of discovery was far too high, likely resulting in renewed conflict with old enemies that perhaps even the praetor did not want.

At least, not yet.

"So, we have a new ship on the surface," she said. "Are there additional life-forms, as well?"

Darjil turned back to his instruments and after a moment replied, "Our scans do indicate a small increase in the total number of life readings, but the continuing interference is such that I am unable to determine a specific number or differentiate between species."

"But someone is there," said Ineti. "Someone who may have interests similar to our own."

This time, the centurion elected to say nothing, leaving the speculation to his superior officers. Instead, it was Sarith who replied, "If so, then we must act." She needed more information about these new arrivals and what, if any, threat they might pose. With her ship's sensors compromised by the energy waves washing over the planet, there was only one alternative.

"Ineti, prepare a scouting party."

14

Come out, come out, wherever you are.

How many times had that teasing thought danced across his subconscious? Riker had given up keeping count. The joke was funny several hours ago when someone, likely La Forge, had made it, but now like his patience was wearing thin. Standing in silence before the bridge's main viewscreen, his arms crossed as he gazed once more upon the Spindrift Nebula, he could not help the feeling of restlessness that had begun to assert itself. While the nebula was beautiful and just the sort of spatial phenomenon his science department could spend weeks if not months studying, it had lost its appeal for him. Riker realized it was not the nebula's fault, at least not beyond the extent that it seemed to be conspiring against him as it stubbornly refused to yield its most tantalizing of secrets.

A little overly dramatic, Captain. Don't you think?

His feelings of agitation, minor though they may be, were only compounded by the fact that he was forced to wait, giving his people the time they needed to complete their work in order to provide him with information upon which he might make a decision. Waiting was not something with which Riker had ever been comfortable, and it was only after his promotion and the ceding of his former responsibilities to Data that he realized just how much a captain was required to do nothing except allow others to do their duties. As first officer, his role had been one of coordination, overseeing the efforts of the crew as they accomplished whatever tasks were required of them. There never seemed to be enough time to manage everything, and that was before a situation's urgency increased all the way to full-blown emergency. All the while, Captain Picard would sit at the center of the maelstrom of activity, silent and stoic as though evaluating every iota of information sent his way. Was it possible that Picard, even just for the briefest of moments when all seemed calm around him, had just been bored? The thought made Riker smile, and he even glanced around to make sure no one was observing him.

I just wish you were here to tell me.

"Captain."

Turning from the viewscreen, Riker saw that Data, who had been sitting in his seat moments ago, was now standing at the rear of the bridge with Geordi La Forge and Wesley Crusher. The pair had become semipermanent fixtures there during the past several hours, and Riker knew that fatigue had to be weighing on them by this point. Two gamma shift ensigns were positioned at the conn and ops positions, while Lieutenant Yar moved between her own tactical console and those forward stations, overseeing the junior officers and leaving Data free to assist La Forge and Crusher.

"Mister Data?" he said as he started moving toward them.

The first officer waited until Riker joined them before replying. "We have made a breakthrough, sir."

"I'll say," added La Forge, before tapping Crusher on

the arm with the back of his hand. "Well, maybe you should say."

Crusher explained, "We've been able to decrypt more of the buoy's communication logs, Captain." He touched a control on the engineering console and Riker was greeted with the familiar graphic of the alien probe's transmission stream, only now it featured several more deviations, each with its own time code.

"It's a complete history of its transmissions, from the time of its original deployment, including each instance of the planet's interaction with this dimension."

Riker smiled. "Now we're talking."

"As our earlier research indicated," said Data, "the logs show a marked deviation in the signal as well as re-corded and transmitted information each time the planet moves to or from our dimension. The largest spike comes during those times when the planet is here, and tapers off after it transitions to another dimension."

La Forge pointed to the screen. "It's like a data dump whenever the planet shows up. The pattern is consistent for that, at least, with a larger data transmission being the first thing that happens following transition. It also receives information back. Most of it is still encrypted, but we're guessing the probe essentially fires off whatever data can't be transmitted between dimensions and then receives some kind of update from . . . well, I guess you'd call it the home base."

"There's more," said Crusher. He tapped another control on the console and the display shifted to show a total of five such graphs, each with their own sequences of peaks, valleys, and markings indicating periods of in-tense data transmission.

"According to the logs we've decrypted so far, there are four other buoys just like this one, each deployed to a different dimension. These transmissions all contain encoded information pertaining to specific quantum signatures."

Data said, "Our conclusion is that the planet is shifting between five dimensions at random intervals and at an irregular rate, and doing so with no discernible pattern for which dimension is visited."

"But why?" Riker frowned. "Why go to all this trouble just to bounce an entire planet around like that. For what purpose? Is it all deliberate, or just a massive accident?" Was what they were seeing inspired by curiosity and a quest for knowledge, or was something more sinister in play? Or, was it simply a bizarre but natural phenomenon of a sort never before encountered? Each possibility warranted further investigation, but it would help to know the motivations of whoever or whatever was responsible for all of this.

"There is the warning we received from the planet to consider," Data offered. "Though only a portion of it was intelligible, the intent of the sender seems rather explicit in their wish to have us stay away from the planet."

"They also said that what was happening was of their own doing." La Forge reached up to rub his temple where his VISOR connected to the port on the right side of his head, and Riker noted the other man's slight frown. "They know what and why this is happening."

Riker asked, "You all right, Geordi?"

The chief engineer nodded. "Just tired, sir. We've

been staring at this stuff for a while now. I'll be fine."
Clearing his throat, he indicated the display screen.
"Here's something else. So far as we can tell based on our
analysis of residual quantum energy readings we scanned
from the planet itself, it's not from any of the five dimensions where a buoy is deployed."

It took a moment for that to sink in, after which
Riker scowled as he began to comprehend La Forge's
meaning. "Wait, you're saying this planet is randomly
bouncing around between five different dimensions, and
none of them are its point of origin?"

"That is correct, sir," replied Data. "Our analysis
shows that since entering this cycle, the planet has not
returned to its own dimension. Based on this preliminary analysis, we suspect the planet was never intended
to be transported in this fashion. Instead, it was meant to
act as the anchor point in what appears to be a rudimen-
tary transdimensional network, with the buoys providing
target locations for any ships or other objects designed to
make the transition."

"And if that's true, it means something went seriously
wrong somewhere," said Crusher.

La Forge managed a tired grin. "He's been working
on his understatements, sir. Data has been coaching
him."

Grateful for the momentary levity, Riker replied,
"Keep up the good work."

An alert from the tactical station made them turn to
where Tasha Yar was leaning over the console.

"Sensors just picked up a deviation in the buoy's
comm signal, sir," reported the security chief.

Having moved back to the engineering station, Crusher

tapped several commands into the console's instrument panel. "We instructed the computer to be on the lookout for that and issue a tactical alert, just in case." After a moment spent studying the sensor readings, he added, "Definitely a spike in the signal, sir."

"This might be it," said La Forge.

Riker asked, "You've got our sensors configured to monitor the buoy throughout the process?"

The engineer nodded. "Yes, sir. If and when it happens, we'll be able to record and analyze the whole process."

Data said, "I am also attempting to maintain a connection with the buoy's signal. I have reconfigured our communications array to compensate for the quantum fluctuations. I cannot guarantee success, but I am hopeful it will provide additional insight into the buoy's role in the transition process."

"Outstanding." Moving away from the engineering station, Riker made his way down the ramp. "Full sensor sweep, Geordi. I don't want us to miss anything." Pausing before his seat in the command area, he returned his attention to the mass of multicolored swirling gases that filled the viewscreen.

"Quantum energy readings are increasing," reported Data, who also had moved to his own seat and now was consulting the console positioned next to his chair. "I am attempting to predict a time for the planet's arrival."

Riker acknowledged the report, his attention still on the screen. Was it his imagination—perhaps fueled by Data's observations—or was the nebula more animated, even agitated, than before? Could the mysterious planet's impending arrival already be having a tangible effect on the space it was set to occupy?

If that's the case, then let's hope it's a good sign.

ELSEWHERE
ChR Bloodied Talon

"You are certain of these readings?"

Standing at the sensor station, Darjil nodded, and Sarith saw the nervousness gripping the young centurion. "Yes, Commander. Scans indicate another quantum shift is imminent."

"But so soon after the last one?" Her concern mounting as she moved around the bridge's central hub, Sarith stepped closer to the sensor controls in order to verify the readings with her own eyes. "Why?"

Darjil replied, "We have insufficient information to . . ." His voice faltered, and he cast his gaze downward before drawing a breath and straightening his posture. "I am unable to answer that question, Commander. I have failed."

"No," countered Ineti. "You cannot be faulted for an inability to grasp something that is beyond all of us, Centurion. Attend your station." He pointed to the officer manning the communications station. "Contact the shuttle *Amidar*. Have them return to the ship immediately."

Angry with herself far more than any of her subordinates, Sarith turned away from the sensors, fuming. It had been her decision to dispatch a landing craft to the planet's surface. Working with the information provided by Darjil, she and Ineti had worked out a rough approximation of the minimum amount of time the planet had been present in this dimension following a quantum shift. Sarith then had cut that number in half, leaving her with a window of time she believed would be more than sufficient to gather more detailed information via direct reconnaissance of the alien structures and machinery on and below the ground.

And yet, the fates have seen fit to smite me.

"The *Amidar*'s pilot is contacting us," reported Centurion Skerius from the communications console. "She reports difficulty with interference from the elevated quantum energy readings. They appear to be affecting all shipboard systems."

"It will only get worse if the planet is heading toward another shift," said Ineti.

Do you not think I understand that?

Forcing herself not to give voice to that initial, unfiltered response, Sarith instead asked, "How much time before the shift occurs?"

"I am unable to determine that with any certainty, Commander," replied Darjil.

"We have *no more time* for your theories, Centurion," she barked. This was no longer an intellectual exercise. Her people were in danger, and her patience was nearing its end. "Estimate, *now!*"

Before Darjil could respond, Skerius called out, "Commander! The shuttle is transmitting a distress message. The pilot is losing control, and reports she will be forced to attempt an emergency landing."

"Open the channel," ordered Sarith, snapping her fingers. A moment later and laced with static, the harried voice of Subcommander Variel, her scouting party's leader, came over the bridge's intership system.

"—periencing turbu . . . able to compensate with shields . . . ulsion system compromi . . . anding on the surface—"

"Shuttle *Amidar*," said Sarith, "if you must land, you need to get away from that area immediately."

Darjil said, "Commander, our sensor readings are being corrupted by the heightened quantum fluctuations. I am unable to maintain a solid lock on the *Amidar*."

"Find a way," Sarith replied. "Draw power from noncritical systems, but I want that lock maintained."

Over the open communications channel, Variel called out, *"Main engines are offli . . . thrusters only . . . ing our descent. Stand—"* A loud pop washed out the rest of the subcommander's report, causing Sarith to glare at Skerius.

"What happened?"

The centurion replied, "Communication lost, Commander. The frequency deteriorated before the signal dissolved altogether. I am attempting to reestablish contact."

"I think the shuttle is on the surface, Commander." It was Darjil, his face almost touching the illuminated screen that provided him with raw data from the *Talon*'s sensor array. "I am no longer detecting evidence of their propulsion system, and there is no indication of movement."

Stepping closer to the sensor station, Ineti asked, "Can you ascertain the *Amidar*'s condition?"

"Not with our current sensor capabilities, Subcommander."

Sarith said, "Redouble your efforts." She was already giving thought to deploying another shuttle in a bid to rescue the first group, but prudence demanded she ascertain the first ship's condition before risking more of her crew. There were also other concerns. "What about the quantum energy readings? Are they still increasing?"

"Yes, Commander," replied Darjil. "Well ahead of our most conservative estimates."

Ineti said, "We are running out of time."

From where he stood at the weapons station, Centurion N'tovek said, "Commander, we could attempt to disrupt or disable the equipment responsible for the shift."

"We do not know what damage that might cause on the surface," replied Ineti. "It could prove hazardous for our scouting party."

"The subcommander is correct," added Darjil. "Any attempt to disrupt the quantum-field generator could produce a variety of unexpected results."

Sarith said, "And being exposed to the quantum shift without protection could be hazardous as well." She harbored no illusions that the shuttle's hull would provide insulation from the largely unknown effects of that much quantum energy in such close proximity. The transition might well be enough to kill the entire scouting party. While circumstances on more than one occasion had forced her to sacrifice the lives of those under her command, it was an action she always undertook with great reluctance and never without weighing any and all contributing factors. Further, she loathed the idea of facilitating the death of any subordinate as a matter of convenience or for some perceived greater good. She needed the reasoning for such a decision to be without doubt or ambiguity.

Likewise, leaving to chance the fates of those who looked to her for leadership was also something she could not accept.

"Target the power source," she said, moving closer to N'tovek and the weapons station. "Only the power source. None of the surrounding infrastructure, or any of the surface structures. We want to disable, not destroy. Am I clear, Centurion?"

After all, there is still the praetor's prize to consider.

15

The waiting was the worst part.

There was nothing more for T'Ryssa Chen or her companions to do except wait, just as they had done the last time this sequence of events had played out. Along with the rest of the away team, she watched as Nelidar and the other Sidrac engineers moved between workstations, checking and rechecking instruments and status indicators. Things were different this time, and with good reason.

"Is it me," she said, "or does everyone look more nervous this time?" Now that their presence had become accepted by the Sidrac, she and the rest of the away team were no longer confined to one corner of the observation room. Taurik and Chen had even offered to assist their hosts, but for now stood with their companions, waiting.

Nelidar, having made a circuit of the observation room to check with each of her colleagues manning a workstation, replied, "This is the first time a transition has happened so soon after a previous shift. We have no precedent for this, and it is the possible cause that is giving us our greatest concern."

"Is there a problem?" asked Worf.

"There has been a change in the signal we are receiving from the probe at target location two. It is unlike anything we have experienced since first deploying the buoys."

Chen frowned. "Location two? Didn't you say that was where you detected another ship?"

"We transitioned from that point before our encounter with you, Lieutenant." Nelidar frowned. "Our scanners alerted us to the presence of a vessel in that region as well, but it took no provocative action. We broadcast our usual warning messages, but did not receive a response before we left that dimension."

Worf said, "If the ship in that dimension found your buoy, they may be attempting to access it in order to understand its functions."

"And that might prove troublesome for us," replied Nelidar. "If they somehow interfere with the signal, there is no way to know what effect that might have on Ushalon during a shift to that location."

Standing next to Chen, Lieutenant Kirsten Cruzen said, "As if we don't have enough problems."

"The Romulan shuttle has landed," reported Taurik, who had moved to stand near the male Sidrac engineer, Livak. The Vulcan was once more consulting his tricorder, taking advantage of its link to the shuttlecraft *Spinrad*'s more powerful sensor array. "Seven life signs. Their current position is approximately five hundred meters southwest of our position and eight hundred meters west of our shuttlecraft. I am detecting a hull breach, and at least one possible injury. Given their current circumstances, it is logical to assume they will attempt to come here, as it is the closer destination."

Standing next to Chen, Doctor Tropp asked, "Should we not attempt to render assistance?" Along with Lieutenant Rennan Konya, the Denobulan had joined the rest of the team once it became apparent that the Sidrac were not a threat and new problems had arisen.

Worf replied, "Not until we can ascertain their intentions." The first officer had already begun consulting with Konya and Cruzen about possible courses of action now that it appeared they were about to have company. "We must assume they will attempt to enter this habitat."

"There are four entrances," said Nelidar. "They can be locked, but they were not meant to withstand a forced intrusion."

That made sense, at least to Chen. After all, Ushalon was an uninhabited planet from an unknown star system, as yet undiscovered by other spacefaring species.

Cruzen said, "Commander Taurik said their technology wasn't as advanced as ours. Can we jam their scanners and communications with the *Spinrad*?"

"An interesting notion." The Vulcan tapped a series of controls on his tricorder. "I believe that is possible."

"I'd hold off on doing that," said Konya. "Wait until we're sure they're heading in our direction and close enough that doubling back looks like a bad idea, then do it. Otherwise, they might decide to head for the shuttle and disable it."

Worf nodded. "Good thinking."

A deep rumbling from somewhere beneath or outside the room caused everything to tremble or rattle. Lights and consoles flickered, and a new round of alert tones sounded from various stations. Everyone, away team and Sidrac alike, looked around for the source of the tremor.

"What the hell was that?" asked Konya.

The only answer he received came in the form of another alert siren, and this time it was one Chen recognized. She turned to see Livak, the male Sidrac engineer, hovering over his control panel. His long, thin fingers moved across his instruments, and his expression was one of near panic.

"Something struck the field generator complex!" Livak did not look up from his console. "A powerful energy burst, unlike anything I have ever seen." A moment later, he added, "Quantum readings are increasing, much faster than expected. Another shift is imminent!"

Taurik said, "The Romulan ship fired on the complex." His report was calm and matter-of-fact, but Chen heard the barest trace of concern in the Vulcan's voice. "It is no longer employing its cloaking device, and I am detecting an energy signature consistent with the disruptor cannons of a *Vas Hatham*–class warship."

"Why the hell would they fire for no reason?" asked Konya.

Chen replied, "They wouldn't. Could they be trying to stop the next shift?"

"Possibly," said Taurik, "but without more information, I am unable to formulate a hypothesis."

"Is there any damage?" Nelidar had directed the question to Livak, but he was looking both to her own people and Taurik for possible answers.

"Aside from some disruption of the surrounding soil and bedrock, I am detecting no obvious damage to the structure itself." Taurik paused, looking up from his tricorder. "If the field generator is itself trapped in a state of dimensional flux, it may have been protected. However, scans are showing significant disruption of the quantum field itse—"

The rest of the engineer's report was drowned out by the return of the alert klaxon, just as Chen felt the first rush of sound in her ears at the same time blinding light washed across her vision. Colors faded as the room around her began to bend and twist, and she thought she caught sight of Rennan Konya reaching for her. His arm seemed to stretch as it drew closer, and for an instant she saw his expression of worry.

Then the light consumed everything.

ELSEWHERE
ChR *Bloodied Talon*

Sparks flew from the environmental control console as yet another overload coursed through the bridge, and the stench of burned circuitry assaulted Sarith's nostrils. Without need for instruction, Centurion N'tovek deactivated the console and initiated a fire suppression protocol. The station's functions were not critical and could be ported to other consoles, and the crew was well trained in such procedures, but that was the least of her problems now.

"Quantum fluctuations are spiking," reported Darjil from the sensor station. "The readings are consistent with a dimensional shift. Commander, if we remain in such proximity to the planet, we may be in grave danger."

"Break orbit." Sarith moved to the helm station at the bridge's central hub. On the console's display screen, she could see the planet beginning to waver and stretch as it had on the previous occasions they had witnessed its vanishing, only this time it was happening while her vessel was much too close for her comfort. "Alert the *N'minecci* and the *Jarax* to retreat to safe distance."

Prall, the centurion manning the helm, reported, "Something is preventing us from maneuvering, Commander. It is not a tractor beam, but the effect is similar."

"Diverting emergency power to the impulse engines and our deflector shields," said Ineti. The subcommander had pushed aside the centurion manning the secondary helm console and had taken the controls himself. With practiced ease, the elder Romulan keyed the necessary instructions and Sarith felt the trembling from the ship's depths as the *Talon* answered his commands. Even with the added power, experience and instinct told her something was wrong.

Ineti confirmed her suspicions. "We are at full power and unable to break orbit." The subcommander looked away from the helm controls "I am routing power from the warp engines, but there is no change."

"Can we engage the warp engines?" Sarith knew the risks of such a dangerous maneuver, both to her ship and even to the planet below, but time and options were dwindling.

"The elevated quantum fluctuations are preventing us from establishing a subspace field. Deflector shield generator output is already exceeding tolerance levels and is blocking but a portion of the quantum energy interference." Ineti input more commands to the console, before shaking his head. "There is nothing more we can do."

Turning from the weapons station, N'tovek said, "The escort vessels are reporting similar difficulties, Commander. We could fire on the complex again. Perhaps a more concentrated bombardment."

"It would require us to divert power from our propulsion or shields."

Sarith asked, "Are we being pulled toward the planet?"

After consulting one of his instrument panels, N'tovek replied, "No, Commander. The effect is more disruptive in nature. If we were able to block or stop the source of the interference, we would be free of its effects."

Another alarm sounded in the confined space, and Ineti moved to silence it. "Our engines are beginning to overheat. If we do not reduce power or break free, they may incur more damage than our engineers can repair."

Before Sarith could answer, the entire ship shuddered around them, protesting as though forced to endure a withering attack. Several of the bridge consoles went dark as the main lighting failed, replaced by emergency illumination that flared to life from points around the room. Then everything around her seemed to spin or bend, and a wave of vertigo washed over her. Reaching for the nearest console to steady herself, she felt Ineti's hand on her arm. She tried to say something but what sounded like a torrent of rain or wind flooded her ears, and she winced at the sudden onslaught. Light pushed in from the edges of her vision, and the dizziness that had come without warning threatened to overwhelm her.

What is happ—

ELSEWHERE
U.S.S. *Enterprise*-D

"Red alert!"

Riker shouted the command just as the entire ship seemed to heave beneath his feet. All around him, the other bridge officers clambered to hold on to anything to anchor themselves to chair or consoles as the *Enterprise*'s inertial damping system struggled to compensate with the abrupt disruption. The main lighting failed, dousing the bridge in near darkness for the seconds it took emergency illumination to activate. Gripping the back of the conn officer's chair was the only thing that saved Riker from being thrown to the deck. For the briefest of instants he sensed the artificial gravity wavering, the change channeling through his body and making his stomach lurch.

"Quantum energy readings are off the scale!" reported Wesley Crusher from the conn seat. "Much more powerful than anything we've seen so far."

"Pull us back," ordered Riker. "I want some extra distance."

Crusher replied, "I'm trying, Captain, but engines aren't responding."

"We are experiencing system overloads across the ship," reported Data from his seat next to Riker's command chair. "Backup systems are being enabled."

The buffeting the *Enterprise* was enduring in response to the planet's unexpected arrival was beginning to ebb, leaving only a slew of alert indicators sounding across the bridge. Glancing behind him, Riker saw a number of illuminated status indicators flashing on the rear workstations, including far too many from the engineering console. Similar warnings were displayed on Worf's ops panel.

Riker pulled down on his uniform jacket as he stepped back from Wesley's chair. Turning around, he caught sight of Deanna sitting in her usual place next to the captain's chair. Her expression communicated her discomfort.

"You all right?" he asked.

Nodding, she replied, "The crew's emotions are running high right now."

"Tell me about it." Riker was sensitive to her empathic abilities, of course, and knew that in the face of the unknown situation they were in, it was a natural reaction to be uncertain if not afraid. Deanna would pick up most of that, he knew, particularly from the people here on the bridge.

Looking to Data, Riker said, "Damage report."

"Updates are still coming in, sir," replied the first officer. "There are a large number of power relays that have suffered overloads. Damage control teams are responding."

At the back of the bridge, Geordi La Forge called out, "I've already got my people rerouting critical systems, Captain, but there's a lot to go through." As though emphasizing his point, the bridge's main lighting flickered back to life.

"What the hell happened?" asked Riker. "I thought you said we could anticipate its arrival?" He paused, catching sight of the dead gray world that now was centered on the bridge's main viewscreen. Though it had erupted into existence, to him it still appeared enveloped by the effects of the transitional shift.

Data replied, "Unknown, sir. There was a brief surge in the buoy's broadcast signal just before the planet's arrival that was inconsistent with anything recorded by our sensors or extracted from the buoy's own communications log."

"The readings aren't dissipating," said Crusher. He looked up from his console, confused. "Quantum energy levels are holding steady. It's like the planet's stuck." He tapped several controls. "Helm is still unresponsive. We're holding position, but I can't get us to move."

"Geordi?" prompted Riker.

"Working on it, Captain." There was no mistaking the irritation in the engineer's voice. "The quantum fluctuations are really doing a number on us."

"Pull power from wherever you have to, but get us some breathing room." Riker turned to see La Forge bent over the engineering console, with Data ascending the ramp to lend assistance.

"It's not a question of power, sir. At least, not just by itself. The quantum energy around us is disrupting our systems' ability to distribute it. I'm trying to modulate our shields to compensate, but even that's giving me fits."

"Captain," said Tasha Yar from the tactical station, "I'm picking up additional vessels in orbit around the planet."

Frowning, Riker turned to the security chief. "What? From where?"

Yar shook her head. "I don't know, sir. They were just . . . *there*. Sensors are still trying to sort it all out." Riker was already moving in her direction when she added, "I've got a lock on one of the ships, sir. It's . . . it's *Romulan*."

That was enough to make everyone look up from their stations, and Riker almost froze in midstep as he climbed the ramp toward her. He caught himself and made his way to stand beside her, eyeing the sensor readings now displayed upon her console.

"Are you sure?"

Yar scowled. "That's just it, sir. Sensors say it's Romulan, but an older class of ship. A *much* older class, as in more than a century out of date." She tapped another series of controls. "The other two ships look to be

Romulan too, and all three have sustained minor damage."

"What the hell are Romulan ships doing here?" asked La Forge, dividing his attention between his own work and Riker and Yar. "We're nowhere near Romulan space."

"And how did they get here without our noticing them?" asked Riker. "Could the nebula have disguised their approach?"

Shaking her head, Yar replied, "I just don't see how, sir. Our sensors weren't *that* compromised, and if these readings are right, that ship is a century old, with cloaking technology to match. We should've seen them coming light-years away."

Another mystery, Riker mused. *Just what we need right now.*

"How are our shields?" he asked.

"Thirty-six percent." Yar glanced over her shoulder. "Engineering's still working on rerouting power to compensate for various overloads."

Without waiting for further prompting, La Forge said, "We're on it, but there are more overloads than I have people to fix them. We're going to need—"

The rest of his reply was cut off by the ship shuddering around them for a second time. Looking up from the tactical station, Riker saw the planet displayed on the main viewscreen, apparently still caught in the midst of the dimensional shift, beginning to quiver again, and he was sure the planet was faded enough for him to see through it to the rest of the nebula and the partially obscured stars behind it.

"It's happening again!" said Crusher.

Data added, "Quantum energy readings are intensifying as before. A dimensional shift is imminent."

From the ops station, Worf called, "Routing emergency power to the shields."

The extra effort seemed to do nothing to alleviate the pounding the *Enterprise* was forced to absorb as a renewed wave of unleashed energy collided against the starship's deflector shields. Riker had just enough time to grab on to the railing before everything rocked to starboard, and he felt himself collide with Yar. The security chief had one hand locked on the railing above her station and had anchored her knee beneath the console to maintain her balance.

"Remind me to ask for a chair up here," she said.

Ignoring her remark, Riker ordered, "Conn, get us out of here!"

His hands moving across his instruments, Crusher shook his head. "I can't break us free, Captain. Helm is not responding!"

When the lights faded this time, they remained out, and backup illumination was even slower to respond. Warning tones erupted from every console on the bridge as the deck disappeared from beneath Riker's feet, and he felt himself slam chest first into the railing. Yar's valiant effort to maintain her footing failed her as well, and he saw the lieutenant thrown over her station and down to the chairs in the command area. She landed hard and clumsily, and Riker heard her cry of pain even as Data and Deanna pushed themselves from their chairs to help her.

"Shields are failing!" reported La Forge.

He started to say something else, but Riker could not hear him over the sound of rushing air that assaulted his ears. In front of him, Worf and Crusher along with the front of the bridge seemed to stretch away from him, and everything was bathed in a blinding white light. Riker reached up to shield his eyes, waiting for the effect to pass, but it only strengthened to the point that he thought he might pass out from the sensory overload.

And then . . .

16

HERE
U.S.S. Enterprise-E

Awareness returned, and with it the realization that every bone in his body seemed to hurt. With great reluctance, Picard opened his eyes to find himself looking up at the bridge overhead, and his wife staring down at him.

"Welcome back," said Beverly Crusher.

"Where did I go?" Blinking several times in rapid succession, Picard raised his head enough to note that he was lying on the carpet in front of his chair. His forehead throbbed with a dull ache that was only slightly more pronounced than the discomfort racking the rest of his body. What had happened? Looking around, he saw Lieutenant Aneta Šmrhová kneeling on his opposite side, her expression one of concern.

"We were hit by a massive rush of quantum energy when the planet reappeared," replied the security chief. "You were thrown from your chair, sir. Commander La Forge and Lieutenant Elfiki took nasty tumbles, too."

"I sent them to sickbay," said Beverly. "He managed to break his ankle, and she has a broken wrist, but it's nothing we can't fix. They'll both be back in no time. There were a handful of injuries around the ship, but nothing serious, thankfully."

Allowing Šmrhová to assist him to his feet, Picard offered her a nod of thanks before asking, "Status?" Even as he asked the question, he took in the sight of the planet now centered on the bridge's forward viewscreen. With the brilliant violet and magenta hues of NGC 8541 serving as its backdrop, the cold, gray world somehow appeared almost beautiful. "Have you been able to contact the away team?"

"Not yet, sir," replied Šmrhová. "Quantum energy readings near the surface are still elevated to the point that they're interfering with our communications. I'm working with engineering to figure out a solution, but we got hammered pretty hard, and they're up to their eyeballs in repairs. Commander La Forge is coordinating everything from sickbay."

Picard could not help the small smile that escaped his lips. "Of course he is." Though not completely satisfied with the report, he knew that his people were—as always—giving their best effort, and time would be needed to carry out the various tasks requiring attention. Still, he could not help thinking of Worf and the others, still marooned on a planet that might disappear before their very eyes yet again.

"Glinn Dygan," he said, noting that the Cardassian had returned to his place at the ops position. "The effect of the planet's reappearance seemed rather more forceful than our sensor data indicated should happen."

Turning in his seat, Dygan replied, "That is correct, sir. The surge of quantum energy accompanying the planet's return to this dimension far exceeded even our most generous estimates. The result was an enormous surge of energy that overloaded our deflector shields before proceeding to affect the ship itself. Several systems were impacted, including sensors and propulsion. Engineering reports they had to deactivate the warp drive so that they could inspect the antimatter containment system. Our shields remain inactive, and there are even issues with our weapons control systems."

Picard grimaced. Without the warp drive, the ship would be relying on the impulse engines to provide power for onboard systems, which might mean compromises and prioritization of resources.

One thing at a time, Captain. Let your people work.

Next to Dygan, Lieutenant Joanna Faur said, "Helm is sluggish, Captain. I'm still trying to figure out if the problem is with the engines themselves, or just the power disruption we're experiencing."

"It is likely that the numerous overloads are the primary cause." Even as Dygan spoke, two sections of his ops console that had been dark and inert came back to life, accompanied by a string of indicator tones.

"It seems Mister La Forge is doing a fine job coordinating his people," said Picard, reaching up to rub his forehead. The ache, though sharp, was an irritant more than anything else.

"Are you all right?" asked Crusher. "I've already addressed the contusion, so there won't be any bruising, and I can give you something for the pain."

His first impulse was to decline the officer, but the sensation of weariness that continued to linger gave him second thoughts. Still rubbing his temples, he replied, "Perhaps that would be prudent, Doctor."

"And here I thought you were going to resist me so that you could look brave and invincible to your crew." Smiling, Crusher pressed a hypospray to the side of his neck and Picard felt the push of air as whatever medication she had chosen was injected into his bloodstream. It took only seconds for the treatment to assert itself, and he closed his eyes for a moment as the sensation of great weight upon his head and neck seemed to evaporate.

"Much better. Thank you." Pulling on the bottom of his uniform jacket, Picard said, "Please tend to the other injured and keep me informed as to their status."

"Of course, Captain, and *you* let *me* know if you have any further discomfort." Though Crusher kept her demeanor professional, there was no denying the concern in her voice, which he knew went beyond the extraordinary compassion she felt for anyone in her care.

"Understood, Doctor." Picard punctuated his reply with a smile that seemed to assure her, and after collecting her medical kit she disappeared into the turbolift at the rear of the bridge.

Looking around at the rest of his officers, he observed that several of the perimeter stations that had been dark were coming back to life, their individual interfaces restarting and reconnecting to the *Enterprise*'s main computer. At the science console, he saw that Lieutenant Paabell had arrived to take over for Lieutenant Elfiki. A Capellan male, Paabell had an imposing build that made Picard sure the lieutenant could rip through his Starfleet uniform merely by flexing his pronounced muscles. The captain also knew that harbored within Paabell's daunting physique was a keen intelligence, as evidenced by his Academy test scores and the recommendation from the commanding officer and science officer of his previous starship posting, the *U.S.S. Hayabusa.*

"Good to have you with us, Mister Paabell," said Picard.

Swiveling his seat away from his console, the lieutenant nodded. "Thank you, sir. I was just about to report that the sensor array is reinitializing. We have partial capability for the moment, but that is only sufficient for short-range scans."

Picard's reply was cut short by the sound of a tactical alert, and he turned to see that Lieutenant Šmrhová had returned to her station.

"Deflectors are attempting to activate," reported the security chief, "but they're only at twenty-two percent. They're firming up, but it's going to take time." She looked up from her instruments. "Sir, sensors are detecting three ships in orbit around the planet. They're . . ." She paused, as though uncertain of the readings as she dropped her gaze back to her panel. Shaking her head, she said, "They're Romulan, Captain. One is a class of ship I haven't seen outside of a history book or a museum, and the other two are smaller escort vessels."

"Older ships, converted for civilian use?" asked Picard.

Šmrhová replied, "No, sir. According to sensors, the warship could've been built a year ago. The smaller ships are a little older, but only by a few years. They're adrift just out of visual range beyond the curve of the planet, and I'm picking up signs of system failures and overloads, similar to ours though not nearly as extensive." She snorted. "I guess they got lucky, but I don't have a clue as to what they might be doing all the way out here. I can't even believe they slipped in here without our noticing it. Sensors should've picked them up long before the planet showed up."

Tabling that thought for the moment, Picard moved to the science station and leaned closer to Paabell. "Are you detecting any life signs?"

"Scanning." The console seemed to all but disappear beneath the Capellan's huge hands. "All three vessels show

Romulan life signs, sir. Numbers are consistent with what the library computer has on file for . . . such older vessels."

On one of the station's display screens, Picard studied the computer-generated schematic of the Romulan vessels. The escort ships were unfamiliar to him, but the *Vas Hatham*–class warship was immediately recognizable, being a class of attack craft that saw extended service during the mid- to late twenty-third century. Such ships had been labeled as obsolete decades before Picard was born, and like Šmrhová he had only seen one at the Starfleet annex to the Smithsonian Space Museum in San Francisco. There were also numerous references to such vessels in Academy history texts, including detailed accountings of several notable meetings between ships of the Romulan Empire and various Starfleet captains.

But what the hell is it doing here?

That the Romulans might choose to expand in this direction was not unreasonable, given the proximity of the Odyssean Pass to the far boundary of space claimed by the Empire. The largely unexplored and unclaimed expanse skirted that territory as well as that of the Klingons and the Federation, and was one of the few directions in which the Romulans could expand without much interference from either of those rival powers. The Empire's involvement in the Typhon Pact only served to complicate its relations with the Federation, but for now, at least, the current Romulan praetor, Gell Kamemor, seemed content not to challenge any Starfleet exploratory missions into the vast region.

Had that changed? If so, why send a relic to carry out such a mission?

What if it's not a relic? What if it is a brand-new vessel, just not from here?

The implications of those wayward questions were just beginning to shape Picard's thoughts when another alert tone sounded from Šmrhová's tactical station. He turned and once again saw his security chief with a perplexed expression.

"Okay, I have to be imagining things. Sensors have picked up *another* ship in orbit, on the far side of the planet. At least this one's Starfleet. Scans show it's a *Galaxy*-class starship, but I don't know how it managed to sneak up on us either. It's making its way toward us. We'll have visual in a moment."

Compared to the Romulan ship, this development at least sounded normal. A number of *Galaxy*-class vessels were still in Starfleet service, constructed upon spaceframes designed with intended life spans of a century or more.

None of that served to explain what the ship was doing here.

Picard watched as Šmrhová tapped a short sequence of keys, then saw her jaw slacken before she looked up at him.

"Sir, I just accessed its registry. It identifies itself as *U.S.S. Enterprise . . .*"

U.S.S. Enterprise-D

"NCC-1701 . . . E?"

His eyes still stinging as a result of smoke from the overloaded console that had exploded at the back of the bridge, Riker turned and regarded Tasha Yar. The side of her face was still reddened from where she had impacted against the deck below the tactical station, and she was favoring her left arm, but she was otherwise uninjured.

"Can we see it?" he asked, still trying to process the information the security chief had given him seconds earlier regarding the appearance of the strange ship now orbiting the far side of the planet, which bore all the marks of a Starfleet vessel that—so far as Riker knew—was still being developed.

Yar replied, "Yes, sir. It's entering visual range." A moment later, the image on the bridge's main viewscreen shifted to display what Riker recognized as a *Sovereign*-class starship. He was only able to identify the vessel because he had seen the technical schematics during a visit to the San Francisco Fleet Yards while the *Enterprise* was still undergoing its own refit at Earth Station McKinley. As he had when first reviewing the construction plans, he marveled at the advanced starship's sleek lines, which suggested speed and power even as it drifted in space.

"That's incredible," said La Forge, and Riker noticed for the first time that the chief engineer had moved down to the command area. "I can't believe what I'm seeing."

Originally conceived as a new version of long-duration, deep-space exploration vessel, the ship design underwent a revision following the *Enterprise*'s initial encounter with the Borg two years earlier. The recent Borg incursion and the heavy losses suffered at Wolf 359 were already having an even greater impact on the *Sovereign* design. People like Lieutenant Commander Elizabeth Shelby were putting those hard lessons to good use in the next generation of Starfleet vessels, ensuring they could stand against adversaries like the Borg while still being equipped to carry out their primary mission of pushing ever outward the boundaries of knowledge and discovery.

That was all well and good, but none of that was supposed to be real. At least not yet, but the evidence on the viewscreen told Riker otherwise.

This, and we still have three Romulan ships to deal with.

"Time travel?" he said aloud. "Is that what happened?"

Behind him, still seated in her chair, Troi said, "If that's true, then who's out of place?"

It was a good question, Riker conceded, but it was not the pressing issue at this particular moment. The planet and its dimensional shift had done its level best to overload every shipboard system. Backup processes were already laboring to lighten the strain on the impulse engines that were now responsible for generating power, as the warp core had deactivated as a consequence of quantum energy bombardment.

He also could not stop one thought from nagging him about the new ship. If that was a future *Enterprise*, then what had happened to his ship? Who was in command over there? Would it be a future version of him? Data? Or, some other member of the crew who had advanced to captain's rank? It might well be someone else entirely, which would beg the question of what happened to this ship's crew?

I hate time travel.

"Captain," said Data. The first officer had moved from his seat to stand next to Riker. "A scan of the ship shows that its quantum signature differs from our own, as well as the planet and the Romulan vessels."

"It gets worse, sir." La Forge, having moved down to the command area, pointed toward the viewscreen. "That *Enterprise*'s quantum signature is consistent with *this* dimension."

At least now it was making a kind of sense. "So, we got pulled along with the planet to here."

"Precisely, sir," replied Data. "The Romulan vessels appear to have suffered a similar fate, having been transposed not once but twice during the planet's shifting between multiple dimensions. Their quantum signatures are also different from the planet as well as our own."

"Time travel, on top of moving between dimensions?" Riker shook his head. "Jellico's going to love this." He looked to Data. "Any idea where . . . I mean *when* . . . we are?"

The first officer said, "I have attempted to access a Federation time beacon, but there are none within sensor range. However, the main computer has ascertained our current position using navigational charts, and we are currently positioned within the nebula NGC 8541, which lies in a region known as the Odyssean Pass. In our time period—and dimension—this area has only been explored by unmanned survey probes."

Riker frowned. He was sure he had read something about the Odyssean Pass, but it had been years. The region had once been highlighted as a promising area for exploration and possible expansion, but that initiative had been set aside as the Federation continued to face an increasing number of interstellar threats. The Klingons, the Cardassians, and especially the Borg, just to name the prominent obstacles, had all seen to it that Starfleet's mandate evolved to incorporate ever greater defense responsibilities. While protecting Federation interests had always been part of Starfleet's mission, there was a time when that mandate had walked in step with its larger focus of exploration. Now it seemed that balance was tipping too far toward more martial concerns, and there were times Riker questioned whether this was still the Starfleet that had so enamored him as a child.

We haven't lost sight of who we are, and we won't. Ever.

Behind him, Yar said, "They look to have suffered damage similar to what we're dealing with, sir. The Romulan ships have some damage, but overall they're better off than either us or . . . the other *Enterprise*."

"That figures," said Riker.

La Forge replied, "It could be that their vessels' less sophisticated technology wasn't as susceptible to the quantum energy fluctuations that hammered us." He released a small grunt. "Lucky them."

"Are they a threat?"

"Toe to toe? No way, sir," said Yar. "However, if they wanted to pick a fight, they might give us some trouble in our present condition. They seem content to keep their distance for the moment, though."

Riker nodded. "They're probably just as confused about all this as we are, and are sizing up the situation and us. It's what I'd do. Data, how much time do you figure we have until the next dimensional shift?"

"Unknown, sir. A scan of the planet shows that the quantum energy output has fallen considerably. Whatever caused the spike and the rapid succession of shifts seems to have dissipated, at least for the time being."

"Keep monitoring. I don't want to get blindsided like that again." There also was the added concern that the *Enterprise* might want to tag along with the planet when it shifted again, in the hopes of returning to their proper dimension.

And time. Don't forget that.

The familiar tone that signaled an incoming communication sounded from Yar's tactical console, and the security chief looked to Riker. "We're being hailed, sir, from the other *Enterprise*."

"I was wondering which of us might do that first," said Troi as she rose from her chair to stand next to Riker.

Still staring at the image of the futuristic yet oddly familiar *Enterprise* on the viewscreen, he replied, "I admit I thought about it, but if we really are from different times, then any interaction we have with each other could be dangerous."

Data said, "As it appears we are from a different dimension, the Temporal Prime Directive would not strictly apply in this instance, sir."

"Besides, they may be able to help us get back to where we belong." La Forge offered a small, humorless smile as he nodded toward the viewscreen. "Assuming their chief engineer is as good as ours."

The comment was enough to alleviate some of the tension of the past few minutes, and Riker grinned. With renewed energy, he looked to Yar. "Open a channel. Let's say hello."

17

U.S.S. Enterprise-E

It was like staring at a photograph, or recalling a vivid memory. The uniforms, the bridge stations, the familiar faces.

Though he had anticipated confronting a somewhat younger version of himself, Picard was unprepared for the sight of William Riker standing on the bridge of *Enterprise*-D, captain's insignia affixed to the collar of his maroon and black tunic. Behind him were other familiar faces—Deanna Troi and Geordi La Forge, the latter wearing the VISOR he had used for so many years before acquiring his more advanced ocular implants. They both looked so young, as did Worf, and Wesley Crusher, who occupied the conn position while wearing civilian attire.

Then there was Data, wearing a maroon uniform, and a commander's rank.

And Natasha.

It was Yar's face that held Picard's attention. Data's death had been traumatic for him and the rest of the *Enterprise* crew, but he had been returned to them. The loss of Tasha Yar, however, still haunted Picard. Her death, during the *Enterprise*-D's first year of service, had been as sudden as it was tragic and useless. That she was killed almost as an afterthought by the cruel alien entity that had struck her down was a wound that had never fully healed.

Now she stood before him and with the rest of her shipmates. The bruise on the side of her face spoke to whatever recent injury she had sustained, perhaps as a consequence of their abrupt transit from . . .

. . . wherever they'd come from?

"Captain Riker, I presume?" Picard offered the greeting with a gentle smile, while trying not to dwell on the obvious question: Where was his own counterpart? "This is an unexpected surprise, but . . . it's good to see you."

Standing ramrod straight at the center of his bridge, Riker nodded. *"It's . . . good to see you, too, sir, even if the circumstances are a little . . . unusual."* There was something in his voice—surprise, certainly—but also another aspect that felt out of place, and one Picard could not identify.

They're dealing with this just like you are. It's strange for all of us.

"By now, I'm guessing Mister Data has confirmed that your ship has journeyed with the planet to our dimension."

On the screen, Riker nodded. *"Yes, sir, and it's obvious that there's a temporal element in play here, as well. That's a wrinkle I'm sure they're going to love hearing about when we get home and file a report to Starfleet Command."* A bit of his trademark humor seeped around the edges of his reply, and Picard noted the almost mischievous glint in the other man's eyes.

Stepping closer to the screen, Picard said, "I can only imagine you have a number of questions." His gaze flickered once more to Lieutenant Yar. "And I'd be lying if I didn't say I had some of my own, but for the moment, I think we can agree we have more pressing concerns. I have an away team down on the planet that we're unable to communicate with, and there are our Romulan friends to consider."

"Agreed. We have damage here, and our sensors show you took a bit of a beating too. As for the Romulans, their ships are a century out of date, but they seemed to come through all of this in pretty decent shape. I was considering an attempt at communication, but I'll defer to you on that."

Picard nodded. "As it's my people on the surface, I'll make that overture, Num . . . I mean *Captain*." He offered another uncertain smile. "Congratulations on your promotion. I have no doubt it was well-deserved."

In response to the praise, Riker appeared uncomfortable, his eyes looking downward for a moment before he returned his attention to the screen. *"Thank you, sir. As you say, it's a . . . long story."*

"Perhaps I'll have a chance to hear it. Right now, however, I think we should concentrate on our repairs while I attempt to retrieve my away team."

On the screen, Data moved to stand next to Riker. *"Captain, if you have been conducting your own sensor scans of the planet, then you likely know that it shifts between dimensions at irregular intervals with little or no warning."*

"We are aware, Commander. We've attempted to devise a means of predicting the shifts, but so far we've been unsuccessful. If it happens again, we may be better off allowing it to transition while maintaining a safe distance. We've acquired enough information to feel confident that it will eventually return."

Riker said, *"Staying here might not be the smartest move for us, Captain, given the time travel aspects of our situation."* He paused, glancing around his bridge as though considering his ship and the space beyond its hull. *"On the other hand, if we hide in this nebula for a few days while we figure this out, we should be able to reduce the chances of our introducing any temporal contamination."*

"Let's just hope the Romulans are feeling similarly charitable."

If the Romulan ships and other *Enterprise* truly had come from different dimensions, then the chances of there being an effect on the timeline, here or anywhere else, seemed to Picard a remote possibility. It was obvious that at least some things had unfolded in quite a different fashion in the reality Captain William Riker called home. The questions he wanted to ask threatened to overload his thoughts, and Picard forced himself to set aside that curiosity.

"For now," he added, "maintain your position while you complete your repairs. That keeps the Romulans between us. As long as they elect to remain in place, at least."

Riker replied, *"Agreed."* It was evident that he had so much more he wanted to say, but also understood the need to maintain priorities. *"I'll contact you once I have an update. Riker out."*

The transmission ended and he disappeared, replaced by an image of the *Enterprise*-D floating within the nebula, and as he stared at the ship, he was gripped by feelings of regret and even longing.

Hello, old friend.

There were, of course, *Galaxy*-class starships still in service, and all of them nearly identical to the vessel Picard now beheld. None of them had ever seemed to embody the majesty and grace that he thought characterized the vessel on which he had served as her captain during its active tour of duty. He had not been with her when she fell from the skies above the remote planet Veridian III, mortally wounded after a brief yet costly battle with a Klingon warship. The *Enterprise*-D—its saucer section, at least—had crash-landed on the planet's surface, damaged beyond any feasible hope of repair. Starfleet instead chose to take the *U.S.S. Honorius*, one of the *Sovereign*-class vessels that at the time were still under construction, and rechristen it as the newest starship to carry on the storied tradition of ships named *Enterprise*.

While grateful for the honor bestowed upon him and his crew, Picard had always felt guilty for the loss of this ship's predecessor. On an intellectual level, he knew it was illogical to assign such powerful meaning to any object, even one as incredibly complex as a starship. Still, it was human nature to form such attachments, particularly to vessels like the *Enterprise*—both the ship on the viewscreen and the one on which he now stood—which served and protected those aboard her with such distinction.

Shaking himself from his reverie, Picard turned to Lieutenant Šmrhová at the tactical station. "Any updates on the away team?"

The security chief shook her head. "No, sir. The quantum energy levels are still interfering with our communications, and our sensor readings are also still muddled, so I can't even get a good fix on the team's position. Engineering reports they've already tasked personnel to solve the issue." She looked up from her console. "Captain, I request your permission to pilot a shuttle to the surface."

"Your offer is appreciated, Lieutenant, but unless or

until we can get a better handle on the nature of the planet's dimensional shifting, I'm reluctant to risk any more of my people." In hindsight, sending Commander Worf and the others had been unwise, even if it seemed, at the time, to be the best way to learn more about the situation on the surface and determine whether assistance could be provided. While Picard knew that any away mission carried with it an element of risk, it did little to assuage his uneasiness at having subjected his people to unexpected hazards such as the one they now faced.

What were they facing down there?

Ushalon

Chen aimed her phaser and pressed the firing stud, but nothing happened, and her surprise was mirrored by the Romulan she had just tried to shoot.

"Well, damn it all to hell," she said, scowling at the misbehaving weapon before throwing it at the Romulan's face.

Her action had the intended effect as the Romulan soldier ducked to avoid being hit, giving Chen the precious seconds she needed to close the distance. She swept her left arm up, catching the barrel of the disruptor in the Romulan's right hand and forcing it away from her. Now within arm's reach, she clamped her right hand onto the muscle connecting her adversary's neck and shoulder and squeezed. The soldier's eyes rolled back into his head, and she felt his body go limp beneath her. He collapsed to the deck, releasing his hold on his disruptor and allowing her to retrieve it.

"Thanks," she said, regarding the unconscious Romulan. His uniform—silver tunic with purple trousers, high black boots, and the gold helmet concealing all but the front of his face—was the very definition of anachronism. Chen had never seen anything like it outside a history text or a holodeck program. It was as though the soldier had stepped out from the shadows of history to confront her.

And he's got friends.

Hearing commotion from somewhere down the passageway, Chen turned and headed in that direction. The Romulan weapon, a form of disruptor pistol that was as out of place and time as its owner, felt large and unwieldy in her hand. Would the damned thing even work? Her opponent had not had the chance to fire upon encountering Chen in the hallway, and a quick glance at its power setting told her the weapon was carrying a full charge.

Your phaser told you the same thing.

Rounding a corner in the passageway, she was in time to see Taurik defending himself against another Romulan. Both men were unarmed, and the Romulan had lunged forward to attack Taurik. Beyond them, Chen caught sight of Kirsten Cruzen flipping another Romulan over her hip and throwing him to the deck. She backpedaled, giving herself room to maneuver as the soldier regained his feet, readying another attack.

Chen raised the disruptor and fired. She was rewarded with a howl of energy as the weapon spat forth a green-white bolt that slammed into the Romulan, forcing him off his feet and driving him into the nearby bulkhead.

"How about that?"

Taurik, still locked in his own fight, blocked his attacker's arm as the Romulan swung at his head before delivering a powerful strike to his opponent's chest. The soldier stumbled back a step, giving Chen a chance to dispatch him with the disruptor.

"Good to know something works around here," said Cruzen as she picked up her adversary's weapon from the floor.

Retrieving a weapon for himself, Taurik replied, "Indeed." He pointed toward another T-shaped intersection in the passageway. "There are others."

The Vulcan's observation was punctuated by the sight of another Romulan appearing in the hallway, flying through the air and slamming into a wall near the intersection. He slid to the floor, clearly unconscious, and a second later Worf lunged into view. Moving to crouch over the fallen Romulan, Worf checked to verify that his opponent was out of commission before turning his attention to Chen and the others.

"Are you all right?" he asked.

Taurik replied, "Yes, sir. We appear to have incapacitated four of seven intruders."

"Five." Worf grunted in annoyance. "This one was not alone. His partner is unconscious near the entrance they used to access the habitat."

Using his purloined disruptor, Taurik pointed past Worf. "The other two are in that direction. Lieutenant Konya and Doctor Tropp were heading that way to investigate." Attempts at communication between the away team members had proven problematic, owing to the still elevated levels of quantum energy being cast off by the Sidrac's field generator. Chen suspected it to be the same issue currently plaguing their phasers, but not—apparently—the older and cruder weapons carried by the Romulans.

There's probably a lesson here about becoming too reliant on technology or some such damned thing.

"Have to hand it to them," said Cruzen. "They did all right, considering there were only seven of them. Sneaky bastards."

"Romulans are without honor."

Worf left that observation hanging in the air as he turned and began moving back the way he had come, gesturing for the others to follow him. Once through the intersection, the first officer grabbed a disruptor lying on the floor near the door Chen knew led to one of the habitat's four entrances. Sprawled on the deck on the corridor's opposite side was another unconscious Romulan, and Worf paused long enough to recover that soldier's weapon, giving him one for each hand.

The sound of disruptor fire from somewhere ahead of them made the Klingon break into a run, with Chen and Taurik following him while Cruzen covered their rear flank. Worf started to turn the corner to his left, only to retreat with such speed that he nearly backed into Chen. There was no time to say anything before a disruptor bolt pierced the air and passed through the space Worf had just occupied, chewing into the bulkhead to their right. More weapons fire echoed in the passageway, out of sight. Chen heard voices and running footsteps.

"I saw both of them," said Worf. "But no sign of Konya or Doctor Tropp."

Taurik reached for his tricorder, and Chen watched his hand brush the empty holster on his left hip. "My last scan showed they were farther away, toward the habitat's southeast entrance."

The habitat that acted as home and laboratory for the Sidrac featured entrances in each quadrant of the cluster of connected structures, each with its own contained pressure lock and storage area for the protective suits used by Nelidar and her companions when venturing outside or below ground to the area housing the field generator. As Nelidar had explained, those sections could be sealed off from the rest of the habitat in the event of a breach, but those measures were intended to contain the structure's internal atmosphere, rather than preventing forced entry by intruders, as the Romulans were now demonstrating. In the immediate wake of the last dimensional shift, the intruders had managed to get through the external doors and into the habitat itself, dividing their team so that each entrance was breached at the same time. This had forced the away team to split up in an attempt to repel their unwanted guests while protecting Nelidar and her people, none of whom possessed weapons of their own.

"They're moving away," said Worf, just before he stepped into the connecting corridor, both disruptors raised. He fired without warning, each weapon unleashing its own energy bolt. Chen winced at the reports in the enclosed space before following after the first officer as he plunged forward. Ahead of him, she saw shadows on the walls forming the next intersection, and heard shouts of alarm echoing in the distance. Worf led the way around the next corner, and Chen chased after him, her eyes widening as she caught sight of the Romulan aiming a disruptor in her direction.

The weapon screamed as Chen and Worf dropped to the floor and the disruptor bolt punched into the wall behind them. Snarling in frustration, the Romulan was adjusting his aim as Cruzen stepped into the corridor, her disruptor grasped in both hands, and fired. A single shot caught the Romulan in his chest, driving him off his feet before landing in a heavy heap on the floor.

Footsteps ahead of them made Chen raise her own weapon, but she elevated its muzzle when three figures appeared at the next junction. She smiled at the sight of Rennan Konya and Doctor Tropp escorting the remaining Romulan. Konya had acquired the soldier's weapon, and for the first time Chen realized their prisoner was a female. She was not wearing a gold helmet like her companions, and her hair was cut in a short style that left her neck and her pointed ears exposed.

"What?" said Konya. "Wasn't everybody supposed to bring a guest to the party?"

Cruzen waved a hand over her shoulder. "They're all back there, sleeping it off." She indicated the prisoner. "She makes seven. That's all of them, Commander."

Stepping closer to the Romulan, Worf eyed her for a moment before saying, "You are the leader." It was not a question. He pointed to an insignia on the Romulan's uniform. "You carry the rank of subcommander. Your companions are all centurions, bound to follow your orders. What is your mission here?"

Her expression one of loathing as she regarded Worf, the Romulan seemed to ignore the question and instead asked, "What is this? When did the Federation allow itself to be conquered by animals such as this? I know humans are weak, but I thought they possessed some self-respect, and would rather die than subjugate themselves to the Klingon Empire."

"You're not from around here, are you?" asked Cruzen.

The Romulan glared at her, but said nothing.

"The lieutenant's statement is crude, but accurate," said Taurik. "At least, if what Nelidar told us is true."

Following the shift, Nelidar had reported that the planet found itself once again in the dimension the Sidrac designated as "location five," which was music to Chen's ears.

We're home again, but for how long?

"Torture me as you will," said the Romulan. "I will answer no questions."

Worf replied, "So long as you cooperate, you will not be harmed."

"I have no intention of doing that, either."

She moved with startling speed, lunging toward Worf with arms extended, her hands aiming for his throat. The Klingon moved with practiced ease, deflecting her attack. His arm wrapped around her neck as he pressed his free hand against the side of her head. Chen gasped at the sudden, unchecked brutality of the move, only then realizing that Worf was restraining himself. Instead of killing the Romulan, he had put her in a hold designed to induce unconsciousness. Fighting to break the hold, the Romulan's hands grappled for purchase on Worf's head and face, but even now her movements were becoming erratic as her strength flagged. Stepping forward, Taurik applied a nerve pinch, accelerating the process of incapacitating her. Her body went limp, and Worf waited an additional few seconds before lowering her to the floor and releasing his grip.

"Thank you," he said, nodding to Taurik.

The Vulcan replied, "It seemed an efficient means of ending the confrontation."

Worf said, "Lieutenant Chen, speak with Nelidar and ask if there is a secure room we can use as a temporary brig." He turned to Konya and Cruzen. "You will have to guard our guests. Secure their weapons and other equipment and keep them in a holding area until we receive instructions from Captain Picard."

"Contacting the *Enterprise* is not currently possible," said Taurik. "The increased output of quantum energy from the field generator is continuing to interfere with our communications."

"And our phasers," added Cruzen. She held up her disruptor. "These seem to work well enough."

Nodding, Worf replied, "For now they are sufficient. Our priority is contacting the ship." He glanced around the area. "I for one have no wish to remain here any longer than is necessary, but if there is a way for us to help Nelidar and her people, we will need assistance from Commander La Forge and Lieutenant Elfiki."

"Any idea how long we might stay in this dimension before the planet shifts again?" asked Konya.

Taurik replied, "Without further information, and until we can determine the scope of any damage that may have been caused by the Romulan attack on the field generator, I am unable to posit an answer to that question."

It was the thought that had been on all their minds since hearing from Nelidar that Ushalon had shifted back to their own dimension. Following the two rapid and violent transitions, the field generator was continuing to emit elevated levels of quantum energy, which implied that another shift could happen at any time. Had the attack from orbit somehow affected the equipment causing the shifts? Already compromised as a consequence of the accident that had plunged Ushalon into its headlong flight across dimensions, was the Sidrac's situation now worsened? Chen sighed as she contemplated their plight.

With their luck? Probably.

18

Though it felt good to just lie down, and he knew he needed the rest, Geordi La Forge could not stay here. Others were counting on him. The captain was counting on him. He could rest later, but now? It was time to get back to work.

"I know what you're thinking, mister, and you can just forget it."

Lifting his head from the pillow of the sickbay bed he currently occupied, La Forge smiled at the sight of Tamala Harstad. Her hands in the pockets of the light-blue medical lab coat she wore over her uniform, she did not return his smile, and he knew the reason. She was in full "doctor mode" at the moment, concentrating on the patients in her care.

"What?" he asked, affecting an innocent air.

As Harstad moved to stand next to his bed, her expression communicated that she was not buying what he was attempting to sell. "I can see it in your face. I can see it in your body language. You want out of here."

"It's that obvious?"

"Maybe not to everyone." For the first time, she allowed the first hint of a smile to tease her lips. "But not everyone knows you like I do."

La Forge glanced around sickbay, including the adjacent bed, where Lieutenant Dina Elfiki was doing her best to pretend she was not listening to the conversation. The science officer was failing in that regard, he decided.

"I need to get back to work." He almost appended that sentence with her first name, but caught himself. She was on duty, and she was overseeing patients, and it would not be fair at this moment to treat her as anything other than a professional colleague. "There's a lot to do, and I need to be down there with my people." He indicated the portable computer terminal that had been brought to him. "There's only so much I can do from here." He bent his right foot, then twisted it from side to side. There was a dull ache at the ankle, but nothing he could not handle. "I'm feeling pretty good."

"I want to check the bone knitting on your ankle one last time, and after that you should be free to go." Harstad started to place her hand on his leg, then seemed to think better of it. "It was a clean break, but still tricky. I want to make sure there's no loss of flexibility or range of motion."

La Forge smiled. "I trust your work, Doc. I'm sure I'll be fine."

Movement to his left attracted his attention, and he looked over to see Lieutenant Gary Weinrib standing in the doorway to the patient ward, as though waiting for permission to enter the room. La Forge knew the conn officer, but he had rare occasion to interact with him, as the lieutenant was assigned to gamma shift. However, everyone not otherwise occupied was being called into service to assist with the various repair efforts under way across the ship.

Looking to Elfiki, La Forge said, "Lieutenant, you've got a visitor."

The science officer, who had been sitting quietly with

her eyes closed looked around before seeing who La Forge meant, and a smile graced her features. Then, just as quickly as it had come, that smile faded as her expression turned to one of puzzlement.

"Wait. Sir, how did you know he was here to see me?"

La Forge stifled a laugh. "What, you think only the junior officers hear the scuttlebutt?" He was rewarded by a reddening of Elfiki's cheeks.

After she waved him over, Weinrib nodded a greeting to La Forge. "Commander," he said, before directing his attention to Elfiki. "I wanted to see how you were doing."

Holding up her left arm, she replied, "Pretty much good as new. Doesn't even hurt." She glanced at Harstad. "The doctor's just getting set to release me."

"You can go," said Harstad, making a shooing motion. "If you have any lingering pain tomorrow, come see me."

"How come she gets to go, and you're holding me prisoner here?" asked La Forge, earning him a look of mock scorn from Harstad.

"Because she does what she's told and doesn't cause a fuss about being let out of here until her doctor authorizes it."

Elfiki grinned. "Sorry, Commander."

"Figures." La Forge watched as she pushed herself from the bed and made a show of flexing the fingers of her left hand.

"Feels fine, Doctor. Thanks."

Harstad replied, "Try not to break it again, at least not for a couple of days."

"I'll do my best." Elfiki offered an informal salute to La Forge. "If you don't get released by dinner time, sir, I'll arrange for a prison break."

Once she and Weinrib had left, La Forge returned his head to his pillow. "I remember being that young once."

"I wish I'd met you back then," said Harstad.

"You still can." He gestured in the general direction of where he believed the *Enterprise*-D—or, *an Enterprise*-D, at any rate—still drifted in orbit on the opposite side of the planet. "I wonder if he's hip deep in repairs over there, or if their doctors are keeping him cooped up in sickbay."

Harstad chuckled. "I said I'd get you out of here." She pulled her left hand from the pocket of her lab coat, and La Forge saw that she had been carrying a tricorder there. Flipping open the compact device, she pulled a small scanner from a recessed port and activated it as she held it over his right foot.

"Sorry for being a pain," he said after a moment. He looked once more around the room. "It's just that with everything that's going on right now, I'm feeling pretty useless."

"Fair enough," replied Harstad. "I know I'd be feeling the same way."

"But would you be badgering your doctor to let you out of here so you could go back to work?"

"Probably. You know how doctors can be such tyrants."

Like nearly everyone else aboard the ship, he had learned about the appearance of an *Enterprise*-D that was all but identical to the ship on which he had once served. According to what Doctor Crusher had conveyed while conducting her last pass through sickbay, the other ship had apparently come from a previous time period as well as a different dimension. It was a lot to process, and of course everyone had questions about this alternate version of a starship with which many members of this crew were familiar. For one thing, there was natural speculation as to the whereabouts of that reality's Jean-Luc Picard. For La Forge, encountering a younger version of himself would be odd, and seeing Yar would without doubt feel awkward, as would seeing Data the way he often remembered his android friend. However, the keen absence of the man who for more than two decades had personified the legacy of starships named *Enterprise* was a question that demanded a response.

But will we like the answer?

U.S.S. *Enterprise*-D

"Will?"

Startled, Riker turned from the port toward the voice, and saw Deanna standing just inside his ready room door. How long had she been there? How many times had she called his name before he even realized she had entered the room?

"Sorry," he said, indicating for her to have a seat before his desk. "I was just . . . lost in thought, I guess."

"There seems to be a lot of that going around." She eased into one of the low-rise chairs situated in front of his narrow desk, her gaze never leaving his face as she moved. "It's natural to feel uncomfortable in a situation like this."

Riker dropped into his own chair. "Is there a lot of precedent for this sort of thing? Meeting people you're supposed to know and yet seem as distant and unfamiliar to you as a total stranger? Not through any fault of their own, obviously, but because they're from another dimension."

"Captain Picard isn't a stranger." She leaned back in her chair, resting her hands in her lap. "He knows who you are. He recognized us as much as you recognized him."

Sighing, Riker reached up to rub his forehead. "It was just so surreal, seeing him standing there, just as he's supposed to. Hell, that should be him standing on the bridge of *this* ship, and while we're talking about where people should be, where am I in that dimension? Where are you? Who else is missing? Are they dead? Are *we* dead?" He paused, shaking his head. "I'm no expert on parallel dimensions, beyond that one module they covered in the temporal theory class at the Academy. I remember the professor talking about a first meeting between two versions of the same person, each from different dimensions."

"I attended those same lectures," said Deanna. "He said that it wasn't like time travel, with the inherent risk of accidentally altering the course of history by interacting with yourself from a point in your own past. This sort of thinking didn't apply when it came to parallel dimensions, because it's reasonable to assume that events will play out in much different fashion than the reality with which we're familiar."

"But isn't there at least some of that risk here?" asked Riker. "Now?" He waved a hand toward the port. "In addition to a different dimension, we're from another time. What if we go over to the other *Enterprise*—the more advanced *Enterprise*—and have a look around? How does going back to our dimension with the information we learn from the other *Enterprise* not impact on our timeline?"

Troi shifted in her seat. "Who's to say that our history

doesn't depend on the acquisition of knowledge that can only come from a vessel of another dimension and time period?"

"Now you're starting to sound like that temporal theory professor." Riker frowned. "What was his name?"

"Bennett."

"Right. That's him." He remembered an intelligent and thoughtful man who never seemed to tire of discussing or otherwise exploring even the finest detail with respect to a theory or question posed by a student. While attending such classes as a Starfleet Academy cadet, he recalled more than one occasion when the class schedule was scuttled because Professor Bennett became so enamored with a particular discussion point dealing with theories about time travel or the ramifications of such reckless cavorting. Often he would extrapolate or expand on the initial thought in ways the cadet offering the original question had never imagined. Rather than being bored by such diversions, Riker usually found himself caught up in the whole process and the professor's unbridled enthusiasm for the subject.

He would enjoy seeing what we've gotten ourselves into.

"I know you're worried about somehow corrupting our timeline," said Deanna, "but there's something more. I'm sensing your self-doubt."

Pushing back from the desk, Riker sank into his chair. "Since the moment Admiral Hanson put me in command of this ship, I've been driven by a single thought: being worthy of the man I replaced." He nodded in the direction of the ship's bow. "And now, he's here. A version of him, at any rate, and as silly as this sounds, I feel like for the first time since I took command, I'm finally being judged by the only person qualified to do that."

"And you don't think you measure up."

Riker was aware that Troi offered that thought as a statement, rather than a question. He forced a smile. "Measure up to Jean-Luc Picard? Is that even possible?"

"Perhaps." Troi shrugged. "Perhaps not, but Captain Picard didn't bring you on as his first officer to turn you into a clone of him, Will. He knew from the beginning what kind of captain you could be, so long as you were given the opportunity to develop your own approach. The two of you did—and do—have very different command styles, but he never saw that as an obstacle." She smiled. "He knew from the moment he first met you that you were a natural leader, not afraid to make the hard choices and with the integrity to stand by those decisions. His job was to prepare you for the day you took your own command, with the skills, experience, and wisdom that all go into making a good starship captain. The rest was up to you."

Now his grin was genuine. "Are you counseling me, Counselor?"

"Yes." Her voice and body language had taken on that relaxed yet professional air Riker knew she exhibited when talking with her patients. "I can understand a healthy measure of self-reflection, particularly in a situation as unusual as the one we're dealing with, but you can't let it control you. If you continue to follow such feelings, sooner or later it will have an impact. It will affect your decisions and even your confidence in your own ability to make those choices."

"I know, and I promise that's not what this is. I'm just . . ." Riker shook his head. "Seeing him brought back a lot of memories, is all. I actually feel jealous of this dimension, because it still has its Captain Picard."

He rapped the desktop with his knuckles. "I'll be fine. Really."

Troi studied him for an extra moment, and he was sure she was trying to read his feelings, before she replied, "I know you will. We all will, particularly once this is over."

"Bridge to Captain Riker," said Data over the intraship.

"Go ahead."

"Sir, we have detected a transmission from the Romulan warship. It is apparently attempting to send a signal to any Romulan ships or bases that might be able to provide assistance."

Instead of replying, Riker chose to return to the bridge. As he exited his ready room, Data rose from the command chair and walked toward him.

"Are they serious?" asked Riker.

His first officer replied, "The signal is on a low-power frequency, perhaps as an attempt to circumvent our ability to scan for such communications. So far as our long-range sensors can determine, there are no other Romulan vessels or installations in the immediate vicinity."

"No, but that doesn't mean somebody won't get lucky and pick up the signal. We're not that far from Romulan territory, remember." He recalled Data's preliminary report about the Odyssean Pass, which in their time and reality had not yet been explored. It was close enough to the Romulan border that the possibility of a visit by a curious warbird or two could not be ruled out.

"Can we jam their transmissions?" asked Deanna.

Data nodded. "Yes, Counselor, though we will not be able to do so without the Romulans knowing we are responsible."

"Do it," ordered Riker. "We'll take our chances." Even in its compromised state, he believed the *Enterprise* could still hold its own against an enemy vessel as out-dated as the nearby Romulan ship. "And let's notify . . . Captain Picard. He's obviously more familiar with the current state of Romulan affairs in this dimension."

That might just qualify as the most bizarre statement I've said today. Then again, the day's not over yet.

Standing behind the captain's chair at her tactical station, Lieutenant Yar asked, "What happens if they're able to make contact with Romulans in this dimension?"

Riker considered that notion, particularly within the context of the peculiar situation in which he and his crew, along with Captain Picard and the *Enterprise*-E and even the Romulans, found themselves.

"Then the party around this planet is going to get a whole lot more interesting."

19

ChR Bloodied Talon

Her engine room was enveloped in chaos.

Around the high-ceilinged chamber that was the heart of her vessel, Sarith saw numerous sections of metal plating pulled from the deck and the bulkheads. Access panels had been set aside and hands, feet, and heads protruded from exposed crawlways and other cavities. Tools, diagnostic equipment, and even ration packets were strewn about the space, everything testifying to the work taking place here.

Though her first instinct was to ask who had destroyed this most crucial area of her ship, Sarith held her tongue. As a Romulan military officer, disorder and untidiness were anathema to her. During her tenure as a cadet at the training academy, even a single article of clothing or other personal item out of place was a disciplinary infraction that brought harsh penalties. Such unruly behavior was quashed from every cadet early enough in the training cycle that by the time candidates graduated and earned their commission, the very idea of conducting oneself in such a slovenly fashion was unfathomable.

Such things were of little concern to Sarith now. This was neither the time nor the place to complain about the disheveled condition of the room or its occupants. A return to proper decorum and order would come soon enough, after the repair tasks were completed, every access panel or deck plate was returned to its proper place, and every tool was cleaned and stored.

"I know how this must look, Commander," said an older, raspy voice, and Sarith turned to see her engineer, Jacius, climbing down a short ladder. Looking up, she saw that he and two subordinates had been working on the catwalk that encircled the room. Intense flickering light from yet another open access panel told her that one of Jacius's junior engineers was hard at work welding or cutting something.

As unkempt as the room around him, Jacius stepped from the ladder to stand before Sarith. His face and hair were coated with grime and perspiration, and his utilitarian coverall uniform had a torn pocket and a ripped sleeve. Sarith even noted that the ragged material along his left forearm was stained dark green.

"You are injured," she said.

Looking down at his arm, Jacius replied, "It is not serious, Commander. Certainly not enough to keep me from my duties."

She should have anticipated such a response. While Jacius might be an embarrassment as a military officer, his technical skill and experience made him an engineer without equal. When she had taken command of the *Talon*, one of her first acts was to replace the officers in key positions with people she trusted or knew from prior assignments. The lone exception to that action was Jacius, who had been aboard the ship as its engineer through its last two commanders as part of a career dating back decades. It was Ineti who had recommended his retention, assuring Sarith that his talents were irreplaceable, and so far the older Romulan had served the ship well.

Until this mission, the demands placed upon Jacius and his staff had been routine, even mundane, and Sarith wondered if the current challenges might be proving too much for the wizened engineer.

"What is the status of our repairs?"

Jacius waved to indicate the room around them. "Proceeding as expected, Commander. Though the damage was widespread, it was not critical. Most of the problems stem from overloaded circuits or burned-out relays. If they cannot be replaced, we can reroute power distribution to compensate. There is only minor structural and hull damage, and my crews report those tasks are also nearing completion. I predict all repairs will be finished by the end of the current duty shift, but critical systems are available to you now."

"Most impressive," replied Sarith, "particularly given the short amount of time. So, weapons and defenses?" She flinched at the sound of a metal plate falling onto the deck behind her, and saw Jacius direct a scathing glare to the subordinate who had dropped it.

"Weapons, defenses," he said. Then, as though studying her expression, he added, "You are planning something, Commander?"

"For the moment, I am considering my options."

Given the proximity of the two Starfleet vessels near the planet, the ability to fight had been the first priority. According to sensor scans, the *Talon* and her two escorts had fared far better during the dimensional shift than either of her adversaries. This was fortunate, as according to those same scans, both Starfleet ships were larger and much more advanced than anything Sarith had ever seen, matching nothing on file in the *Talon*'s memory banks. How was that even possible? Had the abilities of

Romulan spies deteriorated to such a degree that entire fleets of advanced starships could be constructed and deployed without the Empire having the first clue?

That seemed unlikely, Sarith decided. Another explanation was that her ships had somehow been pulled along with the planet during its last dimensional shift. There also existed the possibility that the Starfleet ships had been brought here. At the moment, she had no way to ascertain who was out of place. Were her adversaries cut off from potential reinforcements, or was she? In an attempt to determine the answers to such questions— after she and Ineti had made their best guess about the *Talon*'s current position—Sarith had ordered an encrypted message transmitted to the nearest Romulan outpost. According to her computer's star charts and if the sensor readings were accurate, help might be several days away. Until then, she and her crew were on their own.

The sound of the internal communications system caught her attention, followed by the voice of Subcommander Ineti over the speakers.

"Commander Sarith, please respond."

Crossing to a wall-mounted communications panel, Sarith pressed the unit's activation switch. "What is it, Ineti?"

Her second-in-command replied, *"Commander, it appears our communications are being jammed by the Starfleet vessels. Our attempt to transmit a message to a support base or other vessel that might provide assistance is being blocked."*

It was not an unexpected development, Sarith conceded, though she at least thought they might have a little time before the Starfleet ships detected the attempt at covert communication. The message, encrypted and sent on a low-power frequency, sacrificing response time for security, should have escaped the notice of the Starfleet sensors. She had obviously underestimated her adversaries and their ability to conduct covert reconnaissance. For all their vaunted proclamations about being forthright and honorable, humans were just as clever and devious as the best Romulan spies.

"Are we able to communicate with the *N'minecci* or the *Jarax*?" she asked. "Or our shuttle on the surface?"

Ineti replied, *"The jamming does not seem to be affecting short-range communications, Commander, however there is still interference from the energy surges on the planet that prevent our making contact with the scouting party."* A series of alert tones could be heard in the background, and the subcommander excused himself for a moment before saying, *"We are being hailed by one of the Starfleet ships, Commander."*

"Of course we are." If there was one thing Sarith knew about humans, it was that they preferred to spend an inordinate amount of time talking. About anything. She could not decide whether it was an inherent trait of their species, or a regrettable habit they had acquired as a consequence of their alliance with the Vulcans, who always seemed to pride themselves on their mastery of the spoken word and their ability to employ it until another speaker or a simple lack of oxygen interrupted them.

"Ignore the hail," she said. Glancing to Jacius, who stood nearby in patient silence, she considered other points of concern. "What are we able to ascertain about their repair efforts?"

"Both ships have compromised defenses. Their deflector shields only seem operable at reduced effectiveness. We are

unable to get an accurate report on their weapons, as those systems are not active."

Anticipating her trusted advisor's reaction, Sarith chose her next words with care. "Ineti, we may have an unparalleled opportunity within our grasp. What if we were to seize the initiative?" When the subcommander said nothing for several moments, she could sense him considering her suggestion from every conceivable angle, weighing the advantages and liabilities of such a brazen action.

"What you suggest, Commander, is dangerous. However, the rewards for undertaking such risk would be vast. If these are advanced Starfleet ships, then the information we obtain about them will be of enormous value to the praetor. Even if they are from another dimension, our sensor scans alone will provide benefit to our research and development efforts."

Sarith looked to Jacius. "Our primary weapon—what is its status?"

"Fully operational, Commander." The weathered engineer held up a hand. "However, our shields are not at full strength."

"We have to drop them in order to fire anyway," said Ineti over the open channel.

Jacius shrugged. "True, but I am considering the moments after we lose the element of surprise, and our enemy elects to return fire."

"As long as the larger goal is achieved," said Sarith, "or at least furthered, then it would be worth it. All we need to do is draw their attention long enough to accomplish our true objective, then we can withdraw." She smiled. "Remember, while Starfleet captains are capable of slaying an opponent in the heat of battle, they usually do not choose to fire upon a disabled enemy or one that withdraws from conflict. We can use that to our advantage."

It was a gamble, Sarith knew, just as she knew that any prospect of capturing an advantage over the Starfleet ships was fading with every moment their repair efforts continued unmolested. If she was going to strike, she would need to do it soon.

No, she decided.

The time is now.

Ushalon

"It's good to hear your voice, Commander."

T'Ryssa Chen made no effort to conceal her sigh of relief as she heard Captain Picard's voice emanating from Worf's combadge. Though static still laced the transmission, any contact at all was welcome.

"Thank you, sir," replied the first officer. "The situation down here has been . . . most interesting."

"I can imagine, and it's probably going to get even more so before this is all over."

All six of the away team members listened as Picard recounted the events that had brought them to this point and the current situation in space beyond the planet. Worf followed that report with one of his own, informing the captain of the team's status and their skirmish with Romulan infiltrators. The most intriguing part of Picard's update was the presence of an earlier *Enterprise*-D, which, like the Romulans, had been pulled from its own plane of existence.

"Another dimension and another time," said Chen. "We just can't do anything halfway, can we?"

Picard replied, *"Despite the disparity in technology, the Romulans do have a minor advantage. It seems their shipboard systems were not as susceptible to the quantum interference, and their vessels withstood the transition in far better shape than we did. We are continuing our repair efforts."*

"What about our Romulan friends down here?" asked Rennan Konya. "We're keeping an eye on them, Captain. Doctor Tropp has even treated the injuries one of them sustained in their shuttle's crash."

Picard asked, *"What is their condition, Doctor?"*

"Aside from the effects of their own weapons and unarmed combat with our people, they are all unharmed, Captain. One Romulan suffered a cracked rib in the shuttle crash, but I was able to treat it, and he is fully recovered."

"Excellent. Thank you for your efforts."

Konya asked, "What if their ship sends more people to look for them?"

"I have attempted to contact the Romulan ship and advise them that their people are unharmed," replied the captain. *"So far, we've received no acknowledgment of our hails. For now, keep them secure. We're attempting to reconfigure the transporters in order to retrieve you, but I'm afraid that priority is secondary to our other repairs."*

Worf said, "Understood, Captain."

"I have Commander La Forge and Lieutenant Elfiki here, Number One. What have you learned about the people on the surface and their role in what's happening to this planet?"

Relying on Taurik to provide some of the technical details for La Forge and Elfiki's benefit, Worf provided information on the Sidrac scientists and their experiments, including the accident that had sent Ushalon on its fantastic journey.

"The Sidrac are peaceful, Captain," added Chen at Worf's prompting. "There's no malice here, sir. They're simply caught up in noble intentions gone wrong."

"But the Romulans obviously think there's something here worth exploiting," said Kirsten Cruzen.

Taurik said, "Like us, the Romulans ventured down here without fully understanding the situation, but I am uncertain as to what they hoped to accomplish by sending an armed party, and their later attack on the habitat. As long as the field generator remains in quantum flux, it is inaccessible. If another attack succeeds in damaging or destroying the field generator, the results could be disastrous for the planet and eliminate any chance of the Romulans or the *Enterprise*-D returning to their own dimensions."

"*I've communicated that to the Romulans, as well, Commander,*" replied Picard. "*No doubt they hope to harness the quantum-field generator for some martial purpose. Hopefully they'll choose not to commit any other rash acts while we look for a solution. The engineering and science teams from both* Enterprises *are working on that now.*"

What must that be like? Chen wondered. It had to be odd enough for the captain and other veteran members of the *Enterprise* crew to be looking at a ship from their own past, but what about the differences? She had not known Data in his earlier incarnation, though she had heard stories about him from Worf and La Forge and even Picard himself. Lieutenant Natasha Yar was someone Worf had mentioned on one or two occasions, always with great respect as someone who influenced him during the short period in which they had served together. She could not help dwelling on the thought that the *Enterprise*-D was commanded by that dimension's version of William Riker. It begged the question as to what had become of Picard in that reality. Had he been promoted to the admiralty, or had fate been less kind to him?

I don't even want to think about that.

"We are also working with Nelidar and her people to devise a solution," said Taurik. "So far, our best option would appear to be finding some way to interrupt the field generator's power source. This is, of course, a rather hazardous proposition, given the numerous uncertainties surrounding the current condition of the generator and the power plant. All attempts to deactivate the fusion reactor have failed, owing to its being in a constant state of dimensional flux."

"I still don't even get how that's possible," said Chen. "If the generator isn't really here, then how is the planet still tied to it? If we're in a state of dimensional phase that allows the complex to draw power from the reactor, then how is the *Enterprise* able to contact us?"

The Vulcan engineer replied, "It appears that the quantum field has created a zone around the generator and the complex that is acting as a portal, allowing for this connection to be maintained."

"Like someone sticking their foot in a door," said Konya. "And the planet is the foot?"

"Your comparison is somewhat idiomatic," replied Taurik, "but not inaccurate."

Konya nodded. "Idiomatic, but not inaccurate. I'm putting that on my résumé."

Over the open communicator frequency, Lieutenant Elfiki said, *"So, to torture this metaphor some more, if the door is stuck open but not far enough for us to walk through, we should be able to find a way to kick it in, right?"*

"If I understand you correctly," said Taurik, "I think we would wish to exercise more restraint. After all, we eventually will need to close the door, once and for all, and preferably after everyone including the Sidrac is returned to their proper dimension."

"Since we're all about doors right now," said Commander La Forge, *"let's not forget that it's also a revolving one, at least to an extent. Our scans of the field generator show that the quantum energy output has stayed at an elevated level after the last transition. So far as we can tell, that level is higher than it should be."*

Taurik replied, "That's correct, sir. Nelidar informs us that this is an unusual occurrence. Their own diagnostic tools have been unable to present an explanation."

"We're guessing it's a result of the Romulans firing on the complex," added Chen.

La Forge said, *"As good a reason as any, for right now."*

Soft yet rapid footsteps caught everyone's attention, and Chen turned to see Nelidar, still in her bare feet, running from the observation room toward them. Her expression communicated obvious concern as she motioned to the away team.

"Commander Worf," she said. "We believe another transition is imminent."

Over the channel, Picard prompted, *"Number One?"*

"It may be another dimensional shift, Captain," replied the Klingon.

"There was no alarm," said Doctor Tropp.

"We're picking up a new set of quantum energy readings," reported Elfiki. *"Yeah, looks like it's about to happen again."*

"Mister Worf," said Picard, *"we're still unable to retrieve you."*

"Understood, sir."

The team followed Nelidar into the observation room, which Chen saw was once again awash in activity. Having observed the Sidrac engineers at work before, she thought she was now able to discern subtle changes in their emotional responses as they confronted the situation evolving before them. Livak in particular was showing signs of uncertainty and even stress.

"Something is different," reported the Sidrac engineer. "The quantum energy readings are inconsistent with the previous shifts."

Moving to join him at his workstation, Nelidar asked, "In what way?"

As though remembering that he also was speaking for the benefit of the away team, Livak looked up from his instruments and addressed his reply to everyone. "There's an element of instability I have not seen before. The only sensible explanation is that the field generator did sustain some kind of damage from the spaceship's weapons."

"Interesting," said Taurik, and when Chen looked to the Vulcan it was to see him examining his tricorder. His fingers played over the device's compact control pad for a moment before his right eyebrow rose, and Chen was certain she even saw him frown.

"What is it?" asked Worf.

Taurik replied, "I have just made an adjustment to the scan field on the *Spinrad*'s sensor array. The instability to which Livak refers was something our own equipment was initially unable to detect. Now, however, I am able to study the readings. Livak is correct, there is a minor instability in the quantum field."

"It was not there before," said Livak. "It is unlike anything we recorded during any of our initial experiments or the previous transitions."

Konya, stepping up to stand beside Chen, said, "I don't understand. Are we shifting, or not?"

Shaking his head, Taurik replied, "I do not know."

"Neither do we," said Nelidar. "According to these readings, we should be on a buildup to another transition. I am at a loss to explain it."

Still sitting at his console, Livak reported, "The instability is still rather minor, but it has increased since the last transition was completed. I am concerned that it will continue to grow."

"You're not the only one," said Chen.

Cruzen asked, "I suppose it's too much to hope that we're staying put?"

"That," said Taurik, "or the next transition, whenever it occurs, could be quite hazardous for all of us."

Chen sighed. "It's always something, isn't it?"

20

U.S.S. *Enterprise*-E

Despite the circumstances that had brought them all together and the situation they now faced, as he stood among the group he had assembled, Picard could not help a wry grin.

"I think we all can agree that this will go down as one of the most bizarre briefings ever recorded in the annals of Starfleet."

His comment elicited the expected round of smiles and a few laughs.

Standing in the middle of holodeck one, surrounded by the room's unremarkable pattern of yellow grid lines, he looked around at the faces of the assembled group. Arrayed around him were Geordi La Forge and Lieutenant Elfiki. Joining them via their ship's own holodeck and communications system were Will Riker along with Data, Wesley Crusher, and the *Enterprise*-D's Geordi La Forge.

"Before we start," said Riker's holographic representation, *"may I ask a few questions? What happened to all the color in the uniforms, and since when do you all like it so dark and moody? What happened to the lights?"*

Smiling, Picard elected not to answer the obvious icebreaker. It was awkward enough, he knew, for everyone to be looking at windows into their own past or future, but he was particularly aware of his chief engineer's reaction to this meeting, as he was the only one in the room faced with looking at . . . himself.

"I was a pretty good-looking guy back then," said La Forge. "Wasn't I?"

Standing next to him, the chief engineer's younger self replied, *"Nice to see I only get better with age."* He tapped his VISOR. *"I like the implants. I'll have to look into those."*

"They weren't developed until about fifteen years ago," said La Forge. "Well, fifteen years ago here, that is." He looked to Picard. "No way to know when you all will get around to them."

"I think our engineers have highlighted one of our biggest concerns about the current situation," said Riker. *"Even though we're from different dimensions, the possibility for a form of temporal contamination still exists. We need to tread carefully here."*

Picard nodded. "Agreed." It was for this reason that he had decided to limit Captain Riker and his crew's exposure to this *Enterprise.* He knew that Riker's people were salivating at the opportunity to walk the corridors of this vessel, which in their reality was little more than a collection of technical schematics even as the keel for the first starship of the *Sovereign* class was just being laid. Everyone participating in this meeting knew that they would have to work together in order to solve their current dilemma. Still, it seemed prudent to minimize as much as possible the potential for interfering with however history might unfold in the dimension from which the *Enterprise*-D had come.

"Anything new from our Romulan friends?" asked Riker.

"No. So far, all our attempts to communicate have gone unanswered, though we know they're receiving our hails." The silence was bothersome, particularly given the status of both *Enterprise*s and their defenses, but so far the Romulan warship and its two escort vessels seemed content to keep to themselves. Picard was familiar with the Romulan penchant for shunning contact with other species in the best of situations, so on the surface the behavior of these ships and their commanders did not seem odd. On the other hand, their attempts to send a landing party to the planet's surface and their attack on the Sidrac field generator were definite causes for worry. What else might they decide to do?

Keep our eye on them, for now.

Picard said, "Our primary concern is the field generator and the instability that now seems to have crept into the quantum energy it is producing. What we need to know is whether it will affect any future dimensional transitions, and what impact those shifts may have on the planet or anyone on it." He paused, looking to Riker and his staff. "There's also the rather important question of whether the *Enterprise*-D and the Romulans can be returned to their proper dimensions."

"*We are examining our most recent sensor readings,*" said Data, from where he stood on the hologrid next to Riker. "*The instability reported by the Sidrac engineers is small, but not insignificant. The same is true for its rate of increase. If this continues and the planet experiences another shift, increased instability in the quantum field could have unpredictable, disruptive, or even catastrophic effects.*"

"Catastrophic?" echoed Picard.

The android nodded. "*Yes, sir, though that might well be a worst-case scenario. Our understanding of transdimensional passages is quite limited, so we are therefore forced to consider every possibility, no matter how dire.*"

"Unless or until we can find a way to penetrate the

quantum field surrounding the field generator and the power complex," said Elfiki, "we're not going to be able to do anything. So far as the rest of the universe is concerned, that area of the planet is in its own bubble that's playing by its own rules."

The *Enterprise*-D's La Forge said, *"So, we need to pop the bubble, but in such a way that it doesn't unleash a torrent of unregulated quantum energy all over that planet."* He shook his head. *"I wouldn't want to be down there if that happened."*

Crusher said, *"I don't know if popping is the best analogy. More like locating or creating a weakened area that might give us access, like finding a hole in a ship's deflector shields."*

"What about a controlled burst of quantum energy?" asked the older La Forge. "Maybe push back against the existing quantum field somehow?"

"An intriguing idea," said Data. *"However, I do not know if either of our ships is capable of creating such a release of energy. It may be possible to reconfigure our main deflectors to generate such a burst, but the power costs would be considerable, particularly in each ship's present compromised condition."*

"What about a transphasic torpedo?" asked Elfiki. "Could something like that be reconfigured to provide this burst you're talking about?"

Riker frowned. *"What the hell is a transphasic torpedo?"*

"A little something we picked up from an . . . unlikely source," said Picard.

For the moment, at least, he preferred to avoid discussions about how, two decades from now, a future version of Admiral Kathryn Janeway from yet another timeline would defy regulations and perhaps even logic and common sense in order to assist her past self and the *Starship Voyager*. As part of her audacious plan to help return the wayward ship from where it had been stranded for years in the distant reaches of the Delta Quadrant, she provided her younger counterpart with several pieces of future Starfleet technology specifically created to fight the Borg. Chief among these gifts was an advanced form of ablative armor as well as transphasic torpedoes, with just a single such weapon capable of destroying a Borg cube.

Following *Voyager*'s return to the Alpha Quadrant eight years ago, Starfleet spent considerable time going over the starship's various "upgrades," not just those from the future Janeway but also as a consequence of its crew having to adapt to their situation in the Delta Quadrant. The use of transphasic torpedoes against the Borg had come during their final, massive invasion of Federation space. While Starfleet scored numerous early victories against their implacable adversary in the opening rounds of that conflict, the Collective managed to adapt to the weaponry.

And yet, we still won.

With the Borg gone, transphasic torpedoes were not typically carried aboard Starfleet vessels, though the specifications for constructing such weapons were available in the memory banks of each starship's computer. Was it possible such a device might prove useful here?

"We'd need to go over the specs again," said the older La Forge, "but if we can reconfigure it to deliver some kind of quantum energy pulse, it could work."

Elfiki said, "Without the explosion and wanton destruction that comes with it."

The *Enterprise*-D's La Forge replied, "*Even accounting*

for the apparent time difference between our two dimensions, this sounds like something that's way ahead of us."

Picard nodded. "In truth, it was advanced even for us." Choosing his words carefully, he said, "Consideration was given as to whether or not the technology was something Starfleet should exploit, and the potential impact of that decision. It was finally decided, given the circumstances under which we became aware of its existence, that it was something we could use so long as we did so judiciously."

It occurred to him that—assuming the *Enterprise*-D was even able to return to its own dimension—that providing information about the transphasic torpedoes and the other advanced anti-Borg technology might just give the Starfleet of that reality an edge it had sorely lacked in this one. Could it be possible for the Federation to take the fight to the Borg far sooner than had occurred here? Perhaps they would even be able to vanquish the relentless foe long before it was able to inflict something similar to the widespread damage from which this reality's Alpha Quadrant was still recovering.

There was also the possibility that if the Borg of the other dimension did launch an invasion of a scope similar to what this reality had endured, Starfleet might deploy such a weapon too soon, and give their adversary ample opportunity to adapt to it. Such a tactical error would leave the Federation all but defenseless. The devastation visited upon the Alpha Quadrant in that dimension might be even more severe. Worse, the Federation itself might well fall to the Borg. The very thought chilled Picard's blood.

What to do?

His momentary reverie was broken as Data said, *"I*

believe I could be useful assisting Commander La Forge and Lieutenant Elfiki with the analysis and reconfiguration required to modify such a weapon." When his comment drew looks, the android added, "*If I am so ordered, I would not be able to reveal any details of the technology to which I would be exposed. Indeed, I could even simply delete that information from my memory.*"

"I don't mind saying I'd appreciate the help," said the *Enterprise*-E's La Forge, "but I get that we're definitely skirting the Temporal Prime Directive here."

Riker said, "*My first thought is to say to hell with the Temporal Prime Directive, along with whatever other crazy regulation Starfleet might trot out as justification for complaining about all of this. They're not here, and the only way they'll be able to yell at us is if we make it home.*" He looked to Picard with a wry grin. "*I can't help you with your Starfleet, Captain. You'll have to deal with them yourself.*"

"It wouldn't be the first time," replied Picard. "First things first, however. For now, Mister Data's assistance is most welcome. We'll deal with the other issues once we're closer to crafting a solution to our immediate problem."

Everyone was startled by the sound of a red alert klaxon echoing through the otherwise empty holodeck, and Riker looked to Picard.

"*I take it you're hearing that too?*"

Picard nodded, just as the ship's intraship flared to life.

"*Bridge to Captain Picard,*" said the voice of Lieutenant Aneta Šmrhová. "*Sir, the Romulans are on the move.*"

Expecting to see a *Vas Hatham*–class warship displayed on the main viewscreen, Picard was instead surprised to see the image of a smaller, less powerful *Mularr*-class escort as he emerged with Dina Elfiki from the turbolift.

"Report."

Standing at the tactical station behind the captain's chair, Aneta Šmrhová replied, "They broke formation two minutes ago, sir. The escorts split and started heading for us and the *Enterprise*-D on attack vectors. Sensors show their weapons are armed and their shields are up, and the bird-of-prey has activated its cloaking device."

Picard approached his seat. "Bring phasers online, place them on ready status. Lieutenant Faur, take us out of orbit and engage evasive maneuvers. Concentrate on keeping our nose to the approaching ship. Glinn Dygan, route all shield power to forward deflectors." Settling into the command chair, he prompted, "Lieutenant Elfiki?"

Having returned to her station, the science officer said, "Ordinarily, we'd be able to track a ship using such an outdated cloaking device. Starfleet cracked that nut over a century ago, but our sensors are still compromised by the nebula, the quantum fluctuations, and the damage we took." She turned from her console. "They can still play games with us, sir, if that's their plan."

"Picard to engineering."

"La Forge here, sir."

"I need all available power to the shields and weapons, Geordi."

"Shields are only at fifty-eight percent. Phasers are at three-quarter power. We're trying to improve those numbers, Captain, but if the Romulans are going to start shooting at us . . ."

"Work faster, Mister La Forge. Picard out."

At the ops console, Joanna Faur reported, "The

Romulan ship is closing, sir. It's locked weapons on us, but I'm not seeing any indication it's readying to fire."

"Lieutenant Šmrhová, target their forward weapons ports, but hold fire until my command." Considering the evolving situation, he asked, "What's the other ship doing with the *Enterprise*-D?"

Behind him, the security chief replied, "The second escort is approaching it on a vector similar to ours, sir. The *Enterprise*-D is breaking orbit, maneuvering to give itself some breathing room. Both ships have clear shots at each other."

And there's still the cloaked Romulan ship.

"Open a channel," ordered Picard. When Šmrhová gave him the go-ahead, he announced in a formal voice, "Romulan vessels, this is Captain Jean-Luc Picard aboard the *Enterprise*. Your actions are unprovoked and unwarranted. Withdraw, or we'll be forced to defend ourselves. Failure to acknowledge this message will be interpreted as further hostile action."

After a moment, Šmrhová said, "No response, sir. Ships still on approach."

"Stand by to fire. Lieutenant Faur, continue evasive maneuvers. Keep them in front of us."

Nothing about this action made sense. Even in their compromised condition, each *Enterprise* could best all three of the Romulan vessels in any prolonged skirmish. The only chance the Romulans had now was surprise, and while their cloaked companion played into that to a degree, that advantage would be lost the instant that ship was forced to decloak in order to fire.

There's something else going on here.

"Fire across the escort's bow, Lieutenant."

Picard saw a single orange beam of energy lancing

across space, well ahead of the Romulan ship. For its part, the other vessel seemed unperturbed by the warning action, its course unchanging as it continued its approach. Then the ship seemed to surge forward.

"They're accelerating to full impulse," reported Šmrhová. "They're locking weapons."

"Evasive," snapped Picard even as he saw the escort's forward weapons ports glow bright green just before twin energy bolts spat forth. An instant later the image on the viewscreen was awash with static. The volley was followed by a second strike that produced a similar effect as the ship maneuvered out of the frame. It returned seconds later as Lieutenant Faur continued guiding the *Enterprise* in a bid to keep the Romulan ship in front of it.

Šmrhová said, "Impact on forward shields, but no significant damage."

"Return fire," said Picard. "Target their weapons." He was not ready to disable the other ship just yet, preferring instead to keep that option in reserve.

A new round of phaser fire crossed space, and Picard watched as the energy beams struck the Romulan ship's forward shields. Without waiting for a new order, Šmrhová fired again as the escort attempted evasion, and the second volley was greeted by an even greater clash of energies followed by an obvious strike on the enemy vessel's hull.

"We breached their shields, sir," reported the security chief. "Damage to front starboard disruptor port, but I'm not seeing any signs of a hull breach." A moment later, she added, "They're moving off, Captain."

Before Picard could issue his next instructions, an alarm signal warbled across the bridge, and the overhead lighting shifted from its normal levels to the softer illumination that accompanied an alert condition.

Šmrhová called out, "The bird-of-prey! It's decloaking to the stern!"

"Bring us about!"

Faur was already acting even before Picard's order, and the image on the screen blurred as the *Enterprise* rotated to port. The lieutenant had guided the starship to spin on its axis, bringing its nose down so that within seconds the Romulan bird-of-prey was centered on the viewscreen just as a brilliant crimson energy plume erupted from the weapon port at its prow.

"All hands!" Picard shouted. "Brace for impact!"

The red mass undulated and glowed with barely restrained fury, growing as it filled the screen.

21

Despite the best efforts of its pilot, there was no escape for the Romulan escort, and Riker could not help smiling as he beheld the vessel's stern.

"Target its main propulsion," he said. "Fire."

A pair of phaser strikes courtesy of Tasha Yar at the tactical station was enough to overload the escort's shields, and a second barrage hit home, slamming into the cylindrical nacelle tucked close to the port side of the ship's primary hull. Plasma vented at the point of impact, and Riker saw the vessel shudder in response to the attack.

"Primary propulsion appears offline," reported Wesley Crusher from the ops position, "but their hull's still intact."

Yar reported, "Captain, the Romulan ship has dropped its cloak. It's closing on the *Enterprise*-E."

Well. It's about time.

Attempting to track the elusive bird-of-prey had been problematic, given the ship's compromised sensors. Yar and Data were able to tune the scanners enough to pick up a faint energy distortion, which could have been the enemy vessel, drifting well below the ship's original orbital glide path as it maneuvered toward the far side of the planet. Then the two escorts had taken their own actions, and Riker's attention was forced to shift.

"Bring us around, Mister Worf," he said. "Let's see if we can't lend a hand."

"The Romulans are firing!"

Yar's warning came just as the viewscreen shifted to show the *Enterprise*-E. The second Romulan escort was maneuvering away even as the bird-of-prey was facing off against the larger starship.

"Target that ship, Lieutenant," said Riker, the words leaving his mouth just as he saw the massive sphere of writhing red energy lurch forth from the Romulan vessel. It crossed the void separating the two ships, the other *Enterprise*'s shields flaring into a warped curve of hellish color and light as they attempted to absorb the attack.

"*Enterprise*-E shields down to twelve percent," reported Yar. "Sensors are showing massive overloads across the ship."

Riker snapped, "Fire! Now, before it gets back under cloak."

He could see the bird-of-prey already beginning to shimmer and waver as its cloaking device reactivated. It was moving off, no doubt planning to alter its course as soon as it was fully masked from sensors, but Yar was faster, retargeting the escaping ship and firing. A pair of phaser beams caught the vessel amidships, and Riker recognized the telltale signs of a hull breach. Yar followed with a second strike and the fleeing ship shuddered in the face of the assault.

From where he sat next to Riker, Data examined the control panel near his own seat's right arm. "Their cloak has failed, Captain. The ship's main engines have also been damaged. There was a breach, but the affected compartment appears to have been sealed off. I am unable to determine if there were any casualties. Their life-support system appears functional."

"They're moving off, sir," said Worf. "Should we pursue?"

Riker shook his head. "Negative. Let them go, but keep an eye on them. Tasha, send a message to the ship and offer our assistance with repairs or casualties, but make sure they understand we're done playing games. And contact the *Enterprise*-E. Let's find out how they're doing."

In short order, Captain Picard's weathered visage filled the viewscreen, and he nodded in greeting. *"Thanks for the assist, Captain Riker. Your timing, as always, was superlative."*

Gripped by momentary nostalgia, Riker offered a small smile. "Always happy to help, sir. What's your status?"

"Nothing our Mister La Forge and his team can't handle. Our scans show a similar situation for you."

Moving to stand between the conn and ops positions, Riker asked, "Damage reports?"

Crusher replied, "Some buckling to the starboard deflector shield generators and several more circuit overloads on multiple decks, sir. Commander La Forge has already dispatched repair teams."

"As if he doesn't have enough to do." Riker sighed. The ship's engineering staff had been working nonstop in a bid to finalize the numerous minor yet widespread repairs that still plagued the crew in the wake of the dimensional shift. He knew that their counterparts on the other *Enterprise* were in similar straits, and he suspected this was the reason the Romulans had elected to attack, but to what end?

Redirecting his attention to the viewscreen, he asked, "Any thoughts on why the Romulans would do something so stupid? They had to know that if push came to shove, we had them outmatched."

Picard nodded. *"My thoughts exactly."*

"If I may, sir," said Worf, and at Riker's prompting, continued, "It was a coordinated effort. They split their attack so that we and the *Enterprise*-E had to divide our own resources, with the bird-of-prey lingering in the background and waiting for an opportunity to strike." He frowned, and a small growl escaped the Klingon's lips. "Typical Romulan behavior. They have no courage."

"Maybe," said Riker, "but if that's the case, why not make a run for it?"

"They have people on the surface too?" asked Yar. "Then again, wouldn't a Romulan ship commander just cut their losses?"

Pacing the expanse of carpet behind the forward bridge positions, Riker let his gaze wander around the room as he considered the possibilities. "They're not above that sort of thing, especially if they thought the odds were stacked too high against them. I don't know if that was the case here. No, they deliberately set out to engage us, and they did it in such a way that we had no choice but to . . ." The rest of the sentence died on his lips as a few more pieces of the bizarre puzzle began falling into place.

"Wait," he said. For Picard's benefit, he added, "Just before the escort ships made their play, we picked up an energy fluctuation we thought might be the bird-of-prey under cloak. It maneuvered around the planet's far side before we could get a lock on it though, but for a minute it looked like it might be dipping closer to the surface."

"A distraction?" Picard turned to the female officer manning the tactical station on his bridge. *"Lieutenant Šmrhová, scan for signs of any new ship activity on or near the planet's surface, and contact the away team."*

Riker asked, "You think the Romulans sent another team down to the planet?"

"They still want the Sidrac technology," replied Picard. *"Perhaps their commander thought this was their best chance to get to it before we could."*

Wesley asked, "But why? They're still trapped here, like we are."

"Assuming they even realize they've been shifted from their own dimension," replied Riker. "Remember, we're still jamming their transmissions because they tried to call for help."

"They may have thought they could disable us and make a run for it after acquiring the Sidrac technology, or at least information about it," said Picard. *"Just one of their ships has to get out of jamming range in order to send a signal."*

That would not bode well, Riker knew, based on what Picard had told him about this region. Though Romulan space was some distance away, the empire would not hesitate to send a ship in response to a distress signal from one of their own, even if the ship calling for help was more than a century out of place and time.

Yar said, "They won't be going too far just yet, sir. All three ships have enough damage that they require immediate repairs."

"We can monitor their progress," said Picard. *"In the meantime, we have more pressing matters. Commander Worf has reported in. Another Romulan shuttle has landed on the surface."*

Ushalon

From her vantage point behind the seat occupied by Nelidar in the Sidrac personnel transport, T'Ryssa Chen tried not to look too closely at the jagged mountain peaks that seemed much too close to the small ship's transit. Her anxiety was not helped by the occasional dip or roll they experienced as Nelidar attempted to compensate for the ever-present quantum fluctuations.

"Can I just go on record as saying I hate this idea?" She shifted in her seat, her movements hampered once again by her environmental suit.

Sitting to Chen's left, Taurik replied over the team's shared communications channel, *"I will be sure to note it in my after-action report, assuming we survive and I am able to file it."*

"Not funny, Taurik. Not funny at all."

For his part, Worf had said nothing since he, along with Taurik, Chen, and Rennan Konya, had accompanied Nelidar on what at first blush appeared to be a mission of near desperation. Chen imagined the first officer's thoughts were consumed with what might happen over the course of the next several minutes as they scrambled to deal with a second attempt at Romulan infiltration.

His attention focused on his ubiquitous tricorder, Taurik said, *"Sensors show their craft has landed, Commander. Seven Romulan life signs, as before."*

"Their pilot must be quite proficient," said Worf. *"The interference from the quantum-field generator is increasing as we get closer."*

Chen said, "And we're sure it's just the one shuttle? I'm surprised they didn't send more people."

"Better with a small team that can move fast," replied Konya from where he sat behind Chen. *"They may be hoping to get in, grab something they think is valuable, and get out quick."*

Thanks to Taurik's continued monitoring of the *Spinrad*'s sensors, the away team had become aware of the second Romulan shuttle attempting to make planet-fall even before Captain Picard alerted Worf. The Romulans were crafty, dispatching their landing craft toward the surface while on the planet's far side, masked from the *Enterprise*'s own impaired sensors. Further, this new group of intruders was trying something different than their predecessors, forgoing an attempt at infiltrating the habitat in favor of an assault on the underground complex housing the quantum-field generator and the power plant.

"They have to be out of their minds, trying to get in there," said Chen. "Surely they understand the risks involved?"

Taurik replied, *"It is possible they do not fully comprehend the danger presented by the quantum field. I find it hard to believe that their sensors are so outdated that they cannot obtain accurate readings of the complex."*

"They tried disrupting the field before," said Konya. *"Makes sense that they'd try again. Maybe this is their restrained approach."*

Chen shook her head. "It's going to get them killed, and maybe the rest of us along with them."

The transport bounced around again, and Chen's stomach heaved as she grabbed the edges of her seat, searching for balance or purchase.

"Wait," said Konya. *"That wasn't turbulence."*

Seated before the large, curved black console that dominated the transport's cockpit and dressed in her own excursion suit, Nelidar replied, *"No, Lieutenant. The Romulans are shooting at us."* She shifted so that she could look over her shoulder, her face partially obscured by the metal of her helmet. *"Our craft has protective plating, but it was never intended to be a combat vessel."*

"I knew I should've stayed behind," said Chen, almost under her breath. "Cruzen and Tropp are so lucky."

Konya nudged her arm. *"But this is where all the fun is."*

The transport shuddered again, and this time Chen felt the multiple impacts of disruptor fire against the outer hull as the craft began descending. To her credit, Nelidar seemed to be doing a commendable job evading most of the incoming fire, and from what Chen could see of the cockpit's control panels, no alarms had been activated.

"I am attempting to land behind a rock outcropping that should provide some protection when you disembark."

The plan was a hasty one, devised by Worf as the team was suiting up and preparing to board the Sidrac transport. With Nelidar to guide them, the first officer hoped to deny the Romulans entry to the underground facility by any means necessary. Concerns were high that any disruption by some foreign matter of the quantum field surrounding the complex might corrupt or collapse it, with unpredictable results. There was the possibility of another dimensional shift, of course, but the main worry was that such a transition would now be unchecked, causing irreparable harm to the facility and the surface complex along with its inhabitants. At worst, according to Livak and the other Sidrac engineers, the stresses of such an unrestrained release of quantum energy might well tear the planet apart, reducing it to dust and casting it into whatever void might exist between dimensions.

So, thought Chen, *let's try to avoid that, if we can.*

There was more weapons fire from outside, though she observed that it was not as intense or rapid as the previous attack. Beyond the transport's canopy, she saw the mountains continuing to rise up as the craft made its descent. Konya, already out of his seat and brandishing one of the disruptors the away team had confiscated from the first Romulan scouting party, had moved to the transport's rear hatch.

One more disruptor hit on its hull made the transport shudder, and for the first time an alert indicator sounded in the cramped interior. Chen saw a bright orange status light activate, and Nelidar reached for a control to silence the alarm even as she fought to maintain control of the small craft.

"They struck a stabilizer unit," she reported, not looking away from her instruments. *"Our landing may be a bit more intense than I anticipated."*

"Just get us on the ground," said Konya, who had braced himself against the compartment's rear bulkhead. *"We'll take it from there."*

"Stand by," said Worf as he moved to join Konya on the other side of the door.

Taurik, still holding his tricorder while wielding a disruptor in his other hand, said, *"We will land fifty meters from the Romulans' current position. They are less than fifteen meters from the field generator facility's access point."*

Out of her seat and shuffling over to stand behind Worf, Chen reached for a handlebar mounted to the bulkhead just as she felt the transport pivoting to port and decelerating. Through the cockpit canopy, she was able to make out the straight lines and angles of the metal wall that formed the surface entrance to the field generator complex.

"When I pop the hatch," said Konya as he looked to her and Taurik, *"use the side of the ship as cover. Don't give the Romulans any free shots."*

The transport shed more speed, and then came a slight bump as Nelidar set down. As she had taught him, Konya activated the control to open the craft's rear hatch. The reinforced metal door dropped without grace, slamming into the soil and providing a ramp. Worf and Konya led the way, disruptors held out in front of them and searching for threats as they descended the ramp, making room for Taurik and Chen to follow. Shadowing Konya's movements, Chen pressed herself against the transport's side and began maneuvering toward its nose.

"Nelidar," said Worf, *"remain with the ship until we have secured the situation."*

At that moment a green-white disruptor bolt slammed into the transport's armored front end, and Chen sensed the reverberation as the hull absorbed the impact.

"Easier said than done, sir," said Konya. He gestured with his disruptor. *"We've got some cover, but we'll be in the open before we can get halfway there."*

Behind Worf, Taurik said, *"The Romulans are using what appears to be a storage building near the entrance for cover, but it is marginal."*

"I may be able to assist with that," said Nelidar.

After directing the team to seek protection among the nearby rock outcroppings, the Sidrac scientist powered up the transport, and it rose just two meters from the ground. Its nose angled downward, the craft began to slowly drift forward.

"I like your style, Nelidar," said Konya, smiling at Chen through his helmet faceplate before he and Worf set off after the transport.

Chen exchanged glances with Taurik. "Stuff like this wasn't in the Academy recruiting brochure."

"Indeed."

Their suits made maneuvering with any kind of speed a challenge, but the away team was able to keep pace with Nelidar as she guided the transport forward. Within seconds Chen saw multiple volleys of disruptor fire as the Romulans took aim at the approaching craft.

"Nelidar," said Chen. "Are you all right?"

The Sidrac replied, *"The canopy is reinforced, but mostly to prevent damage from collisions. I do not know how long it can withstand this sort of punishment."*

"We can help with that," said Konya.

Chen watched as the security officer stepped to his left, out from behind the transport and the cover it provided. Nelidar had paid the away team the courtesy of using the craft's forward lights to illuminate the ground ahead of them, and Chen caught sight of dark figures hunkered near a small freestanding structure less than ten meters from the field generator's surface entrance.

"The hatch is open!" shouted Konya before he unleashed several shots with his disruptor.

Joining in the action, Worf fired his own weapon at a fleeing figure, and Chen saw the disruptor bolt strike its target. The Romulan, dressed in a dark-gray environmental suit, fell to the ground. Two of his companions emerged from cover to return fire. Konya dropped to one knee, sighting on another of the Romulans just as Chen sensed movement ahead and to their left.

"Rennan! Look out!"

There was no time to react, and Chen aimed her disruptor and fired. Her single shot struck the Romulan's suit helmet, snapping his body back and sending him tumbling over a portion of exposed rock. The figure crashed to the soil, and she saw the wisps of vapor escaping from his helmet's cracked faceplate.

"Thanks," said Konya after dispatching his original target. He grabbed her arm and pulled her back behind the transport.

"I count only five Romulans," reported Taurik, dividing his attention between his tricorder and the terrain before him. *"Two have entered the structure."*

Over the channel, Nelidar said, *"They cannot be allowed to access the complex."*

More disruptor fire made Chen flinch as an energy bolt hit the ground to her left. Konya pushed her ahead of him, making sure she stayed within the cover provided by the transport.

"To the right," called Taurik, and Chen turned to see the Vulcan aiming his disruptor at what at first appeared to be a collection of boulders in proximity to the nearby hill. He fired the weapon, and the flash of its energy bolt illuminated the figure crouching in shadow. Taurik's shot caught the Romulan in the chest, spinning him around and dropping him to the dusty ground.

"The other one's ahead of us, near the entrance," said Konya. He pointed toward the open portal, and Chen caught sight of someone silhouetted and crouching in the lighted entryway. The figure's arm moved up and over his head, and then Chen saw something else.

"Look out!"

Lunging at Konya, Chen grabbed his arm and yanked him toward her. Both of them tumbled to the ground as the dark spherical object she had seen arcing through the air hit the ground less than five meters from their position before rebounding off the dirt and sailing even farther away.

"Grenade!"

The object bounced over and beyond a large rock that

jutted out of the parched soil, and a second later light erupted, followed by the shockwave of the deflected explosion. Chen winced as she felt something peppering her back and she held her breath, waiting for the alarm announcing the breach of her environmental suit. Only when that did not happen after several seconds did she dare to open her eyes, and found herself staring through her faceplate at Rennan Konya.

"Hi," he said.

Chen blinked. "Hi."

"You could've just warned me, you know. I usually move pretty fast when explosives are involved."

"I'll remember that for next time."

"Deal." He smiled as she rolled off of him before extending a hand to help him to his feet. *"And before I forget: Thanks. Again."*

Looking ahead of them, Chen saw that the Sidrac transport was settling to the ground near the entrance as Worf and Taurik moved in that direction.

"All five Romulans on the surface are disabled," reported the first officer. The first one to reach the doorway, he paused at the threshold, his disruptor trained on the fallen Romulan there. Only after verifying that the enemy soldier was out of action did Worf proceed.

Rushing to keep up, Chen was the next to reach the entry, pointing her disruptor ahead of her as she followed after Worf. She found herself not inside an airlock, but instead at the head of a long, narrow cylindrical tunnel that sloped downward from ground level, descending perhaps fifty meters before leveling out. According to Nelidar, there was an airlock at the passage's far end that led to the quantum-field generator itself, as well as other work areas and support facilities. Recessed lighting at regular intervals provided ample illumination. She could feel a low, omnipresent hum that seemed to reverberate through the tunnel's metal walls and coursed even through her suit's protective material. Sensing movement behind her, she turned to see Nelidar coming through the doorway.

"*The quantum energy levels are elevated,*" said Taurik. Standing just inside the entry, he eyed his tricorder. "*Even though we are still well outside the complex's protected areas.*"

Nelidar replied, "*During our first investigations after the accident, we realized that the quantum field had formed a bubble around the generator and the neighboring facility. We tried to pass objects through the field, to see what would happen, but they just . . . disappeared.*"

Konya, his disruptor aimed down the tunnel as he searched for threats, asked, "*Even Romulan tricorders have to be telling them they can't get inside, right? So, what's the point, unless they're thinking they can scan the field generator if they get close enough?*"

"*That,*" said Taurik, "*or they are hoping they can obtain a piece of the relevant technology to take back with them.*"

Worf grunted. "*That would require them getting past us. We will not allow that to happen.*"

Tricorder in hand, Taurik replied, "*The quantum field is interfering with my scans.*"

"*Is the entrance to the generator secure?*" asked Nelidar.

Taurik nodded. "*Yes, at least so far as my readings indicate.*"

Motioning for them to follow her, Nelidar led the way down the tunnel. As the passage leveled, they found the airlock permitting access to this level of the complex. Nelidar was first inside, and once the large hatch was sealed, she and the away team were able to remove their suit helmets.

"Finally," said Konya.

Placing her helmet on one of two shelves set into the bulkhead, Chen asked, "Any sign of our friends?"

His attention once more on his tricorder, Taurik replied, "Twenty meters ahead, at the end of the service corridor leading to the quantum-field generator."

Opting not to remove their environmental suits, the away team moved through the airlock's inner hatch and into another passageway, which Chen saw was wider than the tunnel leading to the surface, with five smaller connecting corridors burrowing into the surrounding rock. Metal panels painted in colors different from the walls suggested access conduits or other workspaces for the Sidrac engineers, and Chen noted a few display screens and workstations set into the bulkheads.

Worf took over leading the group, leaving Nelidar to follow the Klingon with Chen at her side as he advanced farther along the tunnel, which proceeded for several meters before ending at sharp bend. Pausing at the junction, Worf glanced around the corner, then directed his gaze to the rest of the team. With his free hand, he held up two fingers, indicating he had spotted their adversaries. Then he pointed to Chen.

Me? Oh, hell.

Without waiting for her to indicate a response, Worf turned and stepped into the corridor. Chen followed, and saw two Romulans, each dressed in charcoal-gray environmental suits with their helmet faceplates raised, standing before one of the open wall panels. They were working on something that was blocked from her view. What did attract her attention was the large pressure hatch at the room's far end. Manufactured from some kind of polished metal, the circular hatch was embedded into the stone. It featured a pair of visible hinges, indicating the door opened outward, toward them. Both the door and its surrounding wall lay behind a shimmering curtain of iridescent energy. Everything beyond the barrier wavered and rippled.

The away team's presence did not go unnoticed. Both Romulans reacted to the new arrivals by moving away from the wall panel with disruptors drawn. Konya was the first to react, firing at one of the soldiers. The disruptor bolt caught the Romulan in the side, spinning him around until he slammed face-first into the metal bulkhead. Though the soldier's companion was able to get off a badly aimed shot, Worf stunned him with his disruptor.

"Is that the quantum field?" asked Konya, pointing toward the door.

Nelidar replied, "Yes, but it is . . . larger than during our previous visit. The last time we inspected the complex, the barrier was inside the door."

"The energy readings are showing a definite increase," said Taurik. "There also appears to be a localized interruption in the complex's power distribution network."

Chen pointed to the open access panel several meters from the barrier. "What were the Romulans doing?" She followed Nelidar, who had also seen the signs of obvious tampering. The Sidrac engineer examined the conduit's interior before pointing to a dark metallic object.

"I do not recognize this component."

Before Chen could move for a closer look, Taurik's voice boomed across the room.

"Everyone back! *Now!*"

There was no time to question, or to argue, and Taurik was offering no information. Instead, he simply grabbed Chen and Nelidar by their arms and pulled them away from the panel, shoving them in the direction of the nearest tunnel. Chen found herself counting seconds as the away team scrambled for cover, making it to six before the explosion.

22

ChR Bloodied Talon

"Retreat, surrender, or die. Those are our options, Commander."

Sitting at her command station on the bridge, Sarith heard Subcommander Ineti's words but chose not to remark on them. She opened her mouth, relaxing muscles and alleviating the dull ache in her teeth from where she had been clenching her jaw. Her eyes stung from the smoke that permeated the air and resisted the valiant effort of the atmospheric scrubbers. The odor of burned wiring and insulation assailed her nostrils, and the tension of the past several hours had now asserted itself as a throbbing pain across the top of her head. She ignored all of that. Her personal discomfort mattered little to her just now. The only thing of importance was her ship and her crew, for which the fates of both now rested in her hands.

"What is the latest damage assessment?" she asked.

Ineti replied, "Our primary propulsion is still undergoing repairs. Jacius informs me that it will be well into the next duty shift before he can offer a proper estimate on the drive's return. The hull breach in section four has been contained, and a crew has been dispatched outside to seal the rupture. Their repairs should be sufficient until we can reach a support base."

"I suspect there will be no such journey in our future, my old friend."

Frowning, Ineti said, "As you observed earlier, the Starfleet ships appear in no rush to move in and finish us off. They certainly possess the advantage, do they not? What is stopping them, beyond their vaunted principles?"

"The planet, obviously." Sarith pushed herself away from her seat and turned to the central hub. "They have people on the surface, and the alien technology attracts their attention as much as ours."

"For vastly different reasons, no doubt," said Ineti.

Sarith shook her head. "Do not be so sure. Despite constantly espousing its desire to explore the stars in peace, the Federation is well aware that its long-term security and prosperity is dependent upon the allies and resources they find along the way. We know from our past dealings with them that they are more than capable of exploiting a tactical advantage and setting aside their dubious notions of morality in order to assure victory. That is the humans' dark secret, even if most of them are unwilling to admit it even to themselves."

She had heard the stories, passed down from those who had engaged the humans and their allies during the Great War. Though many from Earth waded into that conflict with some sense of honor and even decency, there were those who were content to cast aside such notions in the heat of battle. It was an all too familiar refrain in any war. A rational mind might think that those unpleasant realities would discourage the practice of war and instead inspire a greater struggle for peace, but such thinking often was in short supply once the fighting started.

"Still no contact from our surface teams?" asked Sarith.

Ineti sighed. "No. We lost track of the second shuttle within moments of deploying it. We are not able to verify that it made it to its intended target, due to interference with our scans." He glanced around the room. "Then we had larger concerns."

"Of which I am aware." It had been Sarith's decision to dispatch a second shuttle to the immense facility generating power for the surface and subterranean complex. She had hoped her team might secure some piece of technology or information that could be delivered to her superiors if not the praetor himself, perhaps as a prize that might one day be used against their Federation adversaries. Had her people met with success or failure? Were they even still alive, or had they been captured? Assuming the Earth captain was being truthful during one of his annoying, relentless attempts at communication, the first centurions she had sent to the surface were now prisoners of the Starfleet landing party.

"Continue our attempts to reach the shuttles," said Sarith.

Ineti nodded. "Of course."

"Commander," said Centurion Skerius, turning from the communications station, "we are being hailed again by the Starfleet captain."

Ineti offered a humorless grin. "The human is persistent."

"A common trait among their species." Sarith turned to Skerius. "Ignore it."

"Forgive me, Commander," said the centurion, "but this message is different. The human is offering as-

sistance not just with our repairs, but also in seeing us
safely returned home." He paused, looking first to Sarith
and then Ineti. "Some of what he says, I do not understand."

Sarith looked to Ineti. "Interesting."

"He could be lying," replied the subcommander.

"But to what end? He can already destroy us if he so
chooses." Moving to the display screen set aside for intership communications, she said to Skerius, "Open the
frequency."

The screen activated, its image coalescing into that
of a human male wearing a type of black-and-gray uniform she did not recognize. It was quite different from
the more colorful variations she had seen depicted in recent intelligence reports. Behind the human, Sarith saw
a small number of officers occupying workstations, but
they and the rest of what must be the starship's bridge
were far more advanced—even luxurious—than anything she had ever seen.

*"Romulan vessels, I am Captain Jean-Luc Picard of the
Federation Starship Enterprise. We renew our offers to assist you with your repairs and casualties, and we have no
interest in further aggressive action."*

Sarith replied, "How can I trust you, Captain Picard?"

"Because you're still here, talking to me."

There was no bravado in the human's voice, no attempt at asserting superiority. He had made the comment as a declaration of simple fact. That he was correct
only served to further aggravate Sarith, but she schooled
her features so as to offer no reaction.

"Fair enough. How do you know you can trust me?"

"I don't. On that subject, further acts of aggression are

not necessary. That includes your sending people to the surface. Their actions have placed the planet's inhabitants and my people in danger, which I will not tolerate any longer." He held her gaze for a moment before his expression softened. *"Commander, we can stand here all day posturing, but by now you should have realized that you are rather outmatched. Instead, we should be working together to accomplish something that may be of some importance to you: getting you home."*

Forcing herself to maintain her fixed expression, Sarith said, "We may be injured, Captain, but we are not crippled. Romulan space is not out of our reach."

"That much is true, but what you apparently don't seem to realize is that it's not your Romulan space."

He stopped himself again, and Sarith's instincts told her he was considering how his next words might be received. Then, as if reaching some decision, he stepped closer to the screen.

"If you've been monitoring the planet that seems to have captured all our interests, then you know it's been subjected to a series of interdimensional shifts that have seen it propelled between several different parallel realities. What you may not realize, Commander, is that you also have been pulled from your own dimension, and deposited into mine."

"That's impossible," said Sarith. This was fantasy; a fiction concocted by the human captain as a bid to distract her.

And yet . . .

She turned to Darjil at the sensor station and saw his own expression of shock and disbelief. "Is what he says true? *Can* it be true?"

"I . . . I do not know, Commander." There was no mistaking the centurion's fear and uncertainty. "We have never encountered anything like this phenomenon before. I am not a scientist. I do not even know how to make such a determination."

Stepping forward, Ineti said, "Subcommander Variel is the one who could speak to such matters."

Sarith frowned. *And she is on the surface. What a fool I have been. All this time?*

"Each dimension has a unique quantum signature," said Picard. *"That signature can be detected at the subatomic level of anyone or anything. It can be used to identify a person or object that has moved from one dimension to another. Scans of your vessels show that your quantum signature is different from this dimension, and further still from the planet we're orbiting."*

Was it possible? If not, then why would this human go to such lengths to perpetrate a ruse?

On the screen, Picard motioned to Ineti. *"If I overheard your crewman correctly, you have someone who can verify what I'm telling you. I would suggest allowing that individual to do so."*

What should she do? Admitting that her science officer was down on the planet and already in the custody of Picard's subordinates might show weakness, an inability to stand on even footing with this human. However, any attempt at deceit would likely be short-lived.

Still, there was something about this man that compelled trust.

"That would be Subcommander Variel," she said after a moment. "At last report, she was on the planet's surface. Your people have taken her prisoner."

"I will arrange for you to communicate with your people,

Commander, and to have them returned safely to you." To her surprise, Picard smiled. "*I suspect she will be of some value to all of us, particularly if you wish to return your people home.*"

Ushalon

"As explosions go, there are worse ones to be caught in."

Chen held up her tricorder as she stepped closer to the scorched, tattered section of bulkhead where the access panel had been. Within the blackened hole that had been enlarged through violent means thanks to the improvised explosive, she regarded the conduit's blackened and metal innards. The blast from the makeshift device had not been large, though still powerful enough to propel shrapnel across the room, and she gave silent thanks once again for Taurik's fast thinking in pushing her and Nelidar down a connecting passageway and out of danger before the detonation.

"*The power readings for the quantum field are holding steady,*" reported Taurik over the open communications frequency. "*Whether that is a fortunate outcome remains to be seen.*"

According to an inspection conducted by Nelidar and Taurik, since verified by the status monitors in the observation center and now Chen's tricorder, destroying a power distribution node outside the barrier created by the quantum field had not adversely affected the energy levels. The field itself remained in place, though Taurik had detected a noticeable spike in the readings as the field generator apparently compensated for the breach in the power distribution network.

"What do we do now?" asked Chen.

Taurik replied, *"For the moment, we will continue monitoring the situation while Commander La Forge and Lieutenant Elfiki finalize their preparations. Taurik out."*

The connection severed, Chen turned to stare at the oblong black cylinder, resting on an antigravity sled, that was the object of those preparations. Even like this, largely inert and with its access panels opened to expose its inner workings, she was still able to appreciate its power.

"These things always give me the creeps."

Having removed his environmental suit's gloves in order to facilitate his work, Geordi La Forge stood at the opposite end of the transphasic torpedo, his hands working inside the weapon's housing. "Well, try flying down here with one strapped to the deck behind you." He sighed. "That's not something I'm eager to try again."

Despite the quantum energy readings that had been much less severe than those experienced by the original away team, they still were sufficient to give La Forge and Elfiki a rough ride as they descended from orbit aboard the shuttlecraft *Jefferies*.

"At least your landing was smoother," said Chen.

The chief engineer could not help a small grin. "Fair enough." He pulled his left hand from the torpedo's open access panel, and Chen saw that he held a green isolinear optical chip between his thumb and forefinger. "On the other hand, nothing says we'll be able to take off without getting smacked around. This is a long way from being over."

"Stay out of his head, T'Rys," said Dina Elfiki. "We don't want him getting distracted and blowing up half the planet."

La Forge paused, eyeing the science officer. "That's not really helping, either."

"Sorry."

Setting the chip next to the tricorder and work satchel he had brought with him from the surface, the chief engineer said, "Don't worry. We're dropping this thing's compression pulse generator to its minimum output level. The effect will basically be a beefed-up electromagnetic pulse, and we don't want to be anywhere near this thing when it goes off."

"Good tip," said Chen. She was only partially familiar with the inner workings of the advanced weapon. The transphasic torpedo functioned unlike conventional missile-based weapons in that it delivered a subspace compression pulse that was transmitted across a spectrum of phase states. This allowed the torpedo's destructive power to overcome most varieties of deflector shield technology, including those that operated on their own subsets of nutational frequency modulation. Chen knew that the key to the weapon's performance was the component that generated a random dissonant feedback frequency that could not be easily predicted, let alone defended against. It was this feature of the transphasic technology that had made it such an effective weapon against the Borg.

But even they adapted to it, eventually.

Chen had skimmed the torpedo's specifications even as La Forge and Elfiki were on the *Enterprise*, replicating the components needed to construct one. There had been precious little time to do so, between assisting Worf, Konya, and Cruzen with escorting their Romulan prisoners to their one functioning shuttle. Captain

Picard had ordered their release, and the commander of the Romulan ship had agreed that there would be no more trouble here on the surface. Chen had completed another quick review of the weapon's technical schematics after the *Enterprise*-E's chief engineer and science officer delivered the device to the planet's surface and down to this work space within the subterranean complex, even as other members of the engineering team worked to repair the shuttlecraft *Spinrad* so that it could be returned to the ship. That they had brought with them Data from the *Enterprise*-D was something of a surprise, but his help in preparing the torpedo for deployment had been invaluable. As with everyone else, he also wore a standard Starfleet environmental suit, sans helmet and gloves.

Having remained silent for the past several minutes, the android looked up from the examination of his tricorder. "My configuration of the compression pulse generator is complete. Readings indicate the component to be operating within acceptable parameters."

"Thanks." Pausing, La Forge looked up from his work. "I have to tell you, it's weird to be working with you like this, but it feels right." He smiled. "I know that sounds silly. I'm sorry."

Data replied, "I believe I can understand your sentiment. I have also been intrigued by the personal dynamics of our current situation. For example, I could not help noticing that my counterpart is not among your crew." He looked to Elfiki and Chen. "And I do not recognize either of you."

"That's because we were in grade school when you were on the *Enterprise*-D in our universe," said Chen.

"Of course. The differences in our respective crews have been the topic of much conversation since our initial meeting."

Elfiki said, "It's pretty much the same on our ship."

La Forge replied, "If we do our jobs right, there'll be time for all of that later." Reaching into his satchel, he retrieved another isolinear chip, this one clear blue. He inserted the chip into the reader on his tricorder.

"Okay," he said after a moment. "Once I slide this in and run through its startup and diagnostic sequence, we should be good to go. Instead of generating a dissonant pulse at random, the compression pulse generator should be able to scan the quantum field and produce an appropriate feedback frequency, and at the level needed to overcome the existing quantum fluctuations."

Elfiki added, "That should be enough to trigger a deactivation of the existing quantum field, and bring the entire generator and power complex back into phase. Then Nelidar and her people can hopefully regain control of the generator."

"And after that," La Forge said, "we figure out how to send everybody back where they belong."

Chen rubbed her temples. "Just another day at the office, right?"

"Commander La Forge."

The new voice and the sound of footfalls on the metal flooring made the team turn to see Taurik and Nelidar entering the room from the underground complex's central passageway. Even with his Vulcan composure, it was obvious to Chen that he was concerned about something, and that worry was reflected on Nelidar's features.

"What is it, Taurik?" asked the chief engineer.

"The quantum field is showing an increase. Slow, but steady."

Nelidar added, "By all indications, we are approaching another transition, which is not unusual. I have verified against our logs that we have now passed the minimum amount of time that Ushalon has spent in any one dimension since all of this began, so a shift is expected. However, the energy readings are erratic. Perhaps it is a consequence of the explosive's effect on the quantum field."

"But there's no way to be sure when the shift will happen?" asked Elfiki.

"I am afraid not," replied the Sidrac engineer.

Taurik said, "There is another matter. I have been running computer simulations on the impact of the subspace compression pulse on the quantum field. Based on my calculations, there is an eighty-three point six percent chance that our attempt to disperse the quantum field will have an adverse effect on the complex's fusion reactor."

"The reactor was designed to operate autonomously for at least twenty solar cycles before requiring any sort of maintenance," said Nelidar.

"But the continued generation of the quantum field has accelerated its decay." Taurik held up his tricorder. "Given that the transphasic weapon will push back against the field via subspace, there exists the possibility that feedback from the pulse will hasten the reactor's deterioration to the point where it will no longer be able to power this facility."

Reaching up to rub the bridge of his nose, La Forge grunted in exasperation. "Well, that certainly changes things."

Chen exchanged glances with Elfiki. "Is he saying what I think he's saying?"

"If the generator can't produce a new quantum field," said the science officer, "then it can't push this planet out of this dimension."

Data said, "It, along with our *Enterprise* and the Romulan vessels, would be trapped here."

23

It was like stepping back through time.

The consoles, the sounds, the uniforms, and even the carpeting that he had hated the first time he saw it all those years ago triggered a torrent of memories as Jean-Luc Picard and Beverly Crusher stepped from the turbo-lift and onto the bridge.

"Oh, my."

Materializing in the transporter room, along with every step along the corridors and even the ride up in the turbolift, had stirred thoughts and feelings he had not considered for years. The sense of nostalgia—and loss—that washed over him was reflected on the familiar faces staring back at him.

"Captain on the bridge," said a familiar voice, and Picard steeled himself as he beheld Natasha Yar. This version was a few years older than she had been the last time he saw her. Though she appeared not to have aged, there was a wisdom in her eyes that had not yet formed in the Tasha Yar he remembered. Cruel fate had seen fit to rob her of the opportunity for the life and experiences that would have given Tasha whatever perspective she now carried within her. He also saw that her own emotions were conflicted in the face of this unlikely meeting.

"Lieutenant," he said, stepping toward her and extending his hand. "It's good to see you."

Taking his hand in both of hers, Yar nodded. "It's good to see you too, sir." Her voice trembled, and she reached up to wipe a single tear. "I'm sorry, Captain. I didn't think I'd . . . I didn't . . ."

"It's quite all right, my dear." Picard squeezed her hand. There was so much he wanted to say. How much was appropriate? From Riker, he had learned the fate of his own counterpart, and that emotional wounds were still fresh. It was a foregone conclusion that the crew of this *Enterprise*, and the senior officers in particular—men and women with whom he had forged a unique kinship, or might have done so in the years that lay ahead of them—had countless questions. He shared their curiosity, and it was a struggle to remind himself that other priorities demanded his attention.

Then why come here at all?

He had asked that question of himself at least a dozen times since accepting Captain Riker's invitation. Both captains had agreed that having anyone from the *Enterprise*-D visit its more advanced counterpart—and successor, assuming events in their dimension played out in similar fashion—was not a sound idea. While absolutely avoiding violations of Starfleet's Temporal Prime Directive was impractical if not impossible under the current circumstances, Picard and Riker had concurred that minimizing such instances was in the interests of both crews. With that in mind and setting all other considerations aside, Picard knew this visit was personal indulgence. That was even more the case with Beverly, who had admitted to her one purpose for accompanying him.

Now that he was here, Picard realized the feelings he was experiencing seemed to run even deeper than when after many years he had walked onto the wrecked bridge of his first command, the *U.S.S. Stargazer*, which had been believed destroyed decades earlier. Picard found the disparity in his emotional reactions interesting, considering the *Stargazer* had been a relic, a representation of a starship class long since resigned to obsolescence. On the other hand, he had traveled aboard other *Galaxy*-class vessels more than once in the years following the *Enterprise*-D's demise, and in many regards those ships were identical to the one he once had commanded.

But they weren't yours.

As Crusher moved to embrace Yar, Picard turned toward Lieutenant Worf, who had risen from the ops station and now stood before the captain's chair, looking up at him. The Klingon offered a single, formal nod.

"Captain. It is good to see you again, sir."

"Mister Worf," said Picard. "The pleasure is mine, Lieutenant."

The emotions threatened to reach a fever pitch as Picard and Crusher descended the ramp to the bridge's command area. Waiting for them were Will Riker, Deanna Troi, Geordi La Forge, Doctor Katherine Pulaski, and Wesley Crusher. Eschewing any sense of protocol, Beverly stepped toward her son and pulled him into her arms.

"I don't mind saying this is a little weird, Mom."

"You need to call more."

"How do you know I don't?"

"Because I'm your mother, no matter what dimension we're in."

Their comments were enough to defuse the tension, eliciting several smiles and laughs from the group as handshakes and hugs were exchanged.

Unable to resist a remark as he took in the sight of Riker and Troi standing together, Picard offered a wry grin. "I always had a feeling about you two."

Nodding toward Crusher, Troi replied, "Same here."

"I must admit that this does feel awkward," said Picard. "I did debate whether to beam over." He grimaced. "It felt . . . inappropriate, somehow."

"We're glad you did," replied Pulaski. "You've been missed, Captain." She looked to Doctor Crusher. "Both of you have."

Riker said, "Livingston is still in the ready room, if you want to take him with you." He shrugged. "I didn't know what to do with him, and he wasn't bothering anyone."

"I think the fish I have might take issue with a roommate." Picard said. It had been some time since he had thought of the lionfish, which in this dimension had succumbed to age some years ago. Its successor now lived in a much larger aquarium in his ready room aboard the *Enterprise*-E.

The odd memory did give way to one of Picard's overriding thoughts since first laying eyes on this version of the *Enterprise*-D. This starship and the people aboard shared far more similarities than differences with the ship he once had commanded. There were numerous minor divergences, such as with instrumentation and layout, or the captain's chair being on a small dais that elevated it slightly from the two seats flanking it, and other subtle deviations with respect to workstations. When it came to the people, the parallels were much stronger. Aside from variations in hairstyles or wardrobe, these could be the same people with whom he had served all those years ago.

Riker said, "I'm sure that someone, somewhere, in some dimension will be upset when they find out about this, but they're going to have to get over it."

"I just don't want to be anywhere near whichever admiral ends up reading about all of this," said La Forge. "In any dimension."

"That makes two of us." Picard would file his report, and whatever happened after that would be up to people who were not there, with him and his crew, facing the vast unknown and the risks and dangers that sometimes accompanied it. For now, he had larger problems.

"I wish we could spend more time together," he said, "but we all know there are more immediate concerns, and a great many people, on our respective ships and on the planet below, will be affected by what we do or fail to do. Even the Romulans stand to be impacted by our actions. Our responsibility is great, but I trust we can answer the challenge put to us, just as we have so many times before."

He realized as he spoke the words how easily he had slipped into the role of being captain over these people—*this* version of *these* people. The differences in time and dimension did not matter. These were still men and women whom he had come to trust, and who likewise had put their faith in him. No measure of distance, either across space or time, could ever erode that bond.

"Perhaps when the current issues are resolved, and we've found a way to help the Sidrac, there will be time for us to indulge the personal aspects of this rather unique situation in which we've found ourselves."

Pulaski said, "We could probably spend the next six months just talking and learning about the other side." Reaching out, she placed a hand on Crusher's arm.

"Where have you been? What have you seen? Who have you met?" She smiled. "I know you can't answer any of those questions, or at least you shouldn't, but the thought is exciting."

"Even though you're only twenty years or so ahead of us," said La Forge, "it's obvious you've made some huge technological advances. What I wouldn't give to crawl around inside your *Enterprise*."

The temptation to tell them what they might expect in the years ahead was all but overwhelming, but Picard checked himself. After all, this *Enterprise* might not even find itself in situations identical or even similar to what he and his crew had encountered over the course of their missions together. Indeed, what wonders might they soon discover that had eluded Picard all these years?

"Captain Riker," said Lieutenant Yar. "I'm receiving a message from the *Enterprise*-E. The away team is asking to speak to you and Captain Picard, sir."

"We'll take it in the observation lounge."

Riker indicated for La Forge and Wesley to follow him, and they along with Picard and Doctor Crusher removed themselves to the main observation lounge behind the bridge. Once there, Picard saw that his Geordi La Forge along with Worf, Taurik, and Data were already waiting for them on the room's main viewscreen.

"Mister Worf?" prompted Picard.

On the screen, his first officer replied, *"We have encountered another potential problem, Captain."* Worf stood silent as La Forge and Taurik explained the new issues surrounding the Sidrac's power plant and the quantum-field generator. Though Picard understood a great deal of the Vulcan engineer's detailed recounting, some of the technical aspects were beyond him.

"Why not just let the shift happen?" asked Wesley. "Our *Enterprise* and the Romulans were brought here, so it makes sense that we could ride the wave—or whatever—and shift again, right?"

"It would not help the Sidrac," said Data. *"None of the beacons are in their own dimension, which is why the planet has never returned there throughout this entire affair."*

The *Enterprise*-E's La Forge added, *"The only way they've got a shot at getting home is by regaining control of the generator."*

Now the pieces were falling into place. Picard said, "And the only way to do that is with the torpedo, which we now think might actually make things worse." He grimaced. "Well, that does seem to present a complication."

"What about the reactor?" asked Doctor Crusher. "Is there a way for us to repair it, or refuel it, or something?"

"Nothing we have would provide sufficient power for a long enough duration," replied the younger La Forge.

"The decay would continue once a new quantum field was enabled and the planet began shifting again," added Taurik. *"And once they leave our dimension, we would be unable to assist them."*

Picard asked, "How much time would the Sidrac have before the reactor was exhausted?"

"There's no way to know that for sure, sir," replied his La Forge. *"Hours, probably less. So, even if our transphasic pulse works and the Sidrac are able to regain control of the field generator, they'll have to initiate at least three dimensional shifts in order to get everybody back where they belong."*

Taurik said, *"Fortunately, we know the destinations for*

the Enterprise-D, *the Romulans, and even the planet itself. Each party's unique quantum signature will allow the Sidrac engineers to program their systems to generate new quantum fields at the proper frequency and initiate the transition with little time needed for preparation."

"The only variable is the energy consumption and the reactor's rate of decay." Picard glanced first to Riker's staff and then his own. "Options?"

Data said, *"Perhaps only a limited amount of power is needed. If we were able to bolster the reactor's output by interfacing with the distribution network that supplies power to the field generator, that might stabilize it long enough to complete the shifts."*

"But the only thing either of our ships has that can transmit that much power is the main deflector dish," replied the *Enterprise*-D's La Forge. "It wouldn't require as much as something like the transphasic pulse, and we'd be able to transmit a continuous stream. We'd need to keep it going and that—" Behind his VISOR, the chief engineer's eyebrows went up. "Oh. Well, *that's* not dangerous. At *all*."

His counterpart on the viewscreen replied, *"At least one of our ships would have to initiate and possibly maintain the connection throughout at least one dimensional shift, perhaps two."*

"Or we stagger it," countered Wesley. He held up his left hand. "This is the *Enterprise*-E. It makes the initial connection and stabilizes the power stream for the first shift. The *Enterprise*-D and the Romulan ships shift with the planet to the Romulans' dimension." Holding up his right hand, he continued. "We need the transphasic torpedo to regain control of the quantum-field generator.

So we trigger the initial pulse the way we planned. Once that happens, our *Enterprise* takes over after the first shift, maintaining the power feed long enough to shift to our dimension, then severs the connection just before the planet shifts one last time, hopefully back where it belongs."

"Such a connection could present issues during a shift if we experienced significant feedback," said Taurik. *"The possibility of overloads would be considerable."*

"Yeah," said the younger La Forge, "but we'd only have to hold things together for a couple of minutes at most. This could work." Then he shrugged. "Or we could all die."

Riker asked, "So, the usual sort of problems?"

The engineer nodded. "Pretty much, sir."

"What of the Romulans?" asked Worf.

"I'd have to check the specs," replied the *Enterprise*-E's La Forge, *"but I don't think their navigational deflectors can project the kind of power we'd need. They'd basically be along for the ride."*

Riker grunted in apparent amusement. "I'd love to hear their commander explain that to her superiors, and how us weak humans helped them."

Still processing what he had heard, Picard replied, "Captain Riker, your *Enterprise* would be at the greatest risk, given your role in Mister Crusher's scenario. Once you're separated from us, we would have no way to provide assistance."

"For the sake of everyone involved," replied Riker, "I don't see that we have much choice." He glanced at the faces of his own officers. "Anybody else have a better idea given the available time and resources?" When no one offered a response, he turned back to Picard. "I say we do it, sir."

The captain realized that everyone in the room and on the screen was looking to him. Nodding in understanding, he offered a small, knowing smile.

"Make it so."

24

ChR Bloodied Talon

Even with her back to her subordinates as she studied the human captain on the viewscreen, Sarith could feel their eyes upon her. She sensed their skepticism, their uncertainty, and even their fear. It was hard to find fault with the conflicted emotions that had to be plaguing them. As soldiers, they had been trained—conditioned—to believe that the Federation was the enemy. Its aims were in direct opposition to the goal of all Romulan people to secure the Empire's borders and to protect its interests while expanding ever outward its sphere of influence. The Federation, young Romulans were told, was a threat to the prosperity due to every citizen of the Empire.

And now here Sarith stood, ready to accept aid from a Federation's representative.

"What we are proposing is dangerous, Commander," said Captain Picard over the communications link. *"Timing will be critical, and it's very possible that additional damage may be inflicted upon all our vessels. While your warship can likely withstand the strain these maneuvers may inflict, my engineers are not as certain about your smaller escort vessels. As they are incapable of landing on the planet, you might well consider relocating their crews to your ship until you transition to your proper dimension."*

It went against her training and everything she had come to regard as truth, but Sarith wanted to believe this human. His every word, and the tone of his voice, elicited that faith. Was it all an act? Could Picard be manipulating her? As she had discussed with Ineti, that notion made little sense. The Starfleet captain already possessed the power to destroy her ships. There was no need for him to waste time with such an elaborate deception.

"What part would we play in this exercise?"

Picard replied, *"Your vessels have sustained damage and are underpowered for the energy demands required to be an active participant in this, Commander. However, monitoring of the process will be necessary to ensure your ships make the transition. The idea is to have some control over the process, rather than simply being caught up in it in the manner that brought you here. To that end, you may need to make adjustments in your orbit or in the communications stream you will be maintaining with the quantum-field generator down on the planet."*

Looking over her shoulder to where Subcommander Variel stood at her science station, Sarith asked, "Does this make sense to you?"

"Yes, Commander. I have studied the information transmitted by his engineer and science officer." She drew herself to her full height. "I believe I can do what is required."

Even Variel trusts this human.

Sarith found that surprising, given her science officer's often militant stance against the Federation, its allies, and most especially its Starfleet. That Variel seemed convinced of Picard's sincerity was remarkable.

"What about relocating the escort crews to our ship?" asked Ineti, who had moved to stand next to Sarith. "Does that sound correct?"

After considering the question for a moment, the subcommander replied, "Though all three of our ships came through the initial transition without significant damage, the subsequent skirmish with the Starfleet ships has had a greater impact on our ability to withstand another shift. We are operating at compromised power levels, which will affect our shields and other critical systems."

Sarith did not really want to discuss the vulnerability of her ships with an adversary listening over an open communications channel, but she suspected none of this was information Picard did not already possess. There likely was no point worrying about such things. As had already been demonstrated, the *Talon* and her escorts were outmatched by either of the Starfleet vessels, let alone both. Attempts to scan the ships had been fruitless, owing to jamming techniques her engineers had been unable to circumvent. Because of that, Sarith would be unable to glean any information about either vessel for her superiors and perhaps warn them, and even the praetor, about the advances in starship design Starfleet would be developing in the years to come.

"There is another alternative, Commander," said Ineti, eyeing Sarith.

He did not have to say anything further for her to know what he meant. Arming the *Talon*'s self-destruct mechanism was a thought to which she had already given consideration. That, at least, would be in keeping with standard regulations when it came to interactions with an enemy. If a vessel was incapacitated or otherwise in danger of being seized, it was the commander's responsibility to prevent that action at all costs. The directives on this were quite clear, with severe penalties imposed on officers who failed to carry out their sworn duty.

Did her crew deserve such a fate, as a consequence of

being caught up in a situation as bizarre as the one they now faced?

No.

"We will not be pursuing that course," she said. Turning back to the viewscreen, she regarded Picard. "Very well, Captain. We will proceed as you have advised."

Seemingly satisfied, the human nodded. *"Excellent. Time is short, Commander, and there are some preparations to be made. My chief engineer will communicate the final instructions. If all goes to plan, you will all be home in short order."*

What would happen after that? Assuming Sarith and her crew survived what was to come and were returned to their own dimension, only she would face whatever punishment might arise from her failure to obey protocol. Ineti might endure reprisals for not relieving her of command, but Sarith doubted it. He was too well respected within the establishment and had more than enough friends within the halls of power willing to protect him. As for the rest of her crew, they would be spared, their actions viewed as obeying the officers appointed over them.

And that is sufficient.

Ushalon

They were as ready as they were ever going to be.

"That should do it," said Geordi La Forge. Stepping back from the portable computer terminal he had brought with him from the shuttlecraft *Jefferies* and that now occupied a worktable in the Sidrac habitat's observation room, he closed his eyes, rubbing his temples. "All that's left is to light this thing and see what happens."

Working at an adjacent terminal, Data replied, "That is an interesting choice of words, Geordi, considering that a malfunction during the deployment of the torpedo would likely result in a massive explosion."

"It loses something in the translation." Sighing, La Forge massaged his neck. Still dressed in his environmental suit, he was growing uncomfortable. He had considered dispensing with the garment, but he did not want to waste any portion of what might end up being a very narrow window of time fumbling with the suit. That would only impede their exit from the Sidrac habitat and back to the *Jefferies*, or in Data's case the *Justman*, the shuttlecraft from the *Enterprise*-D he had flown down to the surface.

"La Forge to *Enterprise*," he said, speaking into his suit's communicator.

Captain Picard replied, *"Go ahead, Commander."*

"We're ready to go, sir. We can throw the switch at any time if everybody's ready up there." Having sent the rest of the away team back to the ship, he and Data were the only ones from either *Enterprise* who remained on the surface.

"The Enterprise-D *and the Romulans are standing by,"* said Picard. There was a pause before the captain added, *"Commander, I would prefer you were not on the surface at the time of detonation."*

This had already been a topic of discussion even prior to the final preparations, and La Forge had made his case that it was important for him to be on site and ready to assist Nelidar and her people in the event the transphasic pulse introduced unintended side effects to the quantum-field generator or the power plant. While the device itself was deployed within the underground facility and near the boundary of the uncontrolled quantum field, it was here in the observation room that the detonation would be carried out.

"Assuming this works and the Sidrac regain control of the generator, Captain, they'll likely be dealing with any number of diagnostics and adjustments. I'd like to stay at least long enough to make sure they've got a handle on everything. After all, whatever happens next will be our fault." Though there was momentary silence over the open channel, La Forge was sure he could hear Picard mulling over what he had just heard.

Finally, Picard said, *"All right, Geordi, but not a minute longer. If we have to move fast, I don't want you down there."*

"Understood, sir. La Forge out." The communication ended, and he turned to where Nelidar and Livak were waiting along with a handful of other Sidrac engineers and scientists. Each of them was regarding him and Data, and he saw no fear in their piercing blue eyes, but rather anticipation.

"I think we're ready," he said.

Nelidar nodded. "As are we."

"The quantum energy readings are continuing to rise," said Livak, and La Forge heard the edge in his voice. "I suspect we do not have much time."

"Then I guess we should get on with it." Once more he engaged his suit's communicator. "La Forge to Taurik. How's it looking up there?"

"Taurik here, Commander. Our configurations are complete and we are standing by. The deflector can be brought online at your command, sir." Taurik had returned to the *Enterprise* along with the rest of the away team and was now overseeing engineering and the employment of the starship's main deflector array.

La Forge said, "That's it." He nodded to Nelidar. "It's your generator and your planet, so I think you should have the final say."

Glancing first to her colleagues, Nelidar replied, "Regardless of what happens, we want to thank you, Commander." She looked to Data. "Thank you both, for everything. The extraordinary lengths to which you and your people have gone to help us will not be forgotten."

Now feeling self-conscious in the face of praise that might end up being premature, La Forge cleared his throat. "Well, there's no sense waiting." He turned to Data. "Ready?"

Having returned to his own portable workstation, the android nodded. "I am ready."

"Let's do it." Stepping closer to his computer terminal, La Forge said into his communicator, "Taurik?"

"Standing by, Commander."

Satisfied that there was nothing left to do, La Forge said, "All right. Counting down from five."

Here goes nothing.

He could not help the lone, taunting thought as he counted down, his finger hovering over the highlighted control he had designated for this task. "Two. One. Activating." His finger pressed the key.

The result was immediate, almost too fast for the terminal's display screen to keep up. La Forge watched the computer-generated representation of the transphasic torpedo's detonation process scroll on the screen, as within the space of milliseconds the device's compression pulse generator scanned the quantum field, analyzing the energy readings and formulating a proper feedback frequency. It took less than two seconds for the torpedo to complete its calculations and execute its programmed response.

There was no explosion, no dull thump or any other audible sign that the weapon had detonated. Instead, every light and console and display screen around the room was plunged into momentary darkness. La Forge even heard the sound of the air circulation system fading along with all of the equipment. Only the two Starfleet portable terminals, shielded from the effects of the torpedo, were spared. Without any other source of ambient sound, his own breathing along with that of the Sidrac seemed to pound in his ears. He started counting, knowing from Nelidar's briefing that in the event of main power failure, a battery-powered backup system would engage, starting with the most critical systems and expanding from there.

Instead, everything simultaneously flared back to life. The lights were first, eradicating the darkness an instant before the various workstations and computer banks reactivated. Even the dull hum of the air system was welcome, but it was quickly drowned out by the shrill chorus of multiple alerts erupting from the different consoles. Livak was the first of the Sidrac to resume his work, and was already examining his instruments.

"Main power is still online," he reported. "There was an interruption in the power distribution network, but everything now appears to be in order. Life-support systems are functioning throughout the habitat."

"What about the field generator?" asked Nelidar.

Data said, "The transphasic pulse was deployed as expected." He tapped a series of commands into his portable terminal. "The quantum-field generator is currently operating in a standby mode. The field itself has dissipated."

"He is correct." Livak looked up from his console, his

expression brightening. "Quantum energy readings are at minimum levels. No signs of spiking, and we are once more receiving updates from all of our status monitors inside the generator complex." His eyes wide, the Sidrac smiled. "The pulse was successful." His last statement evoked a round of cheers along with a few sighs of relief from his companions around the room. La Forge could feel the tension of the past hours already beginning to ebb.

"*Enterprise*," he said into his communicator. "Are you getting this?"

"*Indeed we are, Commander,*" replied Picard. "*Well done.*"

"As anticipated, the reactor's power levels are not holding," said Data. "Power output is at sixty-eight percent and falling."

"*This is Commander Taurik. We are initiating the interface with the power reactor's power distribution network. Activating main deflector . . . now.*"

A noticeable increase in the lighting and the low hum of some of the equipment accompanied the Vulcan's announcement. La Forge could see on Data's terminal that the power transfer was already having a positive effect.

The android said, "Power levels have risen to eighty-one percent. I predict that the *Enterprise* will be able to achieve an increase to ninety-three percent, but it will be able to sustain that level for a maximum of eleven point four minutes before Commander Taurik will be forced to deactivate the deflector."

"That'll have to do," replied La Forge. Conscious of the time constraints, he turned to Nelidar and Livak, who, along with the rest of the Sidrac, seemed to be moving about the room in a sort of trance as they gripped one another's hands and offered embraces. There was an air of relief permeating the group, and while he could understand it, celebration would have to wait.

"Livak," he said. "Are you able to create a new field with the correct quantum signatures?"

Returning to his console, the Sidrac engineer nodded. "Yes, Commander. As we discussed, I am making the calculations for target location three. That should be completed momentarily."

"All right, Geordi," said Picard over the open comm channel. *"That's it. Time for you and Mister Data to return home."*

"Aye, Captain. We're on our way."

Retrieving the last of their equipment as they readied to return to their respective shuttlecraft for the flights back to their ships, La Forge and Data moved from the observation room to the airlock entrance. They were escorted by Nelidar, who was flanked by the rest of her fellow Sidrac.

"We cannot ever repay our debt to you," she said.

La Forge smiled as he prepared to don his suit helmet. "Well, we're not there just yet. That's what the next step is for."

Nelidar gestured upward. "Then you certainly must go. We cannot allow you to risk being trapped in our dimension or whatever final destination awaits us."

"You'll make it home," replied the engineer. "I can feel it."

Turning to Data, La Forge saw the android regarding him with that same placid expression that had been so ubiquitous during their time on the *Enterprise*-D. Was it really so long ago, before Data had installed the chip developed by his creator, Doctor Noonien Soong, and gained access to the full range of human emotional responses? Here and now, it was just his friend as he had been during their first meeting, and how La Forge often chose to remember him.

"I wish we had more time," he said. There definitely would be none once they were outside the habitat and on their way to their shuttles.

Data nodded. "As do I." He extended his hand. "It is good to know that you are alive and well in this dimension as well as my own."

Taking the android's hand in both of his, La Forge felt a small lump forming in his throat. "Same here. Good luck."

"To all of us, my friend."

25

Try as he might, Picard could not stay in his chair. It was as though it burned him whenever he tried sitting in it. His only recourse seemed to be pacing that expanse of deck between his chair and the conn and ops positions. He did so in slow, deliberate fashion, taking advantage of the motion to inspect each of the workstations within his field of vision. Status indicators provided him with all he needed to determine the condition of the ship. Those things that were not at full capacity concerned him, but there was nothing to be done about those issues now. For better or worse, he along with the *Enterprise* and everyone else aboard her were committed.

On the viewscreen, Ushalon drifted within the violet maelstrom that was NGC 8541. Though Picard knew it was ludicrous, he could not shake the feeling that the pallid gray world somehow seemed more alive now. How much longer would he be able to gaze upon it? Once it was gone, would it ever return? He hoped not, for the sake of the people who called it home.

"Reactor power levels at eighty-four percent," reported Glinn Ravel Dygan from the ops console. The Cardassian had taken over monitoring the status of the Sidrac fusion reactor and quantum-field generator, providing constant updates about the facility deep beneath the planet's surface. This left oversight of the ship's deflector shields and the main deflector array to Lieutenant Aneta Šmrhová.

From the bridge intraship, Geordi La Forge said, *"That's probably as good as it's going to get, Captain."* The chief engineer had only returned to the *Enterprise* moments ago, and Picard could hear the tension in the other man's voice.

"Understood, Commander," replied Picard. "Stand by."

"We're ready here, Captain," said Will Riker over the open communication frequency shared by both *Enterprise*s and the Romulan warship. *"We've linked into the signal buoy's transmission stream just as we did before, and adjusted our proximity to the planet in line with our previous shift. Here goes nothing."*

Sarith, her voice taut, added, *"We are in position, as well, Enterprise."*

Halting his pacing, Picard centered himself between Dygan and Lieutenant Faur at the conn position and said, *"Enterprise* to Nelidar. What is your status?"

On the viewscreen, the image of Ushalon was replaced by that of the female Sidrac. *"Our calculations for the transition to target location three are finalized, Captain. We are preparing to generate the new quantum field."*

"Good luck, Nelidar. Perhaps one day our people will meet again."

Nelidar bowed her head. *"I look forward to that day, Captain. Stand by. We are initiating the new quantum field."*

Uncertain as to what to expect, Picard remained in place as the Sidrac disappeared from the screen and the image of Ushalon returned. The planet looked as unremarkable and even uninviting as it always had.

"Picking up elevated quantum fluctuations," reported Dina Elfiki from the science station. "The increase is steady. Matching the quantum signature." Her hands moved across her science console as she divided her attention between sensor readings and the monitors providing her with additional information she extracted from the ship's computer banks. "It's a match, sir. Target location three confirmed."

"Captain," said Worf from where he stood to the right of the command area. "Look."

On the screen, Ushalon was beginning to waver, and portions of the planet were fading, to the point Picard could see the nebula behind it.

"We're starting to get some feedback from our power transfer, Captain," said La Forge over the speakers.

Glinn Dygan reported, "Power levels in the reactor are starting to drop, sir."

"It's the shift, Captain." La Forge's voice sounded harried, and Picard waited as the chief engineer issued a series of terse, indecipherable commands to one of his people.

"We're losing our connection to the power distribution network."

Glancing over his shoulder to Šmrhová, Picard asked, "Shield status?"

"Holding at sixty-one percent," replied the security chief. "Even though we're not supposed to be going anywhere, it could get bumpy for us."

Picard returned his attention to the screen, feeling his jaw tighten as he watched the planet Ushalon trying to disappear.

What was taking so long?

ChR Bloodied Talon

Something was wrong, Sarith decided.

"This is not working," she said. Her fists clenched at her sides, she stalked a circuit around the bridge's central hub. The illumination had been reduced to tactical mode, freeing up extra power for the ship's deflector shields and also eliminating glare on the various display screens arrayed at stations around the room.

"The quantum field is increasing," reported Subcommander Variel, who now stood beside Centurion Darjil at the sensor station. The science officer had been tasked with monitoring the quantum energy readings throughout the upcoming transition. "Energy readings are rising rapidly."

"Our shields are at half strength," reported Centurion N'tovek from the weapons station. "The quantum fluctuations are already straining the generators. If this continues, they may overload."

Sarith asked, "What about the *N'minecci* and the *Jarax*?" On the advice of the human captain, she had ordered the crews from their two support vessels transferred to the *Talon* to ride out the transfer. At this moment, all available berthing and cargo space was allocated to supporting their new guests. It would be a tight fit on the lower levels, but it was a minor inconvenience while pursuing the greater prize.

"Their shields are already approaching the overload point, Commander," reported Darjil. "If we continue to tow the vessels, that is power we do not have for our shields."

"I am aware of our ship's power needs, Centurion," said Sarith. "And our link to the beacon?"

Standing before the communications station, Centurion Skerius replied, "Our connection to its broadcast signal is holding steady, Commander."

"Look at this," said Subcommander Ineti, and when Sarith turned in his direction it was to see her second-in-command scrutinizing the image of the planet depicted on the viewscreen. Stepping closer, Sarith saw that the gray, dead world was shimmering while parts of it faded in and out of sight.

"It begins," she said. All around her, she could hear the *Bloodied Talon*'s mounting protests at the stresses being placed upon it. She saw anxiety in the faces of her subordinates, who were doing their best to present a brave front as they forced themselves to attend to their individual responsibilities.

"*Commander Sarith,*" said the voice of the human captain Riker over the active communications frequency currently being shared between the *Talon* and the two Starfleet vessels. "*The shift is starting. Hold your position and maintain your link to the buoy.*"

Everything had come down to this; waiting while others worked to secure the *Talon*'s return to its own dimension. Assuming this gambit was successful, how would she explain it all to her superiors? What would Toqel, her mother and trusted advisor to Praetor Vrax, think or say when she learned that her daughter had allowed her ship and crew to be assisted by humans? Would Sarith's decisions and action—or lack of same—bring disgrace to Toqel and perhaps their entire family?

None of that mattered just now.

"Our shield generators are beginning to overheat," reported N'tovek. "Shield output at one-third strength."

"The *Jarax*!" It was Ineti, manipulating the viewscreen controls to change the monitor's image. Sarith looked past N'tovek to see that the subcommander had called up an image of the escort ship from the *Talon*'s sensor array. She was in time to see the smaller vessel's hull starting to buckle under the unseen forces being heaped upon it.

"Sever the tractor beam," she ordered. There was no sense diverting energy to preserve a ship that obviously could not stand up to the strain they were experiencing, and Sarith knew they might still need the power for her own ship's defenses. Noting that the second escort was also showing signs of succumbing to the escalating quantum fluctuations, she said, "Do it for the *N'minecci* as well. Divert energy from the tractor system to the shields."

Ineti replied, "Yes, Commander." His response came just as, on the screen, the *Jarax* starting to drift now that it was free of the *Talon*'s tractor beam.

"Shield strength improving, Commander," reported N'tovek, "but only slightly."

Based on their past experience with this phenomenon, Sarith knew that the shields operating at that capacity would not be sufficient to protect the *Talon* from the effects of the dimensional shift. Indeed, the ship might end up suffering even greater damage than it had before, and this time it might be too much for her engineer to repair.

"Stand by to break all connections," she said, turning back to the central hub. "Prall, plot a course away from the planet and the Federation ships."

Turning from the viewscreen, Ineti eyed her with concern. "Commander? If we abandon this course, we may never see home again."

"And if we continue as we have, we may die." In her mind, there was no choice. They would find Romulans here, in this dimension, who would provide support. For all she knew, the Empire of this reality had developed the sort of technology required to accomplish what she and her crew were now witnessing.

"*Sarith!*" It was Riker again, blaring over the open channel. "*What are you doing?*"

U.S.S. Enterprise-D

Pushing himself from his chair, Riker moved to where Wesley Crusher once more manned the conn position. "What are they doing?" On the bridge's main viewscreen, the planet Ushalon was becoming more indistinct with every passing second. The dimensional transition was well under way, and there was no turning back now.

"Their shields are failing, sir," replied Wesley. "They might be panicking."

"What's our status?"

At the tactical station behind Riker, Tasha Yar said, "Shields holding steady, sir, along with our fix on the targeting buoy. We're pretty much right in line with what we had the last time." She shook her head. "Captain, without shields the Romulan ship is going to get pounded pretty hard."

"We could extend our own shields as a means of protecting the Romulan vessel," said Data. "We would lose some strength in the transfer, but it would only be needed for a short time."

Riker nodded. "It's better than anything I'm going to come up with. Bridge to engineering. Geordi, we need to extend our shields around the Romulan ship. Can we do it?" There was a brief pause, and Riker imagined he could hear his chief engineer swearing under his breath as he considered the unorthodox maneuver.

"*We can do it,*" replied La Forge, "*but it's going to weaken the whole bubble around both our ships.*"

"But only for a minute or so, right?" asked Riker.

La Forge said, *"Sure, but that's all it takes to blow us up."*

"Do it." Moving to Worf, he tapped the Klingon on his shoulder. "Take us in closer. Maybe we can cheat this a little bit."

"We're extending shields," reported Yar. "Total shield strength now at sixty-eight percent."

Riker grimaced, unhappy with the number. "That's just going to have to do." This was no time to play it safe.

"Picard to Captain Riker," said the *Enterprise*-E's captain over the shared channel. *"We see what you're doing. We may be able to—"*

His voice faded in the midst of what to Riker sounded like the rush of oncoming water. Vivid white light pulled inward from the edges of his vision, and a wave of vertigo washed over him. He grabbed the back of Worf's chair for support. Squinting, he could just make out the image of Ushalon on the viewscreen, mere seconds before it and everything around him dissolved into nothingness.

26

HERE
U.S.S. Enterprise-E

All around him, the ship shuddered, struggling to come to terms with the strain to which it was being subjected. Picard ignored the wails of alarms that sounded due to overloaded circuits and burned-out relays, trusting his people to address whatever issue had caused a particular alarm. Instead, his attention was riveted to the viewscreen, and he watched as Ushalon disappeared. Within seconds, the planet was gone, leaving behind only the silent beauty of the nebula.

"Discontinuing main deflector beam," reported Lieutenant Šmrhová at the tactical station.

Pivoting away from the viewscreen, Picard asked, "What about those Romulan escort vessels?"

The security chief replied, "Both of them took pretty decent beatings, sir. Neither ship was occupied."

Picard allowed himself a small sigh of relief, thankful that Commander Sarith had heeded his suggestion to transfer the crew of the two smaller, more vulnerable ships to her own vessel. "Any change in the buoy's transmission beam?"

"Nothing yet, sir."

Commander La Forge had told him to expect a delay in any sort of confirmation that Ushalon's transfer was successful. Owing to the power drain of the Sidrac's fusion reactor and the need to continue with the process of targeting and shifting to the next dimension, Picard knew there might not be time for Riker or Nelidar to dispatch the messages all had agreed to send upon reaching their destinations. There might also be other, unanticipated effects from the transition that Riker and his crew would now be forced to address in order to bolster their chances of returning to their own dimension.

And there's nothing we can do to help them.

"Glinn Dygan," he said. "Damage report."

The Cardassian exchange officer turned in his seat. "Nothing serious, Captain. Overloaded circuits and power distribution nodes. Commander La Forge reports his teams are already addressing those issues."

Small favors, Picard decided. The ability to prepare for the effects of the quantum fluctuations and the dimensional shift had played a large role in the ship being able to weather the event, but he knew that the *Enterprise*-E was the vessel least impacted by the entire affair. For the rest of this bold plan to succeed, its counterpart would bear the brunt of the punishment. The task had become that much harder after Captain Riker's daring maneuver to protect the more vulnerable Romulan warship with his ship's deflector shields. What effect might that have on the *Enterprise*-D's ability to withstand whatever it might endure in the midst of successive transitions?

There was no way to know. All that remained for Picard and his people was the waiting.

Good luck, Will.

ELSEWHERE
ChR Bloodied Talon

The disorientation, not nearly as severe as during their previous shift, faded. Realizing she was still holding on to the edge of the sensor console for support, Sarith released her grip and stepped away from the central hub. A hint of smoke lingered in the air, signaling some kind of overstressed power conduit or other component. Around the cramped bridge, several of her subordinates were already removing access panels and examining the innards of different consoles and equipment. Sarith noted that there were no audible alarms.

"Report," she snapped. "Is there any new damage?"

Subcommander Ineti was already consulting the instruments dedicated to monitoring the *Talon*'s shipboard systems. "Our shield generators have automatically deactivated in order to avoid overload. There are numerous circuit burnouts across the ship, but nothing critical."

"Commander," said Variel from the sensor station. "I have scanned for the targeting beacon in this dimension, and it possesses the proper quantum signature." The subcommander looked away from her controls, her expression one of surprise. "We are home."

Ineti said, "So, the human captain was being truthful after all."

"It would seem so." Sarith could not help looking to the viewscreen, where an image of the planet was once more displayed. Beyond the dead world was the welcoming sight of the Lirostahl Nebula, where this entire bizarre journey had begun. She did not think she would ever be happy to see the familiar yet mind-numbing clouds of blue-green gases. "What of the *Enterprise*?"

Darjil replied, "Their shield strength is down considerably, Commander. Extending their screens to protect us was a dangerous maneuver, but their ship appears to have escaped serious damage. They have activated their deflector array and the *Enterprise* is channeling power to the quantum-field generator."

The next phase of this audacious plan, Sarith knew. Without the other Starfleet ship to provide assistance, this *Enterprise* was now responsible for helping the Sidrac power their facility long enough to complete at least two more dimensional shifts. The situation would grow more precarious following the next transition.

Only for the most fleeting of moments did Sarith consider the tactical situation. As a Romulan soldier, evaluating an adversary and seeking a strategic advantage came without conscious thought. Despite training and instinct attempting to assert itself, she halted that line of thought as she considered the true danger the Starfleet captain had accepted to protect her ship and crew. The human, Riker, had done so without hesitation, placing his own vessel in harm's way as though they were allies or even trusted friends rather than enemies. Sarith wondered if, with the circumstances reversed, she might have acted in similar fashion. She was surprised, and somewhat ashamed, to realize she had no answer to her own question.

If it were only so easy for all of us to trust one another, to undertake risk on behalf of one another.

"Is the communications link still open?" she asked.

Centurion Skerius replied, "Yes, Commander."

Moving to the console for the main viewscreen, Sarith tapped the control and the image of the planet was replaced by that of the bearded human, Riker. Behind the Starfleet captain, she observed the number of alarm indicators flashing along the back wall of his ship's bridge.

"Commander," he said. *"Our scans show you came through the shift largely unscathed."*

Sarith replied, "Thanks to you, Captain. I must confess that I am somewhat at a loss for words. In my reality, such cooperation and assistance is . . . unprecedented."

As though sympathizing with her uncertainty, Riker nodded. *"Well, if you ever have the opportunity to repay the favor, I won't turn you down. Since that'll probably never happen, I hope you'll save that marker for some other occasion where it might be useful."*

Though the human's use of odd language confused her, Sarith was sure she comprehended his larger meaning. "I will . . . remember that, Captain. Thank you."

"Commander," said Variel from where she still worked with Darjil at the sensor station. "We are detecting renewed quantum fluctuations."

"The Sidrac are making the calculations for another shift," said Riker. *"That's our cue."* He raised a hand and touched the edges of his fingers to his forehead in what Sarith recognized as an informal gesture of respect. *"Safe journey home, Commander."*

"And to you, Captain." To her surprise, Sarith heard and felt the conviction in her words.

Riker's image vanished from the viewscreen to show a fresh image of the planet. Already she was seeing it beginning to flicker as the unreal forces of the dimensional shift seized it once more. Within moments, the world faded from sight, leaving behind nothing but void.

"The probe, Commander," said Ineti. "We can retrieve it and take it back with us. Even that technology would be a prize for the praetor and keep research scientists occupied for quite some time."

Instead of replying, Sarith tapped a control and the viewscreen image changed to show the Sidrac's targeting beacon, drifting alone within the nebula. Moments later, the device erupted in a brief, brilliant white light that dissolved into an expanding cloud of debris.

"What?" Ineti stared with open shock at the screen before turning to Sarith. "You knew this would happen?"

She nodded. "Captain Picard told me. The Sidrac are pulling back the tethers anchoring them to these other dimensions."

Centurion Skerius said, "Commander, prior to the explosion, there was a surge in the beacon's communication stream. The Sidrac must have sent some form of self-destruct command."

"That's correct," replied Sarith. "They will not be back, and neither do they wish us to follow."

Though unhappy with this revelation, Ineti said nothing. Instead, his eyes narrowed. His expression became almost serene, and he nodded in apparent understanding.

"So shall it be." The subcommander looked around the bridge, his eyes as always scrutinizing everything taking place around him. "What are your orders, Commander?"

The tension and fatigue of the past days were already beginning to close in around her, emboldened by the relief Sarith felt upon having returned her ship and crew to their proper place in the cosmos. That she had done so with assistance from those her leaders might call enemy was immaterial. There would be time later to discuss and dissect her actions, but for now she did not care.

"Let us go home, my friend."

ELSEWHERE
U.S.S. Enterprise-D

Now things were getting interesting.

"Shields are down to thirty-four percent!" shouted

Tasha Yar over the latest in a string of alarm sirens howling across the bridge.

His fingers digging into the arms of his command chair, Riker pressed himself against the seatback, trying to anchor himself as the ship trembled around him. The second dimensional shift had been rougher than the first, with the *Enterprise*-E's absence keenly felt as his own ship was forced to carry the load of protecting itself and augment the Sidrac reactor to provide power for the quantum-field generator. His vision was only just clearing from the effects of the shift, and the buzz in his ears lingered to the point that he almost felt the need to shout in order to be heard.

"Where are we?" he asked, feeling the turbulence from the transition subsiding and the ship settling down as artificial gravity and inertial damping systems reasserted themselves. "Did we make it?"

Sitting in his customary place to Riker's right, Data was poring over the information streaming across the compact display next to his own chair. "Scans of the Sidrac targeting buoy's quantum signature is a match, sir. We have arrived in the proper dimension."

Riker tapped a control on his chair's embedded control pad. "Captain to all hands. We've made it. We're back in our own dimension, but we're not finished yet. We still have to help the Sidrac make one more jump. Engineering, how are we holding up?"

"It's getting crazy down here, sir," replied Geordi La Forge. *"I don't know if we'll have enough power for the shields and maintaining the power transfer."*

Data said, "Captain, if Nelidar and her people are able to make the calculations for the final shift, we can suspend the transfer and augment our shield strength as we move to a safe distance."

"What about the power drop-off?" asked Deanna Troi from where she sat to Riker's left. "Will the reactor be able to sustain enough energy for the final shift?"

From the ops position, Wesley Crusher replied, "Total power being fed to the field generator is eighty-one percent of capacity, Captain, but that's with our helping it. The rate of decay is continuing to accelerate, and it'll plunge as soon as we sever the power transfer."

"If we maintain the power transfer until the moment of transition," said Data, "then make our withdrawal as the quantum field is forming, that should be sufficient to facilitate the transition."

Frowning as he processed what he was hearing, Riker said, "Sounds like we're going to take one last kick in the ass before this is all over. At least we're being consistent."

Yar said, "Captain, we're being hailed from the planet."

"Put it on-screen." Riker pushed himself from his chair as Ushalon disappeared from the viewscreen and was replaced by an image of Nelidar. The Sidrac scientist's already pale complexion seemed to have lightened even further, and Riker noted her troubled expression.

"Captain Riker," she said. *"I trust your ship is undamaged?"*

"For the most part." Riker stepped closer to the screen. "Have you finalized your last set of calculations?"

Nelidar nodded. *"Yes, but we are concerned about the reactor power levels. If they fall below what we need for the field generator, all of this will have been for nothing."*

"We're not done yet," replied Riker. "We're maintaining our power transfer until the last possible second, then we'll retreat once the transition starts." He grimaced. "It'll be tight, but I'm confident our shields will protect us."

"The risk you are undertaking is considerable, Captain."

Crusher said, "It's only going to get worse the longer we wait, sir."

"Nelidar, we're out of time. It's now or never. Initiate the shift. We'll take care of our part up here."

The Sidrac's expression softened, her eyes widening. *"We will not forget you, Captain Riker. Any of you."*

"Just be sure to send a message or something, letting us know you made it." Riker recalled what he had been told about the plan for Nelidar and her people once they returned to their own dimension. "You're ready to evacuate once this is all over?"

"Yes. Our transport vessels are already standing by. The habitat's reserve power systems will be sufficient until we depart, and the journey to Elanisal is of short duration."

Riker smiled. "Then I guess this is goodbye. Thank you for everything, Nelidar."

"It is we who are forever in your debt, Captain. May your future journeys be safe and enlightening." Nelidar held his gaze for an additional moment before the connection was severed and her image disappeared, leaving Riker to stare at the dull gray surface of Ushalon highlighted by the brilliant hues of the Spindrift Nebula.

"All right, people," said Riker, returning to his seat. "Let's do this. Worf, plot us a course away from the planet and be ready to engage the instant we cut the power transfer. Wesley, stand by to route power from the deflector array to the aft shields. Let's try to cushion that kick in the pants we're about to get."

"We'll be ready, sir," replied Crusher.

Dropping into his chair, Riker raised his voice and called out, "Geordi, we're going to need everything you have."

The chief engineer's voice sounded harried as he answered, *"We're on it, Captain."*

"Sensors are showing a new quantum field being generated," reported Data. "Energy fluctuations are increasing."

The evidence of this development was visible on the screen, with the planet Ushalon already fading as it was caught in the grips of the transition effect. All around him, the *Enterprise* had started shuddering again as the starship's deflector shields absorbed the brunt of the ever-increasing quantum energy field. His arms vibrated along with the reverberations being channeled through his chair.

Yar said, "Shields are at twenty-nine percent."

"That's as good as it's going to get, bridge!" shouted La Forge. *"We need to break off now!"*

Crusher said, "Cutting the transfer. Routing power to aft deflector shields."

"Initiating withdrawal course," reported Worf.

The Klingon exchanged fleeting glances with Crusher as each set to their respective tasks, and seconds later Ushalon shifted right, disappearing past the viewscreen's edge as the ship maneuvered away from the planet. Without being asked, Yar changed the angle on the screen and Ushalon returned, now further gripped in the throes of dimensional transition.

"Shields are overloading, Captain," said Yar, just as everything seemed to tremble in response to the assault on the ship's defensive screens. Lights and workstations flickered and dimmed before returning to their normal illumination levels, and for the briefest of moments Riker felt his stomach heave as the artificial gravity wavered.

On the screen, the lifeless gray orb slipped away, disappearing into nonexistence or—Riker hoped—existence elsewhere. As soon as the turmoil had come calling upon the ship, it was gone, and he felt the vibrations subsiding.

"Transition complete, Captain," said Yar. "Scans are detecting no sign of the planet and only residual quantum fluctuations." She tapped a string of controls on her console. "The targeting buoy is still online and functional."

From the intraship, La Forge said, *"Please tell me we're done."*

Riker could not help the laugh that escaped his lips. The welcome release of tension made him slump into his seat, and he could feel the weight of the past hours lifting from his shoulders.

"Yes, Geordi, we're done. Nice job down there. Nice job, everybody." Glancing up to Yar, he said, "Tasha, transmit our message to the buoy." If all went according to plan, Captain Picard would soon be notified of the mission's success, at least so far as the *Enterprise*-D was concerned.

Yar said, "Captain, I'm picking up a signal from the targeting buoy. It's a compressed data packet, and I'm running it through our decryption algorithms now." A moment later, she looked up from her console and smiled. "It's from Nelidar, sir."

Deanna turned in her seat. "They're home?"

"Yes," replied the security chief. "It worked. Nelidar says we should continue to monitor the beacon for a while longer. They're sending a more detailed message later, after they secure everything."

It was tempting to bring the beacon aboard and store

it for later transfer to Starfleet Research and Development, but Riker knew that Nelidar's ultimate goal for the device was to destroy it once she had transmitted her final message. She and her fellow Sidrac had decided not to leave behind any traces of their technology, preferring instead to go back to the drawing board and find ways of making such dimensional shifts safer and easier to control. Perhaps Nelidar and her people would succeed, or they might decide the rewards of such efforts did not outweigh the risks.

It was their call, Riker conceded, and one he had no desire to argue. For now, he was grateful for two things: his ship and people were safe, and they were *home*.

27

The drink seemed to have no flavor, which T'Ryssa Chen thought odd considering the crew lounge's bartender, Jordan, had made it based on her exacting specifications. Certain it would taste no better with the next sip, she set her glass on the bar and pushed it away.

Sitting next to her, Dina Elfiki asked, "You okay?"

Chen nodded. "Just lost in thought, I guess."

Pointing to the drink, Elfiki asked, "What is that supposed to be, anyway?"

"A *tolik* sour fizz. It's made from a Vulcan fruit, the *tolik*." Chen shrugged. "Ensign Scagliotti took shore leave there before we left for the Odyssean Pass the first time. She said she found it in a tourist-friendly club near Lake Yuron after reading about it in a travel guide." Tapping the edge of the glass with her fingers, she added, "I don't think I got the recipe right."

"This is why I stick to vodka martinis," said Elfiki, holding up her own glass. "It's almost impossible to get them wrong."

"I'll remember that." Swiveling her seat, Chen took in the rest of the lounge. Alpha shift had ended less than an hour earlier, which meant that the Happy Bottom Riding Club—as named by William Riker before accepting his promotion to captain and departing the *Enterprise* to assume command of the *U.S.S. Titan*—was on its way to reaching capacity. It was a nightly tradition to gather here at the end of a normal duty day, or what might constitute "normal" considering the events of the past few days. Chen could not help noticing that the atmosphere, though relaxed and even jovial, felt subdued. Perhaps everything that had transpired was finally catching up, and everyone was only now beginning to decompress.

Works for me. I could use the company.

Elfiki turned in her seat so that like Chen she could face away from the bar. "You've been pretty quiet since you got back to the ship."

"I know. It's a lot to process, I guess." Chen leaned back in her seat. "It's one thing to study about parallel dimensions and alternate realities in class when it's just some theory. It's another to read the mission logs from ships like this one where the crew had actual encounters with such things, but none of that compares with coming face-to-face with the evidence that they really, truly exist." She blew out her breath. "It's pretty weird."

"That's one word for it." Elfiki sipped from her own drink. "And as weird as it is for us, imagine how it must be for the captain or anyone else who served on the old *Enterprise*-D."

Following that ship's destruction, Chen knew that the majority of its crew had asked to remain with Captain Picard when he eventually took command of its *Sovereign*-class successor. Many of those people had since moved on to other assignments, or left Starfleet altogether, or perhaps met unfortunate fates as could happen from time to time, but there was still a core of personnel who had remained with the ship throughout everything. Aside from Doctor Crusher and Commanders Worf and La Forge, fully a third of the *Enterprise*-E's current contingent had carried over from the starship's forerunner or had returned here after serving on other ships or starbases.

She had overheard snippets of conversations following her excursion to the planet. The common questions and speculation all ran toward the obvious differences between the two ships' senior staffs, including the conspicuous absence of Captain Picard. Answers had not been forthcoming and likely would remain out of reach, in keeping with the captain's decision not to reveal details about how events had unfolded in much different fashion in the other reality.

"They're sure staying tight-lipped about the whole thing," said Chen. "I mean, *really* quiet. It's not like I expect Captain Picard to lay it all out over the intraship, but I guess I figured I'd hear . . . something. I was down there when Data arrived from the other *Enterprise.* He certainly didn't offer anything, and he was the only one who had any interaction with any of our people."

Elfiki replied, "Not counting the captain and Doctor Crusher going over there. Talk about out of the blue."

The decision by Picard to visit the *Enterprise*-D had sparked its own set of rumors. That action would almost certainly trigger an investigation by the Department of Temporal Investigations. It would not matter that the other starship had come from a different dimension; the mere mention of a time-related incursion would be enough to set off agents within the mysterious organization. Those agents would doubtless be thrilled to be talking with the captain so soon after their last discussion following the *Enterprise*'s encounter with the Raqilan weapon ship from the future.

"Even Taurik doesn't know what's up," said Chen,

"or if he does, then he's not saying." She made a note to ask him, wondering if the planet Ushalon and the Sidrac had appeared in any of the computer data the Vulcan had accessed from the Raqilan vessel before sealing all of that information and giving it to DTI. Of course, Taurik had been sworn to secrecy about whatever knowledge of future events he might possess.

"Maybe it's better to just not know," said Elfiki.

Chen giggled. "Knowing what you know about me, do you see me leaving this alone?"

"Yeah, I didn't really think that through."

Movement behind them made both women turn to see Jordan emerging from the work area behind the bar. Chen saw that he was carrying a silver frame, and it was obvious that the bartender was looking to mount it along with the eclectic collection of memorabilia that covered the bar's back wall. In keeping with the lounge's namesake—a bar on twentieth-century Earth frequented by military test pilots—an assortment of photos and other curios decorated the walls, featuring replicated items from the original establishment as well as Starfleet mementos dating back more than two centuries. Jordan, a human with a penchant for his planet's ancient history, had taken to Captain Riker's naming of the lounge with great enthusiasm for carrying on the tradition of the original Riding Club. He was forever adding or exchanging various pieces of bric-a-brac around the room in accordance with his shifting tastes.

"Finally found something new?" asked Chen.

Holding up the frame, Jordan replied, "Not me. This is from the captain." He paused for a moment, studying the wall, and eventually selected a frame in which was mounted a white trapezoidal patch originally worn by men and women assigned to Earth's first permanent moonbase in the twenty-first century. In its place, Jordan hung the new frame, and Chen got her first good look at the photograph it contained.

"I'll be damned," said Elfiki.

Jordan smiled. "I know, right?"

It was a picture of Captain Riker and his senior staff from the *Enterprise*-D.

Chen said, "That's going to raise some eyebrows." She gestured to the photo. "Wait. Does this mean the captain told you the story behind it?"

"Yes," replied the bartender.

"So you can tell us?" asked Elfiki.

Now the man's smile turned mischievous. "One day. Maybe."

Rolling her eyes, Chen tapped her glass. "I need a drink."

"We can fix that."

Her attention caught once more by the photograph as the bartender set to work, Chen could only wonder about what might have been and what might still be.

The nebula was, in a word, beautiful.

With everything that had transpired since their discovery of the planet, Picard had somehow allowed himself to forget about NGC 8541's simple splendor. Even without the mystery it had harbored, the nebula offered numerous research opportunities for the ship's science department. On the other hand, after the events of the past days, he knew it would not be easy for them to return to such mundane work, no matter what else they might find here.

It's hard to blame them.

"Captain?"

Only upon hearing Worf's voice did Picard realize he had allowed his mind to wander, and that he had done so not while sitting alone in his ready room, but in the ship's observation lounge, with his senior officers and most trusted friends waiting in apparent silence for him to stop daydreaming.

"I'm terribly sorry," he said, straightening in his chair before looking at Worf, Geordi La Forge, and Beverly. "I have to admit that I've been prone to the occasional bout of distraction these past few days." He leaned forward in his chair, resting his forearms atop the polished obsidian conference table. "I'm finalizing my report for Starfleet Command and wanted to know if any of you wished to add anything. I value your perspectives and opinions on what we all experienced."

La Forge replied, "I've organized information from our sensors and our tricorder readings while we were on the surface, sir. Everything we were able to learn about the quantum-field generator is in there. Starfleet R and D will love that."

"Indeed. Particularly since we can include in our report that Ushalon and the Sidrac returned safely to their own dimension." The final transmission from Nelidar, transmitted through the dimensional barrier via the targeting buoy deployed to this reality, had detailed the planet's safe arrival and the Sidrac's evacuation to their home world, Elanisal. This, preceded by the message from Captain Riker that the *Enterprise*-D and the Romulan ship had also made it to their proper places in space and time, would ignite the imaginations of countless engineers and scientists back home. Starfleet Research and Development was always on the lookout for some new specimen of alien technology to study, be it something offered by a modern society or some ancient remnant of a lost civilization. The *Enterprise* had presented those scientists and scholars with a fair number of such specimens over the years, and they would spend months if not years poring over this new data. Picard imagined he would hear something about the fact that no practical examples of the quantum-field generator would be delivered, and even the targeting buoy was gone, having been obliterated thanks to a self-destruct command sent by Nelidar.

Oops.

"It's not R and D you have to worry about," said Crusher. "What about your report for DTI?"

Picard offered a wry smile. "As you might imagine, that will be somewhat longer and more detailed."

And that's before they find out everything.

"I hope you realize that I didn't call you three here to discuss these particular matters," said Picard. "Despite the extraordinary circumstances in which we found ourselves, these post-mission activities are mundane, if important. Instead, I invited you to this meeting because I need to confess something to you." He placed his hands flat on the table and lowered his gaze to study its surface. "Captain Riker—Will—confided in me details about . . . some . . . of the differences between our two realities. As you might imagine, I was most curious as to what happened to my counterpart." He briefly described the *Enterprise*-D's first year with Riker in command after the abduction of that dimension's Jean-Luc Picard and the destruction of the Borg cube that had assigned him as their spokesperson, Locutus.

"The Borg remain a threat in that timeline," he continued, "which means they will launch further attacks against the Federation. There's no way to know if those future campaigns will mirror what we experienced, but there's also no reason to assume they won't." He looked up from the table in order to look at his friends. "I gave Captain Riker the schematics for a transphasic torpedo."

Picard was uncertain what reaction to expect from the others, with one exception. There was Worf, sitting ramrod straight in his chair with an unreadable expression while Beverly and La Forge exchanged glances.

"That's going to get someone's attention at DTI," said Crusher. "I guess we'll find out once and for all whether the Temporal Prime Directive has rules to govern this sort of situation."

"I'm okay with it." La Forge clasped his hands and rested them on the table. "If the Borg do ever show up in force, the Federation will need every advantage it can get. If they get started now, they'll have years to figure out how to make a better version of the torpedo. That might be all the jump they need to help take out the Borg before they can inflict the sort of destruction we faced."

"Precisely," said Picard. "That, and luck for the interstellar dominoes to fall where needed. Easier said than done, of course."

Worf asked, "What do you plan to tell Starfleet Command, sir?"

"The truth, Number One. I've found that's always the best course." There would be innumerable questions and no small portion of hell to pay, but that did not concern Picard. If he could spare that other version of the Federation the same level of tragedy they were still working to repair, then his actions were worth it.

And what if you only make things worse?

It was a possibility, Picard knew. By giving Riker the schematics, he risked that dimension's Starfleet developing and deploying the weapon against the Borg at a point in time well in advance of when it was first used in this reality. What if the Collective adapted to the technology far earlier? Would that Federation be able to devise some other means of defense? There was also the possibility that the Borg in that dimension could be destroyed earlier. Picard realized he could spend days, if not weeks, contemplating the various scenarios and their outcomes. It was enough to drive a person mad.

"Do you need us to do anything, sir?" asked Worf.

Picard rose from his chair, signifying the meeting's conclusion, and his officers followed suit. "Just what we always do, Mister Worf. We shall continue our mission and let destiny take its course."

After dismissing his staff to return to their duties, Picard was alone in the observation lounge. He swiveled his seat so that he could look out the windows, free once again to regard the nebula. He tried to lose himself in its simple beauty, but it was difficult, consumed as he was by thoughts of what might have been, and what might still be.

Make it so, Will.

EPILOGUE

Will Riker paused just before the door sensor would be aware of his presence. One more step, and the occupants of the room beyond the door would know he had arrived, after which he would be committed to this course of action. There would be no turning back.

Amused at the silliness of his own hesitation, Riker smiled. He did not want to turn back. He did not want to retreat. This was something he wanted to do. Moreover, it was something he had to do.

He stepped forward, allowing the door to register his arrival. Though muffled, the sound of the chime was still audible, and a moment later the door slid aside.

"Good evening, everyone."

Sitting at the octagonal poker table in the center of his first officer's quarters were Data, Geordi La Forge, Deanna, Doctor Pulaski, Tasha Yar, Worf, and Wesley Crusher. Sitting in his customary place on the table's far side as he shuffled a deck of playing cards, Data wore his familiar dealer's visor. Glasses of various shapes and contents sat in front of a few of the players, namely Pulaski, Yar, and La Forge. An eighth chair, opposite the android and next to Deanna, was unoccupied. Everyone started to stand, but Riker held up a hand and indicated for them to keep their seats.

"Please, as you were. We're all off duty." He paused in the doorway, exchanging glances with each of his colleagues. "If it's all right, I thought I'd join you."

Data replied, "Certainly, sir. Welcome."

"Now it's a party," said La Forge, punctuating his comment with an unabashed smile.

Pulaski gestured to the empty chair. "Your credits are absolutely good here, Captain."

Grinning, Riker settled into the proffered seat. He took another moment to regard everyone at the table. More than crewmembers and friends, this was the closest thing he had to a family.

What the hell was I thinking, staying away from this for so long?

"Tasha," he said, "when did you start playing?"

The security chief replied, "I'm not a regular, sir, but I do drop in from to time." Looking around the table, she shrugged. "After everything we've just been through, it seemed like a good idea tonight."

La Forge grunted, shaking his head. "You can say that again." For Riker's apparent benefit, he added, "Except for the minor stuff that can be taken care of during a standard duty shift, we've finished our repairs." He rapped the table with his knuckles. "Perfect timing."

"It is agreeable to have you return to the game, Lieutenant," said Worf, before looking to Riker. "And you, Captain. I have longed for a worthy opponent with the courage to enter this arena." Riker could not be sure, but he thought he saw a hint of mischief in the Klingon's eyes.

"Worf," said Crusher, "it's just poker, not a fight to the death."

"Then I shall make do."

The remark solicited a few chuckles before Data began dealing cards, with each player receiving the first card facedown.

"Five-card draw. Nothing wild."

It was not until each player had received five cards and was looking at their respective hands that Riker paused again. After a few seconds, everyone at the table realized he was looking at them. Glances were exchanged, and he even saw concern on the faces of Troi, Pulaski, and La Forge.

"Will?" prompted Troi. "Are you all right?"

"I was thinking how much I'd missed this." Riker placed his cards facedown on the table. "I want to thank each of you again. Not for what we all just got done dealing with, but also the last several months. I know the transition hasn't been easy for anyone. I couldn't have gotten this far without all of you. I haven't come out and said it the way it needed to be said before now, and for that I apologize."

He paused, his gaze lingering on Data, Yar, and even Crusher just a bit longer than the faces of the others. "Recent events have reminded me that life is short and that we don't know what the future and fate have in store for us. I need to remember that every day, every *moment*, is precious."

"Hear, hear," said Pulaski, holding up her glass of water in toast.

Crusher said, "Seeing the other *Enterprise* . . . seeing Captain Picard standing there, was definitely an eye opener. But it was seeing who *wasn't* standing there that really got to me." He dropped his gaze to the table and swallowed an apparent lump in his throat. "That's what really drove home the point."

"Exactly," said La Forge.

Glancing to Yar, Riker said, "It's worth remembering that their future's not ours. They've already traveled a different path than we ever will. Just how different is that path?" He frowned. "No idea, and I'm not even sure I want to know, if for no other reason than I'm afraid it might affect how I make some future decision."

"I don't think that's unnatural," said Troi. "After all, it's hard to deny that for all the subtle differences that seem to exist between our two dimensions, there also are a great many similarities."

It was a point Riker had pondered almost from the first moment he had seen the other *Enterprise*—an *Enterprise* that had never known a master other than Jean-Luc Picard. Perhaps there were too many of those parallels? What experiences had that man and his crew endured over the years? Picard had offered precious few hints, taking great pains not to reveal too much about the disparate paths their ships had traveled. While he understood the other man's caution—there might still be some permutation of the Temporal Prime Directive that required heeding, after all—it had not stopped Riker from considering the myriad possibilities. How many of Picard's tantalizing insinuations might come to pass in this reality? There was no way to know, just as there was no way to predict just how divergent the courses of the two disconnected dimensions might become.

And I'll go crazy trying to sort it all out. Maybe it's better to just leave it alone.

"You do have to wonder, don't you?" asked La Forge. "I mean, will we see any of the same things they've seen?"

Riker was not prepared to rule out that possibility, and neither—it seemed—was Picard. His former captain had even defied his own orders to say nothing of the Temporal Prime Directive by giving Riker an isolinear optical chip containing full schematics for the transphasic torpedo they had used on the planet. Picard's explanation had been cryptic, but there could be only one reason to provide such valuable information.

The Borg. They might come back. We need to be ready. A lot more ready than we are right now.

Yar, quiet to this point, said, "If so, will we be affected the same way?" As though realizing her comment might cast a pall over the room, she added, "Sorry. I'm not usually so pessimistic."

"I think you're allowed this one," replied Pulaski. "We'd be lying if we said we haven't thought about any of this, and what it means to each of us." She reached across the table and patted Yar's arm. "But you're here, so obviously things are and will be different." Then she looked to Riker. "Some good, and some less so. As for you, Captain William Riker, here's what I know as immutable fact: In any dimension or reality, Jean-Luc Picard would be very, *very* proud of you, and he would take great comfort in the knowledge that the welfare of the people he cared about most in his life were in your hands. Do not ever—even for one second—forget that."

Feeling somewhat self-conscious in face of such effusive praise, Riker wondered if he might blush. Instead, he said, "Thank you, Doctor. I appreciate that."

"Maybe it is better to not know," said Worf. When the others turned to him, the Klingon said, "I believe it would not be beneficial, as I do not believe that our fate is already decided. Just as careless time travel can in theory alter the course of our history, I believe that it is our actions that forge our destiny. Our values and our choices are what define us. There is no honor in relying upon random chance. It is how we employ the gifts with which we are born, and the skills that we acquire over the course of our lives, that allow us to be the architects of our own future."

His words sparked a chorus of agreements, as well as raised glasses in the case of La Forge, Pulaski, and Yar. La Forge shifted in his seat to regard his friend.

"Worf, is that supposed to be a Klingon warrior's way of saying we should play the hand we're dealt?"

The lieutenant seemed to ponder this notion for a moment before offering a satisfied nod. "Yes."

Troi added, "I think that might also be Mister Worf's way of saying it's time to play some poker."

"Sounds like a plan," said Pulaski, leaning forward and resting her elbows on the table.

Crusher pointed to the doctor. "Watch out for her, Captain. She's a shark."

"I remember," said Riker as he picked up his cards. "All right, let's play."

The room grew quiet as Crusher started the initial hand with the opening bet, with the rest of the table throwing in. Relaxing in his seat, Riker felt the tension and uncertainty, which had burdened him for far too long, beginning to melt away. This was where he belonged; not just in this room but on this ship. He had spent more than enough time wallowing in contemplation during the last few days as well as the past several months as he second-guessed and questioned himself and his abilities. It was well past the point for him to cast aside feelings of doubt or indecision.

This ship carried a rich, celebrated history. Its heritage was a sacred trust, passed down for centuries from every ship christened with its storied name, and now in Riker's hands. He was the captain of this *Enterprise*, and he was morally bound to preserve its legacy just as everyone he had succeeded.

But he would have to do it his own way. Riker knew in his gut that Jean-Luc Picard, wherever he might be in this reality or any other, would expect nothing else and accept nothing less.

Play the hand you're dealt.

ACKNOWLEDGMENTS

As always, thanks to my editors at Pocket Books, who keep asking me to carry forward with the adventures of Captain Picard and the *Enterprise*-E. 2017 marks the thirtieth anniversary of *Star Trek: The Next Generation*'s premiere on television. I still remember where I was that night in the fall of 1987, watching "Encounter at Farpoint" with a bunch of Marines on a very subpar barracks rec room TV. Back then, I had doubts that the show would even last, let alone step up to carry as it has the banner first unfurled by Gene Roddenberry in 1966. Now here we are, three decades later, and Picard and his crew are still our friends and guides through the final frontier. Pretty cool, huh?

Thanks once again to Doug Drexler and Ali Ries, who teamed up to provide yet another gorgeous cover to wrap around my words. I have benefited from their talents on several occasions, and this is no exception. Bravo Zulu, you two!

And no acknowledgments are complete without tipping my hat and raising my glass to you, dear reader. Thank you for your continuing support of my work. I get to do what I do within these pages by your good graces, and I never let myself forget that fact.

Let's do this again soon, all right?

ABOUT THE AUTHOR

Dayton Ward has been modified to fit this medium, to write in the space allotted, and has been edited for content. Reader discretion is advised.

Visit Dayton on the web at
www.daytonward.com